LET US GO

To Donald
Mentor
[signature]

Let us go

The narrative of

KAMEHAMEHA II

KING OF THE HAWAIIAN ISLANDS

1819–1824

by

WALTER F. JUDD

TOPGALLANT PUBLISHING CO., LTD.

HONOLULU, HAWAII

1976

Library of Congress Cataloging in Publication Data
Judd, Walter F.
Let Us Go
Bibliography: p.
1. Kamehameha II, King of the Hawaiian Islands,
1797-1824—Fiction.   I. Title.
PZ4.J913Le [PS3560.U35]   813'.5'4   76-14386
    ISBN 0-914916-16-5
    ISBN 0-914916-17-3 pbk.

FIRST EDITION

Printed in United States of America

Design and typesetting by ParaGraphics, Inc., Bloomfield, NJ
Printing and binding by Thomson-Shore, Inc., Dexter, MI

ACKNOWLEDGEMENT AND SOURCES

In an effort to recount the story of Liholiho more accurately and meaningfully, some previously published dialogues, chants, eye-witness reports, and letters have been included.

Grateful acknowledgement is expressed to Kamehameha Schools for their permission to use certain quotations from the rich source:

Kamakau, Samuel M. *Ruling Chiefs of Hawaii.* Honolulu: The Kamehameha School Press, 1961.

Significant dialogue quotations are from:

"History of Hawaii, written by Scholars at the High School, and Corrected by One of the Instructors. Lahaina-luna: Press of the High School, 1838." *The Hawaiian Spectator.* Vol. 2 No. 2. Honolulu: 1839.

Jarves, James J. *History of the Hawaiian or Sandwich Islands.* Boston: Tappan & Benney, 1843.

Lydgate, John M. "Ka-umu-alii, the Last King of Kauai." *Twenty-fourth Annual Report of the Hawaiian Historical Society* (1915).

A prayer is quoted from:

Malo, David. *Hawaiian Antiquities.* (Bernice P. Bishop Museum Special Publication 2) 2d Edn. Honolulu: Published by the Museum, 1951.

Significant eye-witness quotations are from:

Bingham, Hiram. *A Residence of Twenty-one Years in the Sandwich Islands . . .* Hartford: Hezekiah Huntington, 1847.

Stewart, C. S. *A Residence in the Sandwich Islands.* 5th Edn. Boston: Weeks, Jordan & Co., 1839.

CONTENTS

foreword

Any crown prince who succeeds a departed conquering ruler is faced with a practically insurmountable precedent to follow. This was the position of the 23 year old Kalani-nui-kua-liholiho-i-ke-kapu (literally, The Great Chief with the burning back kapu) who ruled the Hawaiian Islands from 1819 to 1824 following the death of his father, Ke Alii Nui (The Great Chief, King) Kamehameha. The new ruler was then known formally as Kalani (The Heavenly One), publically and familiarly as Liholiho (Shining or Glowing), and known by westerners and today as King Kamehameha II.

When Ke Alii Nui Kamehameha died in 1819, he had conquered six of the eight major islands of the Hawaiian Group, and the remaining two acknowledged his overlordship. A number of feudal island rulers had previously endeavored to conquer all of the islands—only Kamehameha succeeded. Success of his military conquests and consolidation of conquered lands and peoples can be attributed to his exploitation of the new weapon, firearms, a receptiveness to westerners and their ideas, and to his tremendous force of character and leadership. He was a remarkable man.

Western influences in Hawaii began in 1778 with the arrival of Captain James Cook of the British Navy, the discoverer of the Hawaiian Islands for the western world. The material possessions and trade goods of this and later western arrivals, plus the vigor of new ideas and standards they brought with them, abruptly caused an accelerated transition of the isolated Hawaiians from the Stone Age to the Iron Age.

Intruded pestilence and diseases had halved the Hawaiian population by 1819. The prior life style was drastically altered by the western demands for foodstuffs and sandalwood. Rum and gin had been introduced. Traditional standards, values, and practices began to be questioned by most Hawaiians. There was considerable social uneasiness.

It was under these rapidly changing conditions that Liholiho ruled the Hawaiian Islands for five brief but exciting years.

Liholiho was severally described by early writers, mostly hard-looking New England Calvinist missionaries, as: frank and humane . . . good natured, except when intoxicated . . . agreeable . . . inquisitive . . . dissipated . . . idle . . . restless . . . indolent . . . heedless and dissolute, wanting in the great qualities of his father . . . etc. His five year reign was dominated by the strong-willed Dowager Queen Kaahumanu, who had been designated as kuhina-nui (regent) by the late ruler before he died, and by his mother, the Sacred Queen Mother Keopuolani.

Albert Pierce Taylor, then Archivist of the Territory of Hawaii, wrote in 1927:*

> Liholiho, born two years after the decisive battle of Nuuanu, or in 1797,** the son of a princess who was regarded as sacred, was reared during long years of peace. He was raised apart from military camps and fierce battle, when there was even no need for being alert, either for offense or defense. He was raised in the lap of luxury. He had no command of troops, nor was ever assigned as governor of an island, or a district. He was never dispatched on a diplomatic mission.

> Yet . . . During Liholiho's short reign:
> He overthrew the Hawaiian religion and attendant kapu (law or forbidden) system which was the core of the Hawaiian way of life and upheld the caste system of the alii (chiefs).†

> He was able to retain the Rule, or co-Rule with the regent, despite dissension and rebellion in the Hawaiian feudal tradition. The Hawaiian Kingdom, which his father had created and established, continued.

> He accepted the One God of Christianity and His Missionaries into the Hawaiian Kingdom. Literacy began in Hawaii.

> He finalized the consolidation of the island of Kauai and its fief-island Niihau into the Hawaiian Kingdom—by guile.

*Taylor, Albert Pierce. "Liholiho: A Revised Estimate of His Character." *Papers of the Hawaiian Historical Society No. 15* (1928).

**See Appendix 1, Liholiho's Age and Geneology.

†See Appendix 2, The Kapu System.

He died almost half way around the world, in London, England, while on a visit to King George IV and the British government.

Let Us Go may be considered part history and part historical fiction—a series of time-vignettes, if you will. An effort has been made to take the bits and pieces of recorded history (sometimes sparse, as little of the Hawaiian side of the story was ever reduced to writing) and apply humble knowledge and imagination in an effort to make Liholiho and the people of his time "come alive" for the reader. Significant source material quoted or referred to is indicated by reference to bibliography [book number: page number].

"LET US GO . . ." Liholiho ordered firmly on May 18, 1819 at Kawaihae, Hawaii, and he left for Kailua to be pronounced king the following day. This with an awareness that he might not survive and retain the Rule. He could clearly see that he was headed for turbulent times and difficult relationships and decisions.

They were.

HAWAIIAN PERSONAGES

the senior alii (chiefs and chiefesses) of the times . . .

KING:	Liholiho (Kamehameha II)
HIS QUEENS:	Kamamalu
	Kinau
	Pauahi
	Kekauonohi
	Kekauluohi, and later Kekaihaakulou
QUEEN MOTHER:	Keopuolani
HER YOUNGER CHILDREN:	Kauikeaouli (son)
	Nahienaena (daughter)
REGENT:	Kaahumanu (dowager queen)
PRIME MINISTER:	Kalanimoku
COUNSELLORS:	Hoapili
	Keeaumoku*
	Koa-Hou
	Naihe
ISLAND GOVERNORS:	Hawaii—Kuakini
	Maui, etc.—Keeaumoku*
	Oahu—Boki
HEAD PRIEST:	Hewahewa
GUARDIAN OF THE WAR GOD:	Kekuaokalani
TRIBUTARY KING OF KAUAI:	Kaumualii
HIS SON:	Keliiahonui
OTHER DOWAGER QUEENS:	Kalakua, Namahana and Piia.

*same person

x

Cartoon of forth anniversary of Ke Alii Nui Kameha-
meha's death, April 1823. (*Eveleth, Rev. Ephraim.
History of the Sandwich Islands . . . Philadelphia: American
Sunday School Union, 1831*)

Honolulu 1821 by C. E. Bensell. (*F. W. Howay (Ed.)
The Voyage of the New Hazard . . . Salem: Peabody
Museum, 1938*)

King Kamehameha II, 1824 by John Hayter. *(Archives of Hawaii)*

Queen Kamamalu, 1824 by John Hayter. *(Archives of Hawaii)*

Kuhina-nui Kaahumanu, 1816 by Louis Choris.
*(Kotzebue, Otto von. Voyage of Discovery in the South Sea
. . London: Sir Richard Phillips & Co., 1821)*

Hawaiian warrior, 1819 by Jacques Arago. (*Arago,
Jacques. Souvenirs d'un aveugle, voyage autour du Monde.
Paris: 1839*)

Kaonee, queen of Hawaii, 1819 by Jacques Arago.
(*Arago, Jacques. Souvenirs d'un aveugle, voyage autour du Monde. Paris: 1839*)

Queen Kamamalu, Keohoua (or Keoua, Kuakini's wife), and Likelike (Kalanimoku's wife), 1819 by Jacques Arago and engraved by Pellion. (*Freycinet, Louis de. Voyage autour du Monde . . . Paris: 1825*)

Woman of Maui dancing, 1819 by Jacques Arago.
(*Freycinet, Louis de. Voyage autour du Monde . . . Paris:
1825*)

I

move on in my good way

"What are your final counsels for us?"[23]

The dying Hawaiian ruler who lay on his red and yellow ahuula (feather cloak) in the dimly lit thatched house at Kamakaho-nu, Kailua district, island of Hawaii, obviously struggled for strength to speak. Slowly, almost inaudibly, he whispered:[23]

"Move on in my good way . . . and . . ."

John Young, the white-haired old Englishman who had served the ruler loyally for almost thirty years and was one of his chief advisors, couldn't resist his emotion and moved forward to embrace the emaciated aged ruler. The staunch High Chief Hoapili embraced him also, and whispered a final message. Others followed.

Time passed. The majestic slowly moving cumulus clouds winked the stars in sympathy with the mortal struggle below. Four hours later the unconscious ruler's breathing slowed . . . slowed . . . stopped . . . started up again . . . slowed . . . slowed . . . and, after a final weak convulsive effort of the strong old heart to keep beating, he died. Ke Alii Nui Kamehameha, the Island Conqueror, passed away at 2 A.M. on May 8th, 1819.

There was a collective sigh from the assembled members of the royal family and the high chiefs. They continued to blankly regard the dead ruler for some moments. It had been a long vigil, and emotions were spent. The once stalwart warrior-ruler, who had been ailing for months, had vigorously fought death for three days and two and a half nights. They looked at each other, and at Liholiho, the 23 year old designated heir to the feudal Hawaiian Rule. As if at a signal, they all rose from their cramped positions and stood silently in respect.

High Chief Kalanimoku, nicknamed "William Pitt" by foreigners because he acted as prime minister, ordered the body carried to a nearby small thatched house in the residence compound. One aged retainer who was there would not leave the dead ruler, and remained, swaying in silent expression of extreme grief.

Dowager Queen Kaahumanu, the heir Liholiho, and the high

chiefs deliberated on the final arrangements for the late ruler. Kahuna-nui (Head Priest) Hewahewa of the Order of Holoae, which dated back to the time of Paao (12th-14th Century), explained the religious requirements due upon the death of such a distinguished personage.

First, the Uko ceremony, the initial deification rite. A pig must be ceremoniously sanctified and offered to the Gods and to the dead ruler with appropriate prayers by the kahunas (priests) and the designated heir, Liholiho. This would announce to the Gods that the dead ruler was starting on the path to becoming a God. All nodded, and the kahunas of the adjoining Ahuena Heiau (Ahuena Temple), which the late ruler had restored, were instructed to prepare the pig.

Then there was the matter of human sacrifices:[23]

> If you obtain one man before the corpse is removed, one will be sufficient; but after it leaves this house (place), four will be required. If delayed until we carry the corpse to the grave* there must be ten; but after it is deposited in the grave,* there must be fifteen. Tomorrow morning there will be a Kapu [Forbidden], and if the sacrifice be delayed until that time, forty men must die.

To this traditional requirement Liholiho said "No," following the precedent of a recent change from traditional practice by his father.

Several months previous, the kahunas had suggested that human sacrifices might propitiate the Gods to prolong Ke Alii Nui Kamehameha's life. He was then reported to have said:[23] "No, the men are sacred for the king (for my successor)." In comparison with earlier practices, when the Sacred Queen Mother Keopuolani was ill at Waikiki some years before, three men were offered to the Gods at Papaenaena Heiau on the slopes of Diamond Head to assist her recovery. Seven more men would have been sacrificed, but fortunately for them she recovered. Just the previous year, 1818, three other men who had broken the kapus were sacrificed by Prince Liholiho at Kealakekua—one for putting on the malo (loin cloth) of a chief, another for eating forbidden food during a kapu period, the third for leaving a house that was kapu and entering one that was not.

---

* The grave referred not to the final resting place of the ruler but to a procedure in the customary final disposition of the remains, later described.

High Chief Hoapili announced that the late ruler had designated to him the honor of performing the hunakele (secreting the final remains so they would not be violated). There were some raised eyebrows at this, as Ke Alii Nui Kamehameha's forebears had had this honor performed by the family of Keawe-a-Heulu who controlled the secret family burial places in the district of Kau. Liholiho confirmed his father's decision, and this was accepted as an inviolable right of the late ruler. (Counsellor High Chief Naihe, the son of Keawe-a-Heulu, said nothing, but his dour expression indicated his annoyance.)

As was traditional upon the death of such an important personage, the heir moved temporarily "from defilement" of the place of death to another district of the island following the initial deification ceremony. The basic reasons for this were twofold: first, the kapus* were not upheld during the kumakena (mourning period) of ten days and the district within which the ruler died became especially chaotic with grief; second, these were feudal times, and the designated heir often did not succeed to the Rule without a struggle, and sometimes died in the attempt. Discussion revolved around Liholiho going either to the district of Kau or the district of Kohala.

The latter prevailed, as it was more heavily populated with strong supporters of his late father and was under the control of High Chief Kekuaokalani. This high chief lived at Kawaihae and was Liholiho's first cousin. Even more important, as a renowned fighting man and the late warrior-ruler's nephew, High Chief Kekuaokalani had been designated by Ke Alii Nui Kamehameha as kahu (guardian) of Kukailimoku. Kukailimoku had been Kamehameha's war god—the war god that had prevailed over the ruler's enemies and the other islands' and high chiefs' war gods. Thus High Chief Kekuaokalani was a very influential person in any succession question. The concept of almost balance of power between a ruler and the "head of the military force" went back many generations. Kamehameha had performed both functions himself until his old age made Kekuaokalani's appointment prudent.

It was dawn before all was decided. The high chiefs and the royal family, led by the heir Liholiho, escorted the body of the late ruler to the Ahuena Heiau. The royal family retainers, whose workday was from dawn to past dusk, were astir and the first of the makaainana (commoners) to discover that their sovereign was dead.

---

* Kapu means law or forbidden. Appendix 2 contains information about the kapu system.

They fell to their knees and prostrated themselves and began to wail—au-we! au-we! au-we! (alas! alas! alas!).

This keening was heard by others who also began to wail. The not-unexpected news that Ke Alii Nui Kamehameha had died spread among the people of Kailua faster than the tradewinds. Messengers were hurridly sent off on foot and by canoe to spread the news to other districts of the island of Hawaii and to the other islands.

James J. Jarves, respected early historian, wrote in 1843 of wailing that:[25:68]

> Night and day was the dismal sound prolonged; its first notes were low, gradually swelling until one full passionate burst of grief filled the air, and resounded among the neighboring rocks and hills, whose echoes threw back the cry. During the night its effect, as thus borne from party to party, from one valley to another, now rising into almost a shriek of bitterness, then subsiding into a low, murmuring sound, was startling and impressive. Watch-fires, surrounded by groups of both sexes, wailing and weeping violently, tearing their hair, and giving way to other and more barbarous demonstrations of their sorrow, completed the scene.

The Uko ceremony began in the Ahuena Heiau. The leading kahuna offered the pig to the Gods and to the dead ruler and made prayers announcing the intent of Ke Alii Nui Kamehameha joining the Hawaiian Gods. He closed with a prayer to purify and cleanse the heir, Liholiho, from the defilement of having come into contact with the corpse:[27:212]

> *E ma ka 'ai ku, e ma ka 'ai alo,*
> Here is the food offered, here is the food offered in your favor,
>
> *E ma ka 'aia', e ma ka hele huna,*
> Here is the food for the sin offering; let him be hidden,
>
> *E ma ka hele pa'ani;*
> Let him go and play;
>
> *E ma ka uwe makena;*
> Here let there be mourning;
>
> *O kukakau a ka ho'oilina,*
> For the dead and for his heir,

Papae'e - A kaluako'i,
Let him be accepted where he is laid to rest,

I hemu' 'oia i heu,
Let him go in peace,

I hemu' 'oia - i hemu'.
Let him go in silence.

Following the Uko deification ceremony, Liholiho with his wives, followers and retainers departed in a small fleet of canoes for Kawaihae, some thirty miles up the coastline.

During the ten day kumakena (mourning period) it was traditional for the kapus not to be observed or enforced. Grief grew to hysterical proportions and many mourners became pure savage. Jarves further described this as:[25:73]

> The ceremonies observed on the death of any important personage were exceedingly barbarous. The hair was shaved or cut close, teeth knocked out and sometimes the ears were mangled. Some tattooed their tongues in a corresponding manner to the other parts of their bodies. Frequently the flesh was cut or burnt, eyes scooped out, and other even more painful outrages inflicted. But these usages, however shocking they may appear, were innocent compared with the horrid saturnalia which immediately followed the death of a chief of the highest rank. Then the most unbounded license prevailed; law and restraint were cast aside, and the whole people appeared more like demons than human beings. Every vice and crime were allowed. Property was destroyed, houses fired and old feuds revived and avenged. Gambling, theft and murder were open as the day; clothing was cast aside as a useless incumbrance; drunkenness and promiscuous prostitution prevailed throughout the land, no women, excepting the widows of the deceased, being exempt from the grossest violation. There was no passion however lewd, or desire however wicked, but could be gratified with impunity during the continuance of this period, which, happily, from its own violence soon spent itself. No other nation was ever witness to a custom which so entirely threw off all moral and legal restraints and incited the evil passions to unrestricted riot and wanton debauchery.

The kahunas were a powerful hierarchy who influenced the way of life of every Hawaiian. They were responsive to but not necessarily subservient to the alii, and were considered to be in the same social order. Kahunas ranged from the reverent men who presided at ceremonies venerating the Hawaiian Gods, the respected professional men of the time (e.g. doctors, herbalists, astronomers, agriculturalists, historians, genealogists, etc.), to the feared lower order of diviners and sorcerers.

The kahuna-kuni (sorcerers) knew that Ke Alii Nui Kamehameha was going to die—had not a kaimimiki (tsunami, seismic disturbance of the ocean) occurred a month ago which portended this dire happening? (And they were also aware that the ruler had been ailing for the past few years and was failing fast . . .)

Later in the day of Ke Alii Nui Kamehameha's death several kahuna-kuni performed the kuni (burn) ceremony in Kailua, the nearby village of some 3,000 people. This ceremony endeavored to discover and destroy the individual who had caused the ruler's death by sorcery (despite any apparent mortal facts). They started a large fire of uhaloa wood and set up four staffs at the corners of the fire. The staffs were garlanded with auhuhu (fish poison plant) and green gourds, and were topped with white kapa (bark cloth) flags. A number of dogs and fowls were offered as sacrifices. The kahuna-kuni offered prayers to Uli, the God of Sorcery, and were watched apprehensively from a distance by a fearful crowd:[33:102]

> *A-a ke ahi, ke ahi a ka po o Lani-pili,*
> The fire burns, fire of the night of Lani-pili (a deity),
>
> *A i hea ke ahi, he ahi a ka po o Lani-pili?*
> Where burns the fire, fire of the night of Lani-pili?
>
> *A i ka lani; make i ka lani;*
> It burns in the heavens; (death in the heavens)
>
> *Popo i ka lani; ilo i ka lani;*
> Death (decay) in the heavens; corruption in the heavens;
>
> *Punahelu i ka lani.*
> Mildew in the heavens.
>
> *Hoolehua i ka lani ka make o kahuna anaana,*
> Heaven speed the death of the kahuna anaana (a kahuna who prayed people to death),
>
> *Me ka lawe-maunu, e Kane.*
> And of the one who got for him the maunu (part of the

6

victim's body required before praying to death), O Kane (a major Hawaiian God).

Ahi a Ku o ke ahi.
It is the fires of Ku (another major Hawaiian God) that burn.

Kupu malamalama o ke ahi o ka po a,
Flash forth light of the burning night,

Ahi a Kulu-a-lani e a ana.
The fires of Kulu-a-lani are burning.

Ku o Wakea, a ke ahi, he ahi no keia pule.
Wakea stands up and the fire burns, fire for this prayer.
(Wakea was the progenitor of the Hawaiians or founder of the atii class)

An incident occurred. High Chief Keeaumoku, brother of the powerful Dowager Queen Kaahumanu, came along, quite intoxicated, and broke down several of the staffs around the fire. The kahuna-kuni immediately inferred and announced that Dowager Queen Kaahumanu had been instrumental in Ke Alii Nui Kamehameha's death.

One can dimly discern political and religious maneuvering behind this occurrence. The kahuna-kuni would not have performed this ceremony following Ke Alii Nui Kamehameha's death unless they were powerfully backed and paid. High Chief Keeaumoku, known to be impetuous, would not have taken this drastic action against the feared sorcerers unless there was considerable provocation.

For more than twenty years Queen Kaahumanu had been granted the power of life over the people; her royal husband Kamehameha had the power of life and death. For at least the last ten years, the declining years of Ke Alii Nu Kamehameha's life, Queen Kaahumanu had acted almost as regent at Ke Alii Nui Kamehameha's direction, and had practically ruled the kingdom assisted by her astute cousin, High Chief Kalanimoku. The alii were closely intermarried and among her relatives were many powerful and influential high chiefs.* Her sister Kalakua, also one of Ke Alii Nui Kamehameha's queens, was the mother of two of the four wives of the heir, Liholiho. Kaahumanu was powerful, politically astute, and to tilt with her was extremely dangerous.

---

* Appendix 3 contains detail about selected high chief relationships.

Hawaiian politics at this time was similar to all feudal countries (e.g. middle ages in England, Europe, Japan, etc.). When there was a strong conquering ruler, such as Ke Alii Nui Kamehameha, he held a tight rein on the powerful nobles. Loyalties were loose, and sometimes changed as the strength shifted. When there was a designated successor of unknown qualities, or a weak one, the powerful feudal lords became restive, ambitious, and jockeyed for position. The kingdom was held together by force—uneasiness followed Ke Alii Nui Kamehameha's death.

There was a difference though, between this Hawaiian succession and previous successions. Ke Alii Nui Kamehameha, in consolidating his rule over the islands from Hawaii to Oahu, had adopted refined methods of government probably suggested by his haole (foreigner) advisors and by Captain George Vancouver, the friendly and influential British naval officer who visited Hawaii several times 1792-1794. Ke Alii Nui Kamehameha kept the most powerful alii in his court, as was traditional. However, he appointed talented and trusted chiefs (regardless of rank), commoners, and even haoles to govern the various islands and districts. When he distributed captured lands to his chiefs, they were parceled out piecemeal, rather than in large areas which might provide geographic blocs of power. Concern was now for more than one island. Thus it was difficult for any strong alii to develop a contiguous group of people to support him, or overlord of a large area from which to levy war supplies.

Many alii had died during the fourteen years of warfare (1782-1795) when Kamehameha struggled to become ruler of the island of Hawaii and conquer the other islands. Many others (some say half), alii and makaainana alike, had died during an epidemic of mai okuu (either cholera or bacillary dysentary) introduced into the Hawaiian Islands 15 years before (1804). This sudden decrease in population aggrevated the social disruption caused by western goods and ideas, and somewhat dampened the ardor of ambitious nobles.

Also of significance was the fact that in this time of changing conditions there were two powerful orders of kahunas, the Holoae and the Kualii. They differed in the Hawaiian Gods they venerated, and in their adherence without-question to the rigidity of the Hawaiian religion and the kapu system. During Ke Alii Nui Kamehameha's last years the moral force of the kapu system had generally weakened. However Kamehameha's dominent will resisted change and he required strict adherence to the old Hawaiian customs.

But back to the death of Ke Alii Nui Kamehameha. The body was taken to a small thatched house entitled the hale lua (house of dead). The body was wrapped (kapa lau) in banana, wauke, and taro leaves and placed in a shallow trench and lightly covered with earth. A fire to assist decomposition was started over the trench and kept burning continuously during the ten day kumakena (mourning period). A relay of kahunas continually chanted the pule-hui (incantation).

The remains were exhumed on the tenth and last day of the kumakena. The bones were cleaned and bundled in correct order with the skull at the top, and then wrapped in kapa (bark cloth). A sennit casket entitled ka'ai was woven around the bundle of bones. This was further wrapped with kapa and covered with red feathers; two round shells were affixed to indicate eyes. When the ka'ai was placed within the anuu (tower) of the Ahuena Heiau and a kahuna had said traditional prayers, the final ceremony of the deification rite (akua maoli) had been completed.

That night, the tenth night of the kumakena, all people were placed under a strict kapu to stay inside their houses. Any violators of this kapu would be put to death. The remaining residue of the body was carefully collected in the hale lua (house of dead) and laid to rest in the ocean.

Around midnight of that night High Chief Hoapili and a loyal follower, Hoolulu, entered the Ahuena Heiau. The high chief made a short prayer and reverently picked up the ka'ai and gave it to Hoolulu to carry on his back. High Chief Hoapili led the way out of the temple, musket in hand. He was a large man, and had proven many times that he was extremely dangerous when aroused or crossed. He was tense this night with his important and secret mission.

All was silence, except for the tradewinds sighing in the coconut palms, as they quietly and cautiously made their way in a northerly direction along the dark deserted path towards Kawaihae. They slowly crossed the lava field of Punaokaloa.

High Chief Hoapili heard a sound, dimly thought he saw something, took quick aim and fired his musket at it. It turned out to be a stone that he thought might have been a person; the sound was perhaps a bird startled in the midst of its sleep. The shot was heard at Kailua and Honokohai; those who heard it dared not investigate, and burrowed deep within their bedding in their houses.

It was said that early the next morning Keopuolani, the Sacred Queen Mother of Liholiho, came by canoe to meet High Chief Hoapili and Hoolulu at Kaloko. It was further said that the ka'ai was placed in a cave that opened "into the side of the pond." It has also been said that in this ana huna (burial cave) are the remains of Ke Alii Nui Kahekili (The Thunderer), an earlier ruler of the islands of Maui, Molokai, Lanai and Oahu, and reputed sire of Kamehameha. His remains had been secreted by Hoapili's father, Kameeiamoku. It has been handed down that in this secret hiding place are also the remains of Kahekili's sister, Kalola, and her daughter, Kekuipoiwa Liliha, the mother of the Sacred Queen Mother Keopuolani. Poomaikalani, who headed the Board of Geneology of Hawaiian Chiefs in 1884, believed that the ana huna (burial cave) also contained the remains of the famous 16th Century Ke Alii Nui Umi.

Years later, King Kamehameha III, also a son of Ke Alii Nui Kamehameha, persuaded Hoolulu to show him the ana huna. When Hoolulu saw a crowd of people following, he refused to go any further. A kahu (guardian) must never reveal the secret hiding place of the ana huna to anyone who might desecrate it. No urging was sufficient to make Hoolulu continue, and presumably knowledge of the location of this hiding place died with him. Presumably, as Hoolulu's descendents, if any, may still be caring for the ana huna.

All hearsay points to the final resting place of Ke Alii Nui Kamehameha being at Koloko . . . and yet, there were many hiding places, and there were many false rumors planted as to the location of ana hunas. One presumes that Ke Alii Nui Kamehameha is in the Kona or Kohala districts, the area from which he leapt to conquer and Rule.

May he continue to rest in inviolable peace.

As the Hawaiians say, only the stars of heavens know the location of Ke Alii Nui Kamehameha's sepulchre.

muse

The early morning sun warmed the pebbled upper terrace of Puukohala Heiau at Kawaihae. The heir, Liholiho, and High Chief Kekuaokalani listened intently to the old kahuna-pule (religious priest) as he finished the prayer to Kane, the major Hawaiian God of Life, Sunshine, and Fresh Water:[11:258]

E u-i aku ana au ia oe,
One question I ask of you,

Aia i-hea ka wai a Kane?
Where flows the water of Kane?

Aia i-lalo, i ka honua, i ka wai hu,
Deep in the ground, in the gushing spring,

I ka wai kau a Kane me Kanaloa—
In the ducts of Kane and Loa—

He wai-puna, he wai e inu,
A well spring of water, to quaff,

He wai e mana, he wai e ola,
A water of magic power, the water of life,

E ola no, e-a!
Life! O give us this life!

The bushy-white-haired kahuna-pule slowly lowered his raised arms and, spent with emotion, serenely looked at the two alii. They were moved by his prayer. This was good. Being an old man, and privy to all the secrets and conjectures of his priesthood, he knew and could see the tugs of conscience in the large young ruler-to-be (perhaps!). A wave of compassion swelled, for the kahuna-pule had loved his father, Ke Alii Nui Kamehameha, for his strong mana (spiritual force), his reverence of the Hawaiian Gods, and his firm upholding of the kapus.

The kahuna-pule considered . . . "Liholiho had good reason to soul-search; for these *were* troublesome times. There were these strangers from far away, men like themselves, who could disregard the kapus and not drop dead. And Ke Alii Nui Kamehameha *had* sanctioned this, all but allowing them to enter the heiaus. They are men, not Gods! There is something here that bothers me . . . why don't the Gods kill them, as our lore has established happens to *all* who break the kapus? Their conduct is upsetting the people and causing them to question what they should not." The kahuna-pule's inner irreligious questioning faintly caught Liholiho's subconscience as he was inaudibly repeating the last of the prayer. He motioned for the kahuna-pule to leave. As the kahuna-pule bowed slightly and slowly backed away, the tall stern High Chief Kekuaokalani looked sharply at Liholiho and also slowly withdrew.

Liholiho stood silently, contemplating the distance, yet not really seeing it. Liholiho was a large young man, over six feet, and he always stood with a great deal of manly dignity. His 250 pound body was well-proportioned; he had a large chest, heavy arms and legs, and was inclined to stoutness due to inactivity. The soft-black cross-hatched tattooing which covered the right side of his body from shoulder to waist blended subtly with the tawny nut-brown color of his skin. Liholiho had surprisingly small but muscular hands and feet for the size of his body. He had a full frank face and a steady expressive pair of eyes that were dark brown or black, dependent upon the light. His mouth was firm, curved up at the corners, and he had a full lower lip. The wavy black hair above his broad brow was thick and long, and covered the nape of his neck. His teeth were perfect. Liholiho was a noble-looking young Hawaiian alii—more than that, he was a prince about to be king.

Liholiho sank to his haunches and began to brood.

"The water of life, life, O give us this life," he repeated the final poetry of the prayer. "Water is life. O give us this life, and give us the wisdom to understand life, interpret life, live life with wisdom, and rule the life of our people sagely and with perfect understanding."

Liholiho mused . . . "Wisdom in these changing times, wisdom is all important. O my Father, I know your feelings, your teachings, your counsels, your examples, your integrity. But, O my Father, I *am* troubled! All things must be pure and meaningful to be true . . . and they are *not!*"

In almost an agony of spirit Liholiho grasped pebbles in both of his hands and clenched them tight, so tight that his hands and wrists turned pale, and yet he felt no pain. "But, O my Father, there *is* a fallacy. Our people live by our way of life governed by the kapus. Others, the strangers who visit our islands, do not . . . and yet live. And we have been advised that there are many strangers across the seas—more people than Hawaiians."

"These strangers with their wonderful ships and possessions, the iron, the cloth, the gunpowder. They are men like us. And they come here and laugh at our way of life. Those of our people who have gone away in ships—they lived as the strangers do and they have come to no harm. The strangers say they have but one God, whom we do not know. We have many Gods. And the yellow strangers, who live far across the sea to the west, have other Gods and different customs. Do the strangers have a better way of life than we do? O my Father!" Liholiho squirmed with the heretic thought.

"The kapus have been our way of life, the way of life for all people, since they were brought by our forebears from far across the seas so many generations ago. Inflexible, inviolable—and now my conscience is forced to question them. Without the kapus there would be chaos, an unthinkable and impossible lack of a way of life for our people. Yet many of our people are questioning them . . ."

"And Father! It was last year that we had those many discussions with some of our people who had just come back from the Mother Country of tradition, Tahiti, and they told us how the Gods had been overthrown and the one God of the strangers accepted. Tahiti! The Source! The far lands our alii forebears came from 27 generations ago and brought with them the Gods we worship and our way of life. The islands of Tahiti that we have always looked up to. And when I was younger, did you not send messages to their Ke Alii Nui Pomare suggesting that he furnish a daughter to be wife to me and you furnish my sister Nahienaena to be wife to one of his sons? Father! Why, oh why did our revered Source overthrow the Gods and kapus?

"Do not the Gods rule *all* men? I have asked you this before, but you shrugged off the question deeply and merely answered that the strangers were different. But they are men like us. The Gods are the Gods. Why, O my Father?"

Aware that he held the pebbles, he released them and allowed them to drop one by one to the terrace. He reflected . . . "Puukohala Heiau. The ancient heiau my Father rebuilt before I was born. The lore of this heiau goes back over 200 years and gave mana (spiritual force) great enough so that my Father consecrated the rebuilt heiau with High Chief Keoua Kuahuula and his ten moepuu (companions in death). It was with this sacrifice that my Father gained the power to first rule over the entire island of Hawaii."

Liholiho raised his arms towards the deep blue sky, and he clearly enunciated aloud in an agony of spirit, "O my Father, I feel you all around me. Your strong self."

He slowly lowered his arms, and reminisced.

"Since I was a child of five, O my Father, I have been at your side, listening to your wisdom, listening behind you when there was council or visitors."

"It was from that time that you directed I learn and practice the ceremonies honoring and revering our Gods. The only Gods. This I have done."

"It was then also that you selected me to be your heir and selected the wife of your heart, Kaahumanu, to be my foster-mother."

"You designated Kaahumanu this last year to be kuhina-nui (regent) to assist me when I succeeded you." Liholiho sat ramrod straight, and he clenched his fists in his lap. "I know I have fought no battles or governed anything—but I know your teachings. I have had no experience in making decisions—but I will be guided by your teachings. I will *always* be guided by your teachings!"

"I respect Kaahumanu's ability, but O my Father, she is pressing me with strong persuasion to yield to the questions the strangers have raised concerning our religion, our kapus, the way of life which is *our* way of life. She especially wants free-eating—for men and women to eat together. She wants all women to have the right to eat the food kapu to women—the right to eat pork, bananas, coconuts, turtle, and the special fishes, that now they would be killed if they ate."

"And if I sanction *this*, *all* the kapus will also be questioned. It will be the *end* of our way of life!"

"O my Father, help me of your wisdom . . ." Liholiho began to rock back and forth, hoping to crystalize his thoughts.

"And my true mother, the Sacred Queen Mother Keopuola-ni, she is beginning to question also. She who is always reluctant to have people sacrificed when they break her lineage kapu. She of the highest rank and the purest of blood who has the kapu moe (prostrating kapu), and from whom I inherit it. O my Father, she of all people should uphold the Old."

Liholiho chanted the last part of her genealogy:

Kalola-nui, a niaupio* chiefess, mated with Kalaniopuu, a niaupio* chief, and had Kiwalao, a son,

Kalola-nui then mated with Keoua, a niaupio* chief, and had Kekuiapoiwa Liliha, a daughter,

Kiwalao and Kekuiapoiwa Liliha mated together and had Keopuolani, a daughter.

Keopuolani mated with you, O my Father, a Wohi Chief, and had Liholiho—me.

"I have followed this plan of pure blood as you know. I have married two of my half-sisters and two of my step-nieces selected by my Sacred Queen Mother Keopuolani, and the wife of your heart, Kaahumanu, and approved by yourself. I hope there will be issue to carry on this great heritage." Liholiho stirred uncomfortably, for lack of issue was not for lack of trying.

"I have had many discussions, O my Father, with our kahuna-nuis (head priests), Hewahewa of the Order of Holoae and Kuaiwa of the Order of Kualii. Hewahewa and I have prayed to the Kunuiakea (Gods of Ku, one of the major Hawaiian deities) and we are both troubled and perplexed. I have prayed with Kuaiwa to the Lononuiakea (Gods of Lono, another major Hawaiian deity) and he is steadfast against any change in our ways. Further, Kuaiwa advocates drastic actions to bring back our old ways completely. This is contrary to your counsels . . . and I know not which way to turn. O my Father, I am perplexed!"

"And Kekuaokalani, the son of your younger brother Keliimaikai, whom you designated to be kahu (guardian) of Kukailimoku the war god. He is the strong one of the alii who upholds the Old. He wants to kill all the strangers and never let any more come to Hawaii. This was *never* your desire! We have grown apart, Kekuaokalani is suspicious, and I know not what I can expect."

"It was you, O my Father, when kahu of Kukailimoku, who overthrew your higher-born cousin and heir-designate, Kiwalao, and claimed the Rule of the island of Hawaii. And Kiwalao's father, Kalaniopuu, overthrew Ke Alii Nui Alapainui's designated heir, Keaweopala . . . and Alapainui had taken the Rule from

*Child of a union between full or half brother and sister. Appendix 1 contains Liholiho's complete genealogy.

Kalaniopuu's father, Kalaninuiamamao, who had been designated as Ke Alii Nui Keawe's successor."

Liholiho straightened. "O my Father! Is this what you have foredestined for me? Am I, your designated heir to the Rule, to be a stick to be broken by Kukailimoku, the war god? If it is so, I am not afraid. If it is not so, I must hearken back to the wisdom, the many discussions which you and the wise men—Kalaikuahulu, Nahili, Haleino, Kaioea, Keaweopu, and Kuhia—had with me in your declining years when we gathered in the evenings at Ahuena Heiau."

"There *must* be something I have forgotten, something that you told me . . . O, what was it?"

Liholiho tensed, and clenched his fists and beat his brow, and almost shouted: "WHAT!? WHAT!!? WHAT!!!?"

There was silence . . .

And then, there was a sudden large gust of the tradewind . . .

But no other answer.

Liholiho sighed and relaxed, and was suddenly conscious that the wind had chilled his perspiring body clad only with a malo (loin cloth). He became aware of the surroundings—the forty huge sacred carved figures on the stone walls of the heiau, the long shadow cast by the tall lananuu (oracle tower), the blue sea glittering in the morning sun, the black lava flows that followed the gentle valleys down the tan and green slopes to the sea, and the shining mountain of Hualalai behind Kailua in the distance. His eyes caught the flash of the sun on the paddles of an outrigger canoe coming up the coast towards Kawaihae from Kailua.

Liholiho sighed again.

"Let us go . . ." he murmured, as he rose to his feet.

"Let us go."

III

kawaihae

As Liholiho emerged from the narrow stone-walled passageway to the interior of Puukohala Heiau his gossiping attendants and followers prostrated themselves. Liholiho gazed at them for a moment and then signed for them to rise. He waved away his attendants who offered his ahuula (feather cloak) and mahiole (feather helmet) as he wanted to enjoy the sun. Liholiho did not go about much in the daytime as the respect required from the makaainana (commoners) disturbed their labors. On order, his retinue formed to escort Liholiho to his residence complex at nearby Kawaihae village.

First was the kapuo (announcer) who carried a white kapa (bark cloth) flag and kept proclaiming Liholiho's kapu: "Kapu moe! Kapu moe! Kapu moe! (Prostrate yourself! Prostrate yourself! Prostrate yourself!)." Then came Liholiho, striding briskly as usual, ramrod straight, and with his head held erect and his chin forward so that he seemed to look down on everything.

At a respectful distance followed the bearer of his spittoon, the bearer of his ahuula, the bearer of his mahiole, the bearer of his tobacco, his pipelighter, messengers, guards armed with muskets, etc. They were followed by his punahele (companions), and the paakahili (kahili bearer) with his tall staff surmounted with feathers forming a large cylinder which indicated who Liholiho was.

The last in line was the stalwart ilamuku (constable or executioner) who kept strict watch that all observed the kapu moe (prostrating requirement), that all within sight and sound, except those of high alii rank, would prostrate themselves and remove all wearing apparel above their waist.

"There's one! There's one!" exclaimed the ilamuku, as the procession entered Kawaihae village. Liholiho emerged from his brown study and saw the tough ilamuku dart ahead (being careful himself not to incur death by casting his fleeting shadow upon Liholiho) and grab a small fat naked boy sucking his thumb, who was standing by one of the small thatched houses.

"Uoki! (Stop!)" shouted Liholiho just in time to arrest the ilamuku's raised fist from clubbing the now scared little boy to the ground. Liholiho walked over to the amazed ilamuku, who was holding the boy cruelly by the arm. At Liholiho's gesture the ilamuku let go of the small boy.

Liholiho looked searchingly at the boy for a long time. The small boy innocently and trustingly returned the gaze of the big man who had stopped the ugly man from hurting him. Liholiho placed his hand on the little boy's head and said, "This man-to-be is sacred to me. Let him go."

The procession continued towards the guarded entrance of the palisade which surrounded Liholiho's residence complex. The squat ilamuku, who was waiting to resume his place at the rear of the procession, saw an arm emerge from the thatched hut and pull the small boy rapidly inside and out of sight. "Soft," he grumbled because he couldn't fulfill his traditional task. This had happened before with Liholiho. "Soft, just plain soft." He spat on the dusty ground and gloomily followed the procession, brooding on a future that just didn't look good.

As Liholiho entered the residence enclosure he was greeted by his waiting wives. He couldn't help smiling, began to enjoy the bright sunlit day, and exclaimed affectionately, "My rainbow!"

Each wore a different color China-silk pa'u* and each had fresh flowers in her hair and leis (garlands) around her neck selected to compliment the color of her pa'u. His halfsister Kinau wore a purple pa'u; his step-nieces Pauahi and Kekauonohi wore green and white pa'us respectively. His favorite wife and comely half-sister, Kamamalu, wore a scarlet pa'u, the color she liked best. What fine large princesses he had for wives!

They crowded around him and touched noses. He enjoyed teasing Kekauonohi for wearing white, as she was the most mischievous of his wives. Kamamalu began to chant a private risque version of Liholiho's mele inoa (song in adulation of a prince) and her body began to slightly move and sway in a hula (dance). Liholiho grinned, and began to follow her movements himself, and in no time at all both, almost of equal height, were fluidly and subtly dancing opposite each other with a beat provided by the handclapping of the encouraging other princesses.

Kamamalu was soon laughing so much that she had difficulty

---

* A skirt. A piece of cloth several yards in length and one in width wrapped around the body from the hips to the knees.

in chanting. She slowly swung around in front of him and he caught an end of her fragrant maile lei. He began to pull the lei, she wouldn't let go or come closer, so he placed his end of the lei over his shoulder and began to march off. Kamamalu followed, mock protesting and resisting, and they disappeared into the hale noa (sleeping house). The remaining princesses tittered, made ribald remarks, and wandered off within the enclosure, chattering away.

Liholiho was a little late for his midday meal. He sat on a mat with his cousin, High Chief Kekuaokalani, in the hale mua, the largest thatched house in the compound which was restricted for men to eat in and hold council. High Chief Kekuaokalani was older than Liholiho, larger too, with the muscular build and coordination of a trained athlete. His reputation as a warrior-chief worthy to follow to success was well-founded. He seldom smiled, and could turn savage quickly.

In front of the two high chiefs was a large bowl of poi (cooked taro which had been mashed and mixed with water to the consistency of paste), some fresh amaama (grey mullet) which had been wrapped in ti leaves and steamed underground, a bowl of coarse salt which had been obtained by evaporating sea water, and a small bowl of dried sliced and salted he-e (octopus) which Liholiho especially appreciated. They ate with their fingers. Each was attended by a crouching servant. A coconut bowl of rum was in front of each; that of High Chief Kekuaokalani had only been sipped, that of Liholiho was now half full.

A short distance away Liholiho's punahele (companions)—Ii, Laanui, Puaa, and Kalaikoa—ate with chiefly followers of High Chief Kekuaokalani. An old man sat in the far corner of the hale mua chanting a legend.

Liholiho's aipuupuu (steward), Manuia, crawled in front of him and awaited permission to speak. When it was granted, he said, "Lord, a messenger has come from your foster-mother Kaahumanu." Gloom settled on Liholiho's face as he bade Manuia to have the messenger enter. The aipuupuu crawled away, and in crawled the messenger. When given permission to speak he said, "Lord, Queen Kaahumanu instructed me to tell you that the kumakena (mourning period) is over today and for you to return to Kailua."

Liholiho glanced at High Chief Kekuaokalani, who was seriously looking at him, and irritatedly replied, "I will think upon it," and motioned the messenger away.

Liholiho stared blankly at the far wall of thatch and became aware of the silence of the men there. "Out! Out!" he ordered sharply, and the room was rapidly emptied, except for High Chief Kekuaokalani. Liholiho took a big gulp of rum, made a face, and leaned forward with his chin resting on his fists.

High Chief Kekuaokalani slowly said with barely restrained passion, "My high-born cousin, you of all of us know what is right, you of all of us best know the history of past Ke Alii Nuis, you of all of us well know what happened to Ke Alii Nuis who allowed irreligious practices and did not uphold the kapus—the Gods caused them to be removed by the hands of their people. As we have talked before, I beg of you to follow the principles of our way of life. In this I will help you . . . all the way."

Liholiho sighed deeply, and took another drink of rum. "If only it was that easy," he replied wearily, "but there are so many considerations in these changing times."

High Chief Kekuaokalani restrained his impatience with an effort and continued sternly, "Liholiho, I swore to my uncle, your father the Ke Alii Nui, to uphold and venerate Kukailimoku (the war god) and this I must and will do. I gave my word. It is my faith and integrity. This my conscience says I must do till death relieves me of the task." He paused for a moment, and said slowly and deeply, "Liholiho, you know me and my thoughts. I hope for our sakes that you can make decisions I can live with. You *must* uphold our religion, our kapus, our way of life . . . or you may not be our ruler."

Liholiho didn't reply, and with furrowed brow continued to stare glumly and bleakly in front of himself. High Chief Kekuaokalani started to continue . . . but instead closed his mouth tightly, stood up, and slowly strode out with a troubled look on his face.

Soon Liholiho got up and began to walk back and forth with his head bent low and his hands clenched behind him. Back and forth. Back and forth, until weary with his motion and thoughts he stopped and leaned against a large pahu (drum). His fingers touched the tough sharkskin cover, and he thumped it softly with the heel of his hand. Its reassuring deep throb reverberated back through his hand and into his body. The frown left his face and he straightened, hit the drumhead savagely, and began to drum a wild percussion. "Rum!" he shouted at a pause in the loud booming, "Rum! Rum!" and was hardly aware of the scared servant who rapidly crawled in and placed a bottle at his feet. Liholiho stopped and took a big swallow of rum and continued drumming (kaeke), at which he was skilled and found considerable solace doing.

Liholiho drummed the remainder of that afternoon with a

large pahu (drum) at his left and a small pahu entitled lapaiki at his right. He wouldn't admit anyone to the hale mua. He drummed sometimes wildly, sometimes softly. Later that evening when his punahele (companions) crept in to take him to his bed they found him seated on a mat, thoroughly intoxicated, and occasionally hitting the drumhead of the lapaiki which he held cradled in his arms.

Mid-morning of the following day, Liholiho was wakened with the news that Chief Eeka had arrived from Kailua and desired to see him. Liholiho groaned, and didn't like the taste in his mouth at all. After drinking part of a calabash (gourd bowl) of water, and pouring the rest over his head, he left his thatched sleeping house.

As Liholiho slowly and reluctantly walked toward the hale mua there was a sudden gust of the tradewind. He stopped, and looked up at the solid cumulus clouds marching in procession across the blue sky.

And . . . a second larger gust . . . a swirly gust that seemed to ruffle the thatch on the houses.

Liholiho straightened, suddenly and strangely feeling better. He pondered for a moment, and then started walking briskly towards his destination.

When he entered the hale mua he found old Chief Eeka, whom he was very fond of, and his cousin, High Chief Kekuaokalani, awaiting him. After appropriate greetings they all seated themselves. Chief Eeka gave his message:

"Kaahumanu urges you to return to Kailua now that the kumakena (mourning period) is over. Any further delay would be disrespectful to your late father. You must be proclaimed Ke Alii Nui by the assembled high chiefs. You must finalize the matter of the traditional division of the lands. You must take up the task that your father, Ke Alii Nui Kamehameha, foredestined for you. It is your destiny."

Chief Eeka repeated softly, "It is your destiny."

"My Father's remains?" asked Liholiho after a pause. Chief Eeka replied quietly, "All is well, Hoapili saw to that."

Liholiho thought deeply for almost a minute, then turned to High Chief Kekuaokalani and calmly said, "Let us go."[23]

High Chief Kekuaokalani pleaded:[23] "O Liholiho, stay here. There are fish in the sea and food on the land. If Kaahumanu seeks you, face her here, for it would be a fearful thing to die in the wilderness."

Chief Eeka interjected softly, "It is your destiny."

Liholiho turned again to his cousin, High Chief Kekuaokalani, and quietly repeated, "Let us go."[23]

High Chief Kekuaokalani looked at Liholiho sternly and sadly, and slowly replied, "Not I . . . I am sick."[23]

Liholiho dropped his gaze to the woven pattern of the lauhala mat for a long moment, and suddenly stood up. "Let us go," he said firmly, and walked to the door. "Let us go" he shouted "LET US GO!"[23]

There was a sudden hubbub of frenzied activity outside as Liholiho's retainers began to rush around gathering various possessions. Liholiho turned and looked at his cousin, High Chief Kekuaokalani, and silently raised a hand in parting salute. High Chief Kekuaokalani soberly and sadly returned the salutation.

Liholiho emerged from the hale mua and watched his people rushing around with satisfaction. He stood imperiously erect as his attendants placed his ahuula (feather cloak) around his shoulders and handed him his mahiole (feather helmet) which he placed firmly on his head. He was joined, slightly to the rear, by old, stooped Chief Eeka, who was smiling. They started off in the usual procession to the shore.

As Liholiho climbed into his double canoe, he was greeted by his favorite wife, Kamamalu. She was well aware of the implications of this journey to Kailua.

Liholiho stood spread-legged on the five-foot wide platform between the two joined canoe hulls and watched the last frenzied scurrying of his people who were completing the loading of the small fleet of canoes for the sudden departure.

"Let us go!" he ordered firmly as he motioned to his conch shell blower to give the signal for departure.

"Let us go," he muttered with sober determination as he resolutely turned to face forward.

The double canoe was urged from shore by the twenty paddlers under the direction of Kapihe, the canoe's steersman. Liholiho did not look back.

IV

accession

Kahuna-nui (Head Priest) Hewahewa, dressed in his usual white kapa (bark cloth) malo (loin cloth) and kihei (mantle), stood outside the entrance of Ahuena Heiau at Kailua and completed his long prayer ending with a blessing of the Kunuiakea (Gods of Ku) upon Liholiho. Many pahus (drums), which had been assembled within Ahuena Heiau, gave a long rumbling roar which shook the ground and the senses and made the huge sacred carved figures surrounding the heiau sway with resonence. Liholiho and his procession emerged from the temple entrance.

"Kapu moe! Kapu moe! Kapu moe! (Prostrate yourself! Prostrate yourself! Prostrate yourself!)" shouted the kapuo (announcer) with his white kapa flag held high as he importantly led the procession into view of the large assembled throng. The alii of lesser lineage and the makaainana (commoners) immediately prostrated themselves. Those on the outskirts who were in the shallow water carefully turned their heads sideways so they could breathe. Those prone koa (soldiers), who were armed with muskets, carefully held them so they wouldn't get wet or damaged. The senior alii (chiefs and chiefesses) remained standing.

Liholiho wore a red military uniform trimmed with gold lace and a cocked hat trimmed with gold lace and feathers which the English King George III had sent to his father as a return present for a feather cloak. He also wore his red and yellow ahuula (feather cloak) draped over his shoulders. Liholiho was escorted by two high chiefs wearing ahuulas and mahioles (feather helmets) and carrying pololus (12-15 foot long spears): Kuakini, Kaahumanu's youngest brother, who at age 28 stood 6'8" tall and whose weight balanced two piculs of sandalwood (266 2/3 pounds); and the older renowned warrior, Kaikioewa, kahu (guardian) of Liholiho's younger brother Kauikeaouli. The latter high chief was even taller than Kuakini, being seven feet tall, and his 54 year old body was still strong and erect, albeit grizzled.

They were followed by Liholiho's paaipukuha (spittoon

bearer), his paakahili (kahili bearer) carrying the tall kahili staff topped with the feather cylinder indicating Liholiho's rank, and his kuauhau (genealogist) who chanted Liholiho's genealogy.

Dowager Queen Kaahumanu and the high chiefs who made up the council were assembled in front of a large newly constructed halau (rectangular house which had a thatched roof and no sides). Liholiho hesitated a moment, despite his aplomb, startled at Kaahumanu's appearance—she wore Kamehameha's ahuula and mahiole and was leaning on a tall spear which Liholiho recognized as having been a favorite of his late father. Behind her were Kalanimoku, the "prime minister", and the four hereditary counsellors: her brother Keeaumoku, Koa-hou, Hoapili and Naihe. Keeaumoku wore a red cloak trimmed with silver and blue ribbons which had been given to his father, also named Keeaumoku, by Captain Vancouver some years ago. The remaining counsellors wore feather cloaks.

Behind them were the slim and thoughtful Sacred Queen Mother Keopuolani (Liholiho's true mother), the huge and motherly Dowager Queen Kalakua (wife of Kamehameha for twenty years and mother of two of Liholiho's wives), Liholiho's wives, and lesser alii, chiefs and chiefesses.

As the procession moved forward and stopped in front of Kaahumanu and the high chiefs, the kapuo (announcer) ceased his warnings for prostration and stepped to one side. The kuauhau completed his recitation of Liholiho's genealogy.

The six foot tall and heavy Kaahumanu appeared even larger in her feather garb. She advanced and said in a loud voice that all could hear:[27:220]

"Kalani, I speak to you the commands of your Kapunakane [literally grandfather, but in this context the expression intended kingly father].

"Here are the chiefs, here are the people of your ancestors; here are your guns; here are your lands. But we two shall share the rule over the land."

Liholiho glanced at the counsellors behind Kaahumanu, but they made no sign. Liholiho calmly replied, "I agree with my Father's will."

Then Kaahumanu said in a low voice heard only by the alii who were close:[2] "Let us disregard kapu."

Liholiho appeared to ponder a moment and then looked at Kaahumanu with a steady stare and said not a word. Finally Kaahumanu tossed her head imperiously and sharply said, "Let us hold council."

Kaahumanu led Liholiho and the council into the new open-sided structure and they sat down on mats in a circle. The alii gathered at the edges of the shelter in order of rank and also sat down. The makaainana (commoners) crept forward to listen, or began to slip away to be among the first at the many feasts which were being prepared for the accession celebration.

As Liholiho sat down, with his two attendant high chiefs privileged to stand behind him, he looked around and asked, "Where is Olohana (*John Young*)?"*

There was a pause as the 77 year old John Young, longtime counsellor of Liholiho's father, Ke Alii Nui Kamehameha, made his way slowly forward with a grateful smile. At Liholiho's gesture he sat at Liholiho's right. Kaahumanu, sitting opposite Liholiho, waited disdainfully and took off her mahiole (feather helmet). Her hair, still black, was as usual cut short with the bristling rim in front freshly bleached white by means of lime made from burnt sea shells. She turned to her cousin Kalanimoku, who was at her right, and made a low remark. He slowly nodded agreement.

"Kalani," Kaahumanu began firmly, "there are certain traditional and other matters which require your and our action at this time."

"First, as your father directed, let it be clear that you and I have equal power to Rule. We each have power of life and death, condemnation and acquittal. You shall not act without my concurrence. Although you may veto my actions, let it be understood now that I have had considerable experience in governing and am guided by wisdom gained from many years at your father's side. To this I am sure that our counsellors will agree, as it was your father's will."

Kaahumanu looked sharply to her right and left—and received nodding acknowledgements of varying enthusiasm, and then stared at Liholiho with her full face set sternly. Liholiho slowly nodded concurrence.

Kaahumanu relaxed somewhat, and continued with her next item. She spoke somewhat thickly, due to recently having half of her tongue tattooed in mourning for her late regal husband.

"The council met while you were at Kawaihae and we discussed the traditional division of the lands. First, we feel that your father's awards of lands to the alii and kahunas should continue."

* Being a former ship's boatswain, John Young used to call "All Hands" when a task was to be done. The Hawaiians called him by the sobriquet of "Olohana".

Liholiho did not hesitate and nodded his head saying, "My Father's awards were appropriate and just, and they should continue." The alii present indicated pleasure, and the air of tenseness relaxed even further.

Kaahumanu continued, "Second, when your father conquered the islands, other than the island of Hawaii, he retained most of the lands and peoples under his own control. Kalanimoku administered them, as you know. We feel these lands should be distributed to the alii, as is traditional. From them you can secure taxes."

Liholiho pondered a moment, and then said slowly, "My Father was very wise, and I must follow his guidance." He repeated his earlier statement, "My Father's awards were appropriate and just, and they should continue."

There was a momentary silence, and the assembled alii did not appear pleased. Kuhina-nui (Regent) Kaahumanu was about to protest, but thought better of it, and shrugged, "This is something we can discuss further at a later time. Meanwhile, Kalanimoku can continue to administer them."

Kaahumanu went on seriously, "High Chief Kalanimoku should continue as our agent (prime minister) but I believe he should be concerned with more than just the island of Oahu which he governs at present. He has become known as the "Iron Cable of Hawaii" among the many foreigners who come here—for his firm representation of us. He should also continue to be chief treasurer; from him you can ask for funds."

Liholiho looked at Kalanimoku carefully, and Kalanimoku returned the gaze impassively. Kalanimoku was of earlier inferior rank and had been brought up as a child with his cousin Kaahumanu. He was 50, eight years older than Kaahumanu. His ability, integrity, and loyalty to Ke Alii Nui Kamehameha, much less his family connections and political sagacity, had caused him to rise rapidly in stature and position of responsibility. Kalanimoku was of medium size, height and weight, and his thin face looked especially wan as he had lost an eye in mourning respect for Ke Alii Nui Kamehameha.

"I can think of no one better suited or experienced to be our agent (prime minister) and chief treasurer," Liholiho said thoughtfully. Kalanimoku slightly bowed his appreciation.

"With Kalanimoku concerned with all the islands," Kaahumanu continued, "we need to appoint a governor for the island of Oahu. I think Boki, Kalanimoku's younger brother who has been working with him, would be an excellent choice."

Liholiho nodded almost immediately and agreed, as he had always enjoyed Boki's bright spirit and dashing energy. He was also a cordial companion for a night's party. Further, Boki's wife Liliha was the daughter of the doughty Hoapili, the counsellor sitting to the right of Kalanimoku. This family relationship should provide desirable checks and balances. High Chief Hoapili sat more erect, if that was possible.

"Keeaumoku should continue as governor of the islands of Maui, Molokai and Lanai . . ." Kaahumanu began, and didn't bother to continue as Liholiho was already looking at Keeaumoku (who was a counsellor) and nodding affirmatively. Keeaumoku's father of the same name had been Ke Alii Nui Kamehameha's most respected counsellor and, of course, also father of Kaahumanu. Liholiho had always appreciated (and almost envied) Keeaumoku's restless spirits and talents. Although Keeaumoku was the eldest son, he was able to work well for and with his first-born sister Kaahumanu whom Liholiho's father had given so much power.

"The island of Hawaii, this our largest island, needs a firm hand," Kaahumanu went on quietly, "and with all due respect to Olohana (John Young), the present governor, time has taken its toll and a younger more energetic governor is needed."

Liholiho started to disagree, but Olohana laid a gnarled restraining hand on Liholiho's arm and sadly said, "Kaahumanu is right. My eyes are dim and they don't see what they used to see. I tolerate what I wouldn't have before. I ask but that now and then I may have your ear." Liholiho's eyes grew emotional, and he embraced the aged Olohana in answer.

"The logical alii to appoint to govern this island," said Kaahumanu very quietly, "is Kuakini, the present high chief of the Kona district. He had proven that he can handle the district well."

Liholiho looked at Kalanimoku, who was not at all partial to Kuakini, as Kuakini had once absconded with his wife. Kalanimoku made no sign. Liholiho then turned his head and looked at Kaahumanu's youngest brother Kuakini who, as one of Liholiho's escorts, stood behind him and was looking at Liholiho with bold and eager eyes. Liholiho almost grinned as he thought of the other amorous adventure which had not worked out well and instead had caused Kuakini to still be lame. Liholiho nodded and smiled (despite a belief that Kuakini had the tendencies of a robber baron of old). Kuakini smiled back, showing the gap in his front teeth where several had been knocked out in mourning respect for Ke Alii Nui Kamehameha.

The thought ran rapidly through Liholiho's mind—Kaahumanu certainly had her relatives in important and governing positions! The "prime minister", Kalanimoku, was her cousin. Her brother Keeaumoku was a counsellor. He also governed the islands of Maui, Molokai and Lanai. Her cousin Boki now governed Oahu; and her youngest brother, Kuakini, had just been appointed as governor of the home island of Hawaii. She certainly had firm controls over the lands and peoples through her family! Ah well, they were as good as other alii, and their selection would probably make relationships and ruling easier.

Kaahumanu motioned, and the late Ke Alii Nui Kamehameha's kahili (tall staff topped with feather cylinder) was brought forward. "It is fitting that you, on this day, have your father's kahili. As you know, it contains the right shin bone of Kaneoneo as well as the bones of Kaiana, Kalanikupule (last king of Oahu), and other important alii who were killed in the final conquering battle of Nuuanu on the island of Oahu—twenty four years ago, before you were born." Liholiho acknowledged with pride, and the paakahili (kahili bearer) carried the tall kahili and squatted by Liholiho's kahili bearer.

"One other thing," Kaahumanu continued with a gleam in her eyes, "you have but four wives, and tradition of island rulers is to have five. I have discussed this with Sacred Queen Mother Keopuolani and members of the council. We feel you should take Kekauluohi to wife. She is the daughter of Kalakua and the older half-sister of your wives Kamamalu and Kinau, having been born when Kalakua was married to your father's half-brother Kalaimamahu. She is my niece, and was brought up in my father's house. Kekauluohi was your father's wahine palama (wife to warm old age) for the past ten years. Perhaps union with yourself will produce issue."

Liholiho reddened at the implication pertaining to lack of issue, and thought for a moment. To be sure, Kekauluohi was older than his present wives, and two years older than himself—but he had always admired her feminine grace, pretty youthful features, fair skin, and fully proportioned figure. Her rather low husky voice always seemed to raise a certain excitement in him. He nodded acquiescence slowly, with a few interesting inner thoughts.

"And the kapus?" Kaahumanu casually inquired, almost as if an afterthought; "During the kumakena (mourning period) for your father all the kapus were not observed, as was traditional, and there was no harm. The women particularly enjoyed eating what and with whom they wanted. The alii prestige did not suffer. Your mother, the Sacred Queen Mother Keopuolani, especially enjoyed eating coconuts."

Liholiho looked at his mother, Keopuolani, who was at the edge of the shelter, and she put her hand to her mouth as a sign for eating. He looked at the counsellors, and saw mostly expressions of interest and minor concern.

Liholiho paled, and abruptly got up and left the council with his procession scrambling for their positions. He rapidly walked back to the Ahuena Heiau and, casting his ahuula (feather cloak) and hat hurridly aside, went into the inner terrace where he knew he would not be disturbed. He began to pray to the Gods for guidance. What pressures!

Late that afternoon his mother, the Sacred Queen Mother Keopuolani, sent for him. When he arrived at her residence compound they greeted each other affectionately, yet with quiet formality, and sat down on mats. Keopuolani wore a fine light pink pa'u (skirt), pure white kihei (mantle), yellow feather lei on her head, and a magnificent lei niho palaoa (ivory hookshaped pendant suspended by many strands of braided human hair) befitting the high chiefess of the highest rank, was around her neck. Unlike almost all of the high chiefesses who were immense, Keopuolani at 39 was slight with almost a girlish figure. Her features were sharp and fine; her personality of almost a disturbing calmness and thoughtfulness. Liholiho had rarely seen her angry or lose her dignity.

After discussing the events and color of the day, Keopuolani brought up the subject that Liholiho was dreading that she would— ai-noa (free eating between sexes) and the kapus.

"Liholiho, my son," she began quietly, "this we have discussed before, so I need not repeat myself. I believe that it has been proven by the others who have come here to visit or live, and our people who have gone elsewhere, that our way and custom is based on what was deemed necessary in the long past. It is not necessary at present. There are other Gods than ours, and they appear to be more powerful—look what their people have! I too resisted change, but I now agree with the far-seeing Kaahumanu. Our way should change."

"But mother," Liholiho began weakly, "this way is in-grained into our lives and all things depend upon it. Should we change, all will change . . . and I fear that the people will not accept . . ."

Keopuolani interrupted sternly, "Liholiho, you know that I am of the highest rank and may have the most to lose. I know that you have been trained since a child to conduct our religious services and venerate the Gods. Courage of conviction, even to the ultimate, is my heritage—and yours, too. Let me give you proof."

She clapped her hands, and Liholiho's good-looking six year old younger brother, Kauikeaouli, came in and sat down beside his mother. An attendant brought in a covered calabash (gourd bowl) and placed it in front of mother and child. Keopuolani calmly uncovered it, reached inside, took out a banana, half-peeled it and handed it to Kauikeaouli. He started to eat the banana. She took out another banana and, after peeling it, began to eat it herself—all the while steadily looking at Liholiho.

Liholiho was aghast at the sight of his brother eating with his mother (free-eating between sexes). He became almost horror-stricken at the sight of his mother eating a banana—a food kapu to women by tradition other than during a kumakena (mourning period). *And that period of time was over!* His mother and younger brother were *breaking the kapu!*

He scrambled to his feet, trembling, but the Gods did not strike down the two who had broken a most inviolable kapu. He almost staggered blindly from the thatched house and walked unseeingly and slowly back to the Ahuena Heiau. Liholiho was almost in a daze.

Liholiho prayed for a long time, hoping he wouldn't hear a messenger who had the onerous task of advising him that his mother and younger brother had been discovered mysteriously dead. None came. After several hours he turned to his pahus (drums) and rum so he wouldn't have to think. This time he drummed entirely softly.

Early the next morning Liholiho returned to Kawaihae where he joined his cousin, High Chief Kekuaokalani. Liholiho sent a message back to Kuhina-nui (Regent) Kaahumanu and the council at Kailua that the kapus, to include no free-eating between men and women and segregated foods, were to be continued.

The old way had won . . . for the moment.

V

kalanimoku

High Chief (and prime minister) Kalanimoku puffed his tobacco pipe thoughtfully and looked around the empty hale-mua (mens eating house) at Kawaihae before he answered Liholiho's question.

"Yes, I think it would be most appropriate and advisable that High Chief Hoapili took your mother, the Sacred Queen Mother Keopuolani, to wife as they both desire. They are both young," he said, with a slanting nod of his head, "he is 44 and she is 39, and man needs woman and woman needs man at that age too."

"Moreover, he is of good lineage, the son of one of your father's counsellors, Kameeiamoku. As you know, your father trusted him even to the ultimate of selecting him to secrete his bones. Hoapili is a noted war leader, and kahu (guardian) of your younger sister Nahienaena. He is some reactionary, and leans towards the teachings of the religious Kualii Order under Kahuna Nui (Head Priest) Kuaiwa, but I suspect that he leans not too far. He is a good man, can and will protect your mother and sister, and, in my opinion, has not too many ambitions beyond this."

Liholiho pondered, and nodded his head approvingly. "A masterly summation. So be it. You mentioned ambitions—have you other thoughts about ambitions?"

High Chief Kalanimoku nodded slowly, and wondered how many of his thoughts he should divulge to Liholiho. He had known Liholiho well since childhood, but this was a very different relationship. He would trust his judgement.

"Ambitions?" said Kalanimoku stoically, "Oh yes, I have lots of thoughts about ambitions, for in my position in life I must play ambition against ambition, strong person against strong person and weak person to achieve what I consider best . . . for the Rule."

Liholiho probed further, "How do you see the future, the future of Rule and ambition to Rule?"

Almost sympathetically Prime Minister Kalanimoku replied, "Kaahumanu will always be the stronger partner of the Rule. She is good and most capable, and you must recognize this. Despite how farseeing and astute she may be she will never be the sole ruler, for her lineage is not high enough, nor is she popular enough, to satisfy the people. She is of the island of Maui, your father and you are of this conquering island of Hawaii. Your father's achievements and name provide the strong leadership tradition you must lean upon. Don't forget that Kaahumanu needs you too—for you are your conquering father's son . . . and your highest lineage mother's son."

Kalanimoku thought for a moment, stroked his lean jaw, and continued, "The other strong ones? Keeaumoku? Perhaps, but I suspect that he will not try to get the Rule despite his ambitions. He would have to depose his older sister Kaahumanu as kuhina-nui (regent), for she would not accept him as equal or higher authority. Could Kaahumanu set him up to Rule? Perhaps, but I doubt it as she would not share authority with him or work for him as I have just mentioned. Hoapili? Perhaps, but your mother, Keopuolani, will restrain him. Koa-hou, Naihe, Boki, Kuakini? Strong, but not strong enough."

"Yourself without a kuhina-nui (regent)? I would be less than honest if I did not say that I believe your destiny appears to be to share the Rule—to be the junior partner, if I may put it that way. You will never be sole ruler as long as Kaahumanu lives—and she is most strong and valuable to you. And if she were gone, I suspect you would have extreme difficulties. Yes . . . extreme difficulties. She holds the kingdom together with her strength, which is most needed during these changing times."

Kalanimoku pondered a moment, and continued, "Would any of these powerful chiefs withdraw and declare themselves independent of the collective Rule your father established over all of the islands for the first time? This *is* a danger . . . and well within tradition. But I think astute concessions to the island governors, such as granting them the prerogative of trading sandalwood on their respective islands, would cause this possibility to become remote. They then would find little advantage in such action and would not permit the alii on their islands to take this action either."

Liholiho thought about this departure from his Father's policy, for Ke Alii Nui Kamehameha had been the sole beneficiary (royal monopoly) of trading sandalwood on all the islands. He began to slowly shake his head negatively, and Kalanimoku quickly said, "Think upon it. Keep an open mind. This is a danger that *must* be avoided." Liholiho considered for a moment, and nodded.

Kalanimoku went on, "Another concession worthy of consideration to the island governors pertains to the order of the foreigners who come ashore and practically go wild after their long periods of time at sea. Your father was very indulgent of this, except if they profaned the sacred places. However, their numbers have increased to such a magnitude that it is causing considerable trouble and disruption, especially at Kou (Honolulu). It would be in our best interests to agree with the island governors and permit them more authority to keep order. The times are changing."

Liholiho nodded, as he had been brought up to respect order in the Hawaiian way of life. He shook his head almost unbelievingly, "Kalanimoku, I have known you for years but you amaze me. I admire and respect your confidence and frankness. I sincerely appreciate it. I admit some of your thoughts are startlingly new, but I will think upon them. As you brought the subject to mind, what thoughts do you have about the changing times?"

High Chief Kalanimoku thought deeply for a long time, and absently accepted another lighted pipe from a crouching attendant who brought it in. He almost spoke twice, and then finally and deliberately said, "I am aware of and can see many things, some more clearly than you, I suspect, for I see them from a differing and perhaps broader perspective than you do. I cannot offer you advice on this. This must be purely up to you. Either you accept the changing conditions or adhere to the Old as you were brought up to do. This must be your decision. It will tremendously affect all of your people, and so it must be yours alone."

"But I will say this—the number of foreigner visitors and residents since Cook, Portlock, Dixon, Vancouver, and so on, are increasing until they are like the waves that break upon our shores. Over fifty ships came to our islands this last year, as you know. They will continue to increase wanting our provisions, water, salt, and sandalwood. You can either accept them, or reject them. Either will be difficult. I can see no halfway position, the decision must be one way or the other way."

"If I were you I know what I would try and do—but I am not you, and it must be your decision, a most important decision. I cannot advise you on this point of far-reaching principle. The decision will decide your destiny . . ."

Liholiho almost stamped his foot in vexation. "Damn!" he said passionately, "Damn! Damn! Damn!"

Kalanimoku looked at Liholiho unafraid and impassively. "I agree," he said with almost a twinkle in his one good eye. Liholiho had to grin in return, and relaxed.

Liholiho became thoughtful again, leaned forward, and queried earnestly, "And my cousin, High Chief Kekuaokalani?"

"It is as you know," Kalanimoku replied directly, "if he agrees with you and Kaahumanu, he will undoubtedly support you. If he does not agree with you and Kaahumanu, he will resist you, and probably try and take over with all of his power, which is considerable."

"And if he does try and take over . . .?" asked Liholiho with studied casualness. Kalanimoku considered for a moment, and then slowly and succintly replied, "With fortune, I believe you and Kaahumanu can prevail."

Liholiho leaned back and regarded High Chief Kalanimoku thoughtfully. What an amazing man . . . and I believe and trust him . . . and yet . . .

There was a pause, and Kalanimoku said softly, "Before you ask, do I have ambitions, I will answer. Yes, I have, but most of them are unattainable. I say unattainable for this reason—no matter how successful I may be I will always follow a higher lineage ruler. I shall never Rule myself, for people may respect me, follow me in someone elses name, but never in my own name. I shall always serve."

Liholiho leaned back even further, and casually mentioned as if an afterthought, "I *had* heard rumors about you . . ."

Kalanimoku nodded with a quiet smile, "I'm not surprised. I'm sure I planted most of them myself . . ."

VI

fReycinet

Louis de Saulces de Freycinet, captain of the French Navy corvette *Uranie*, stood on the afterdeck and closely watched the Hawaiian king's pilot, who had been introduced to him as Jacques (his Hawaiian name was Kapihe). Jacques had guided the ship up the coast from Kailua during the night. He glanced narrowly at Kawaihae Bay, which they were slowly entering. Everything appeared safe for his ship, especially as his men were heaving the depth line at the bow.

He raised his glass and looked at the shore. What a dry and desolate place! The small village of some 200 thatched huts was huddled by the shore on which a number of canoes were beached. There were but few coconut palms fringing the bay. The strange new Hawaiian flag was waving near what appeared to be a battery behind stone walls. Above it was a large rock mass (Puukohala Heiau). After his few days at Kailua, verdant with coconut palms and other vegetation, he just couldn't imagine why the king chose to live at this inhospitable appearing place. It wouldn't have been his choice! Perhaps it had something to do with the rumors he had picked up at Kailua that the new king wasn't firmly seated on his Hawaiian throne—if there was such a thing!

A large double-canoe, which had been paddled rapidly from the shore, was almost alongside. The 40 year old captain put his glass down and quickly looked around his ship. A bit weatherbeaten, but she still looked trim and neat after this long scientific voyage around the Cape of Good Hope from Toulon, France. What a number of strange and different places they had been to! August 12, 1819—nearly two years from the start of the voyage . . . Two men came aboard from the double-canoe, two men of such disproportion that Captain Freycinet almost smiled. The briefly clad Hawaiian was obviously a chief by virtue of his physical stature—he must have been around 35 years old, at least 5'10" tall, was stout yet muscular, and had an agreeable expression on his face. The second was about a 25 year old European—very thin, not much over four feet tall, and wore an old satin suit too large for him which had been pinned to make it fit. His yellow-topped boots were fairly clean. A tuft of his scraggly hair had been plaited and hung down to the level of his mouth.

The latter addressed the captain in not very good French, and the captain immediately inferred that he was a Gascon. "I have the honor to salute you with the most profound respect. Honored Captain, my name is Jean Rives. I am Interpreter for the king. Allow me to present High Chief Keeaumoku, brother of High Chief Kuakini whom you met at Kailua, and also brother of Kuhina-nui (Regent) Kaahumanu. The western traders at Honolulu also call him Cox."

Captain Freycinet shook hands with High Chief Keeaumoku, and made some pleasantries, which Jean Rives translated into Hawaiian. The High Chief spoke, and Rives translated, "King Liholiho bids you welcome, and is most anxious for you to come ashore and visit with him."

The captain nodded, and motioned to his first lieutenant. The ship was brought to the wind, the anchor was let down with a huge splash, and seamen began to rapidly furl the few sails still set. "Mr. Lamarche," the captain said loudly to his nearby first lieutenant, "my gig, and fire a salute of eleven guns. And come with me."

All was bustle as the guns rumbled forward to peer through the gun ports on the flush deck. The gig was swayed over the side of the corvette. The salutes began, and were answered, gun for gun, from the shore. The captain, Mr. Lamarche, High Chief Keeaumoku, and Jean Rives got into the crowded gig which started to pull for the nearby shore. The salutes were finished when the rowers tossed their oars, and two immaculately white-clad sailors sprang out into the shallow water and smartly drew the gig onto the dingy-colored sand beach. The two French naval officers stepped out onto land—both wore their dress uniforms (that were very warm in this Hawaiian August weather), blue naval coatees with high collars, white pantaloons, black boots, fore-and-aft bicornes, and both wore their plain swords.

Captain Freycinet led the way to the top of the beach where a group of Hawaiians were awaiting him. He surmised that the large Hawaiian wearing the dress uniform of a British naval captain, who was standing erectly in front of the group, was King Liholiho. Behind him were a number of men whom he guessed were chiefs. Most of them wore magnificent red and yellow feather cloaks, a few had scarlet European cloaks, some had shorter feather capes, and some wore feather helmets. Scattered around in the background were what appeared to be soldiers, as they carried muskets—but in whatever fashion seemed convenient. They moved to and fro as the spirit seemed to move them and without order. These men were clad in malos (loin cloths) and most of them also wore Kalmuck-type heavy cloaks of coarse material of a brownish color. Still further in the background were gathered the village residents.

His eye was caught by movement in a nearby open thatched-roof shelter. A number of young men were waving what appeared to be fly whisks over five elegently-clad (below the waist!) young Hawaiian women. He guessed they were the king's wives.

When Captain Freycinet reached the king, he bowed, and shook the offered hand. Jean Rives interpreted greetings and acknowledgements, and advised the captain that King Liholiho would salute him with seven guns. As the captain was about to reply, the king turned away from him, and the captain's slightly pock-marked narrow face set and reddened. Rives hurridly interjected that the king was not familiar with European etiquette and honors. Captain Freycinet relaxed, and watched the king signal vigorously with his arms. Both the captain and the king watched the seven sudden white clouds of the cannon salute which appeared from behind the nearby stone wall. The booms were slightly-off-interval.

King Liholiho turned to Captain Freycinet with an inclination of his head and a big delighted grin after the last of the salute. The king invited the captain to come and relax in his house. The captain acquiesced, and asked if he could first pay his respects to the queens. Liholiho led Captain Freycinet to the shelter and Rives interpreted the introductions. Each young queen shook hands with the captain. He was impressed with their height, which appeared to average over five and three-quarters feet, and especially with the beauty of one who was about 17 years old and was named Kamamalu.* They were all vivacious, and had bold and dashing eyes.

The king led the party of men into a thatched house about two fathoms long (12 feet) and not quite as wide. They all sat down

---

* Kamamalu was then about 18 years old. Jacques Arago, artist on the *Uranie*, described her as: [3:94] ". . . she is about five feet six inches high, her shoulders are broad, her bosom small, and her eyes amorous; her limbs are plump and well formed, and her hands and feet extremely delicate. She is remarkably clean in her person. On her body are some round marks caused by the burns she inflicted upon herself on the death of her father; but I observed with pleasure that not a single tooth had been extracted."

on mats. The captain in his heavy dress uniform was pleasantly surprised to find the house cool after the suffocating heat outside. Although built of different materials and in a different shape, the hut reminded him of shepherds' cabins found in French provinces. Just inside the door stood a large malo-clad Hawaiian holding a long reddish-colored spear—the captain assumed he was the king's bodyguard. Through the door he could see the nondescript soldiers roaming around; occasional tinkling of bells somehow changed their directions of movement.

The captain immediately repeated the request for provisions that he had made to High Chief Kuakini back at Kailua, especially fresh fruit, vegetables and water. Jean Rives interpreted. There was some discussion among the Hawaiians, and the captain gathered that King Liholiho did not have absolute authority. Finally the king promised that what could be provided from the island of Hawaii would be forthcoming within the next two days, and the remainder could be obtained on the nearby island of Maui.

During this conversation the captain noticed that King Liholiho kept eyeing his sword, and appeared to remark about it in Hawaiian to the chiefs. The king finally asked to see the blade. He admired it with many exclamations and asked if another like it was aboard the *Uranie*. Captain Freycinet replaced it in its sheath and presented it to the king, saying that he offered it with pleasure and a sign of friendship. King Liholiho at first hesitated, and stated that he did not wish to leave the captain unarmed. Freycinet immediately replied that he did not need arms when he was with friends, and the king accepted it "without more ado." He insisted on giving the captain the spear that his bodyguard was holding as a return gift.

Following this, the king asked if Captain Freycinet would like a little wine, and all adjourned to a nearby larger thatched structure. Two chairs were provided for the captain and first lieutenant, the Hawaiians sprawled on the mats that covered the floor. (The French captain felt that the wine was of poor quality, and was probably adulterated Madeira.)

The next order of business suggested by King Liholiho was to visit Kuhina-nui (Regent) Kaahumanu and the other dowager queens of the late Ke Alii Nui (The Great Chief, King) Kamehameha. The captain of course replied that he would be most pleased to do so.

King Liholiho led Captain Freycinet, Mr. Lamarche, Jean Rives, and Dr. Quoy (chief surgeon and naturalist of the *Uranie*) whom they met enroute, to another thatched house. The king remained outside, saying the house was kapu for him to enter. (If he had entered the house, it would ever after have his high lineage kapu, and entry would be forbidden to those of lower lineage.) The Frenchmen were introduced to the dowager queens. Captain Freycinet was impressed by Kuhina-nui Kaahumanu, but the whole amazed him. That evening, Dr. Quoy recorded his impressions:[15]

> It was a really strange spectacle, to see in a restricted apartment, eight or ten veritable mountains of flesh in human form half-naked, and the least one of whom weighed at least 400 pounds,* all lying upon their stomachs on the floor. It was not without trouble that we managed to find a spot in which we also stretched out so as to comply with the customs of the country. Servants everywhere held in their hands feather kahilis, or a lighted pipe, which was passed around from mouth to mouth, and from which each one took a few puffs; others were massaging the princesses. These female colossi, who appeared as though they existed only that they might eat and sleep, looked upon us mostly with a stupid air. Kaahumanu, whose interesting history has been set down for us by Captain Vancouver, and who was the favorite of Kamehameha, did not yet appear to have reached the decline of her age, even though since that time, twenty-five years had passed by. She was a very large woman, and as all the others, overburdened with embonpoint. At this particular moment she was not feeling well, and was complaining of general pains, she was sighing and wailing in a way as to make one believe that she was about to die, which her chubby neck and shoulders and her general air of prosperity, seemed to give the lie to. I prescribed some medicines, which Mr. Rives undertook to see that she should take.

Subjects of conversation were difficult, and Kuhina-nui Kaahumanu was not inclined to discuss the state of affairs of the Hawaiian Kingdom. Captain Freycinet paid particular attention to her, as she was such an important person. He noticed that her legs, the palm of her left hand, and her tongue were "elegantly" tattooed. When queried about the great number of burns and scars on her body, Jean Rives advised the captain that they had been inflicted by herself or by her order in mourning respect for her late regal husband.

* One suspects not quite this heavy.

The Frenchmen gratefully partook of some juicy watermelon with the dowager queens, which helped to cover the lags in the sparse conversation. Jean Rives did not eat anything, as he was required to respect the kapu which did not permit free-eating with the opposite sex. Kalanimoku, the prime minister, was expected, but did not come. The king had already become bored, and left. Captain Freycinet and his party bade their adieus and departed to visit with John Young.

Captain Freycinet took off his bicorne and wiped the sweat from his brow. He paused to catch his breath after the long walk up the narrow path to the top of a small hill behind the village of Kawaihae. He looked with pleasure at the stone house in front of him that appeared well-ventilated and sanitary. The only passable house at Kawaihae! He turned around breathing deeply on this very hot day—what a delightful view! His beautiful ship in the bay below, the high island of Maui and the low dry-appearing island of Kahoolawe across the deep blue sea to the northwest, to his left the arid coastline that chased in-and-out to distant Kailua below Mount Hualalai, to his rear the two cool-appearing high mountains of Mauna Loa and Mauna Kea. Despite the beautiful clouds and sea Kawaihae was *still* a desolate location—nothing but black lava rocks and scrub growth pushing their way up above the tan-colored dry grass.

Jean Rives went into the house to announce their arrival. John Young. What an interesting life he must have lived! He had been forcibly restrained from returning to his ship way back in '90, had assisted Kamehameha to become king of this island and of all the islands, and had become his chief advisor. The old Englishman was way up in years now, he had heard that he must be in his seventies.

Rives beckoned from the doorway and the captain entered, immediately appreciating the coolness of the whitewashed interior. He was introduced to a frail white-haired old man who appeared not well, and who was sitting at the foot of a bed. Captain Freycinet dismissed Rives with a wave of his hand as, being a civilized Frenchman, he could speak English well. The remainder of the captain's party remained outside. The captain sat down in a nearby hide chair that looked Spanish and was surprisingly comfortable.

John Young was soon at ease with the French navy captain whose station in life was so much higher than his previous position as boatswain on a trading vessel (time, authority, and contact with many ship's captains had closed the great gap). He slowly briefed

Captain Freycinet on the events following King Kamehameha's death, and then talked about his apprehensions for the future.

"Captain, I served Liholiho's father for almost thirty years. He was a good man, a great man, and was certainly good to me. Why, he even arranged that I marry his younger brother's daughter! Kamehameha was mostly a savage man, yet I loved and respected him, and gave him my all. I *am* very concerned for his son, poor lad."

"I fear for the future . . . The lad even called a council here at Kawaihae just before you arrived and agreed to allow the island governors to gather and sell the sandalwood found on their islands, less a much-too-small percentage to Kalanimoku, the chief treasurer. This to include sandalwood on the king's lands. The young king has been pressured into giving up other of his father's perogatives and seems desperately trying to consolidate his authority by this line of politics. That is why so many of the chiefs are here. The whole kingdom is in danger of going backwards and again becoming a maze of feudal petty holdings fighting among themselves. I'm *afraid* that control over *all* the islands *will* be lost."

"I'm sure that High Chief Kekuaokalani of this district is plotting some mischief. I've heard that he is gathering and training men for conflict. He's a bad one, that Kekuaokalani, and no friend of white men—he wants to get rid of us all! But that cannot be, for the world is growing smaller, and there are more and more traders and visitors stopping here—such as you are doing."

"You can help, Captain Freycinet," said John Young, and he sat straighter and the dimness seemed to leave his eyes, "show him a friendly interest, create a diversion in his favor, and publically offer your protection."

"It is my fervent hope that peace among these people will be maintained—not for myself, for my tenure is almost at a close—but for the sake of the son of my old departed benefactor. The son should have the heritage his father established for him. "As for myself henceforth useless in the world, I would look upon approaching death without regrets, if one may die without regret far from one's own homeland."[15]

John Young stopped, and tears began to flow down his tired lined face. Captain Freycinet impulsively leaned forward and sympathetically patted the old man's hand. There was silence, until John Young pulled himself together again and continued.

"My own people, the British, have abandoned us. Captain Vancouver, who did so much to bring civilization to these islands, Lieutenant Broughton too—what happened to the reports they took back? Three years before Kamehameha died he received a letter dated *four years previous* from the Earl of Liverpool for King George III promising to promote the welfare of the islands! A small ship was supposed to have been built for Kamehameha at Port Jackson (*New South Wales, Australia*), but nothing has ever been seen or heard of it!"

"The American traders here are becoming more and more powerful and influential—and you know how traders are and what their motives are! Oh Captain Freycinet, give this young king and these islands with such a promising future your protection . . . your civilized protection!"

John Young stopped, and slumped wearily, spent by his emotion. The captain was moved, again sympathetically patted John Young's gnarled old hand, and stood up saying that he would do what he could do. John Young nodded slowly with a weak smile, and softly said, "Adieu."

The captain left . . . thoughtfully.

Captain Freycinet stopped again at the thatched house of the dowager queens to see if High Chief (prime minister) Kalanimoku had arrived. He had . . . was stretched out on his stomach like the huge dowager queens, and all were fast asleep! Jean Rives gently wakened the prime minister with some apprehension. Kalanimoku could speak passable elementary English, and the Captain invited him to dine aboard the *Uranie*. This was accepted with pleasure, and the prime minister asked the captain to meet him in front of his house at the beach. Captain Freycinet then set off to pay his final respects of the day ashore to King Liholiho.

When the captain arrived at the beach he was met by High Chief Kalanimoku, who had not bothered to change his attire—a malo (loin cloth) and a European shirt "which was not even particularly clean." He asked if his favorite wife, Likelike (daughter of High Chief Kaikioewa), could accompany him. The captain agreed, and they went in the gig to the anchored corvette.

Dinner that late afternoon was interesting. The captain, his wife Rose (who had been smuggled aboard just before the ship left France), High Chief Kalanimoku and Mr. Lamarche dined together. High Chief Kalanimoku would not allow his wife Likelike to dine with them, saying she was kapued to eat with the opposite Hawaiian sex. She remained on deck, and the captain sent her some preserves, which she ate with enjoyment.

Kalanimoku was intrigued with Rose Freycinet, one of the first European women he had ever seen (and she wore so many clothes!). Rose, on her part, was amazed at Likelike when she came to eat after her husband had left the table. Likelike's attire was extremely loose and scanty! Likelike made up for lost time by drinking several full glasses of brandy.

High Chief Kalanimoku strolled on the afterdeck with Mr. Lamarche, watching the sun go down, and was introduced to the greyhaired 57 year old Abbé Florentin-Louis de Quélen de la Villeglée. Kalanimoku inquired what function Abbé de Quélen had on board.

When told that he was the ship's priest, Kalanimoku relayed through Mr. Lamarche that he had long wanted to become a christian. He added that his mother, on her death-bed, had become a christian by having some water sprinkled on her head by a foreigner.[6:158] The wise Abbé was not at all sure that he believed Kalanimoku—but could see the advantage of this important person becoming a christian, especially a Catholic. And after all, a soul saved was a soul saved. Ad majorem Dei gloriam. After conferring with Captain Freycinet, who agreed, the baptism was set for the following afternoon.

The evening came to a close with the setting off of some rockets from the ship. The Hawaiians at Kawaihae exclaimed with delight, "Maikai! Maikai! (Good! Good!).

The following day (August 13, 1819) Captain Freycinet began to set into motion the request that John Young had made to him. He conferred with King Liholiho (Queen Kamamalu was with him) who agreed, and asked that the captain address the council on the subject. Captain Freycinet concurred, and the king sent messengers announcing the council. The captain then discussed his intention separately with High Chief Kalanimoku, Kuhina-nui Kaahumanu, and with John Young. They each heartily approved.

The council meeting was held under a shelter which extended from one of the thatched houses. King Liholiho, clad in a malo (loin cloth) and kihei (mantle), stood just outside, with the explanation that kapu was involved. High Chief Kekuaokalani, Liholiho's cousin, did not attend. No one rose or payed any particular respect to Kuhina-nui Kaahumanu when she arrived, dressed in a flowing silk garment the color of a pigeon's throat. Jean Rives interpreted Captain Freycinet's address.

> We all know, and my country knows, of the great
> friendship of the British for you, for your people, and for
> your islands. The late respected King Kamehameha sought

and obtained the protection of the British government and entered into this agreement with Captain George Vancouver of the British Navy.

My country is a close friend and ally of the British. Both countries think alike in concern for your prosperity and well-being. As the commanding officer of a French man-of-war, I take great pleasure in advising you that I, representing the great nation of France, have a great interest in your ruler, King Liholiho, who was designated ruler by his late father, King Kamehameha. I wish his reign well, and hope there will be peace and good order in the Hawaiian Kingdom.

I would like to advise you that, should disorder occur, the many merchant and trading ships will no longer stop to visit with you and buy your sandalwood. They will no longer bring the many fine things that you obtain by trading, and which you enjoy. British and French warships, and other men-of-war of friendly civilized nations, will vigorously act in behalf of, and in support of, King Liholiho against any and all who fail to recognize and respect his authority.

Rally around your king! He has the prosperity and well-being of you and your people at heart. Happiness can be only obtained when there is peace, when there is commerce, and when there is progress, using the new things that make life more interesting and better for your people.

The assembled chiefs had not appeared to pay very close attention to what he was saying, but Captain Freycinet felt that he had created the impression that he intended. He hoped that Jean Rives had properly translated his words, word for word! He was somewhat surprised and amazed when Kuhina-nui Kaahumanu raised her head and spoke. Jean Rives translated.

This great interest in our king and our affairs arouses in me apprehension that the sly rumors I have heard, and are being spread about to others, are true. Have you demanded that our islands and people come under the control of your contry, France? Has such been agreed upon between you and Liholiho? If so, our longtime friend and protector, Great Britain, would not only be annoyed, but would question our good faith. For we are first *their* friend.

Captain Freycinet became very agitated, and looked hard at Kuhina-nui Kaahumanu. He protested so fast that Jean Rives had difficulty in keeping up with the translation.

> I object most strenuously to this dastardly insinuation! It is not true! There is not one bit of truth in these crazy rumors you say you have heard. Even if King Liholiho had wished, of his own initiative, to enter into a preferential agreement with my country, and place your islands and people under France's protection, I neither could nor would wish to lend myself to such a transaction.[15]

King Liholiho had been listening and watching intently. He spoke, "I am sure that there is no question of Captain Freycinet's intentions. He speaks the truth. I have not entered into any agreement with him. He has taken a sincere interest in our welfare . . . now it is time to consider his welfare."

There was discussion concerning the whereabouts and timing of provisions for the *Uranie*. The king stated that he would present the captain with twenty pigs and advised that other pigs could be obtained, six piastres for large ones and two piastres for small ones. He regretted that Captain Freycinet would be obliged to pay for the provisions, but they belonged to others than himself. High Chief Keeaumoku, governor of the island of Maui, would accompany the captain there, and assure that the *Uranie*'s needs would be well satisfied.

As the council meeting broke up, King Liholiho asked the still agitated captain if he could bring some of his court to witness the ceremony of High Chief Kalanimoku becoming a christian late that afternoon. (The news of High Chief Kalanimoku's intention had spread like wild fire.) The captain stated that he would be most pleased, and would send his boat for the king prior to the appointed time.

As the captain returned to the shore he thought and thought, but could not figure out the rationale of the reverse twist Kuhina-nui Kaahumanu had placed on his remarks. He wondered, were my words translated correctly? He would never know! Captain Freycinet shrugged, and muttered, "Advienne que pourra! (Come what may!)."

"The party has just left the shore, Sir," the officer of the watch reported to Captain Freycinet. The captain raised his glass and saw his gig starting the short pull to the *Uranie*. The passengers were King Liholiho, his favorite Queen Kamamalu, Kuhina-nui Kaahumanu, and the young Prince Kauikeaouli (Liholiho's younger brother). The gig was followed by two double-canoes and five single outrigger canoes filled with chiefs and chiefesses and their retainers. More observors than he had expected! He quickly glanced around the afterdeck to see that his carefully considered staging had been carried out.

The cloth-covered altar was to the port side of the mizzen mast. The Virgin was in the center, and flanked by two candles in their tall and heavy metal candleholders. Behind the altar was hung a large Hawaiian flag that the sailmaker had fabricated overnight. Two sails had been tautly rigged above this flag for an awning. He could see the gently moving Tricolor hung from the gaff through the opening where the two sails had been lashed together. On the deck in front of the altar was a huge American flag. Subtly symbolic for European influence, he hoped! Too bad the hard-working sailmaker had erred when he made it, also last night—the rumored twenty stars and thirteen stripes instead of the official fifteen stars and fifteen stripes. They wouldn't know the difference anyway!

Two chairs had been placed on the flag near the altar for the king's queen and the regent. He wasn't going to be party to this strange Hawaiian custom of subordinating women—especially one as good-looking as Kamamalu! He saw his wife Rose waving her handkerchief from their cabin aft of the mizzen mast, and waved back. Poor girl, she was weak today, and would watch from there. She had been bled from the foot last night by Dr. Quoy to help her constant headaches.

The captain glanced around the deck. It had been holystoned to white perfection. Good. The cannon were clean and freshly blackened and ready for the planned salute; the gun crews were standing easy at their stations. The remainder of the 100 man crew were mustered forward in their best appearing clothes. His small Marine contingent came marching aft towards the starboard entry in cadence to the rat-tat-tat of the drummer. His critical eye approved of their dress uniform appearance: blue coatees with red collars and Marine epaulettes, white shoulder sashes from which hung their short swords, white pantaloons, and white-gaitered black boots. Their tall black shakos had short stiff plumes in front, the highly polished bayonets fixed to the held muskets gleamed high above in the late afternoon sun. His officers in their dress uniforms were assembled near him. The Abbé in his vestments and High

Chief Kalanimoku (who had been with the Abbé for the past two hours) were just moving to their positions in front of the altar. All was ready. Good.

All were at attention, the officers with their bicornes in their hands, and the snare drum was snarling a military salute by the Marines at rigid Present Arms, when King Liholiho led his court aboard. He wore a blue Hussar short jacket with gold braid and the epaulettes of a colonel, green pantaloons, and a black straw hat.[3:109] When his party was finally assembled aboard, immediately behind him stood a retainer who carried his sword (the one that Captain Freycinet had given him), another carried a fan, others carried a spittoon and a pipe which was kept lighted all the time, and two bodyguards with huge blunderbusses.

King Liholiho insisted on walking forward to closely observe the eleven gun salute. When it was over, the captain escorted Queen Kamamalu and Kuhina-nui Kaahumanu to the two chairs, and was not aware of the raised eyebrows of the king and the chiefs. The king stood just behind. The remainder of the visitors, in Hawaiian attire or European attire or a mixture of both, stood and sat around in a semicircle.

The dignified Abbé de Quélen began the baptism ceremony. He deliberately kept it simple, and impressively slow. Captain Freycinet acted as godfather, M. Gabert, the captain's secretary, acted as godmother. During the ceremony the king began to smoke his pipe, and was not aware of the raised eyebrows of the Frenchmen. The Hawaiians murmured as the holy water was sprinkled on Kalanimoku's head. High Chief Kalanimoku appeared strongly moved throughout the entire short ceremony, and thanked Captain Freycinet profusely at having been baptised with the captain's first name, Louis.[6:158]

Following this, a collation was served to the king and his chiefs, the chiefesses were served separately. The latter, especially the queens, were "astonished at the brilliant costume of the priest, and at the beauty of the image of the Virgin on the alter, requesting that they might be permitted to kiss it."[3:110]

Drinks were served upon the mounting request of the Hawaiians and all were soon merry. The visitors inspected the entire ship. The chiefesses especially appreciated the "convenient little beds."[3:111] The Hawaiians left at dusk. Captain Freycinet observed that in two hours they consumed enough drink to have provided for a ten-man mess for three months! Upon their departure another salute of eleven guns was fired—the merry

Hawaiians delighted in the sudden red flashes and loud booms.

The winds were fickle, and it was not until just before dawn on the 15th that the *Uranie* got under weigh for the island of Maui.

NOTE: High Chief Kalanimoku's younger brother, Boki, was also baptised when the *Uranie* later visited Honolulu, island of Oahu. [6:169]

48

VII

kaahumanu and hewahewa

Liholiho, Kuhina-nui Kaahumanu and Kahuna-nui Hewahewa were talking together under the shade of a coconut palm near
the beach at Kawaihae. They lay prone on their stomachs with their
chins resting on their hands. They closely faced each other, like
some strange three-pointed star. Several attendants with wands
tipped with white kapa (bark cloth) were just out of ear-shot; their
insignia warned the people that this location was temporarily kapu.
There was a light tradewind fluttering the coconut palm fronds, the
only other sound aside from the constant surf was that of some
distant children playing at the water's edge on the beach.

Kaahumanu was speaking—"Liholiho, my keiki hanai (foster
son), you know how much I love you. You know how much I loved
your father. And you know how much I want your father's Rule
over all of the islands to continue. We must work together towards
this end. I have asked you and Hewahewa to meet me here so we
can express our manao (feelings) freely and frankly. We must come
to grips with the weakness of our kapu system . . ."

"Liholiho, you are concerned as our ruler. Your kapu moe
(prostrating kapu), which you inherited from your mother, the
Sacred Queen Mother Keopuolani, combined with your position
makes you equal to the Gods. Only you have the power to release
the kapu of a God."

"Hewahewa, you are the head priest of the Holoae Order
which reveres the Kunuiakea (Gods of Ku, one of the major
Hawaiian deities), and thus are vitally concerned in any matter
which is connected with religious practices. The Order of Holoae is
by far the most important of the various religious orders, and is
preferred by the alii. You are the most powerful of the religious
leaders."

"Let us be logical. Liholiho, let me ask you some questions—
and do not answer them—just reflect upon the questions and take a
careful look at your reactions."

"Captain Freycinet, who was just here, is a pukaua (war

49

leader) of his country, larger than ours so they tell me, and rules the complexity of his warship. Do his men prostrate themselves before him as our people are required to do to you? No . . . and he is a great captain with many men and guns."

"If the many other peoples in far off lands do not prostrate themselves to those of highest lineage, why should it be required here? And it was just a short while ago that I heard that you had absolved a small boy who violated your prostrating kapu . . . why?"

"Does Captain Freycinet go about usually at night, such as you usually do? No. If someone casts their shadow upon you, our lore says that the culprit must be offered to the Kunuiakea (Gods of Ku) by being burned to death for defiling your kapu. We all know that you dislike this, and this is the reason you are seen in daylight so seldom. Is Captain Freycinet, and other captains of ships like him, so much more, or less, a ruler than you are?"

"Your father pronounced the mamalahoa (law of the splintered paddle) many years ago—Let the aged men and women and little children lie down in security in the road. How can they lie down in safety if they must be afraid of breaking your kapu or the Gods' kapus?"

"Captain Freycinet had his woman with him. They ate together. There was no harm . . . and it is foreign normal custom to eat with their women. Our traditional way of separated eating between the sexes is stated to avoid harm. Why, and for what harm of lore? How can eating with women weaken the mana (spiritual force) of men? Was it not perhaps just caprice that started this kapu?"

"Look at that fisherman's home," Kaahumanu pointed to three very small adjacent thatched houses which were nearby. "That man and his woman must eat separately. Why should this be? Is this not burdensome, from a purely logical point of view? How can love flourish and be sustained when man and his woman must be arbitrarily separated like this?"

"We insist that those foreigners who come here and work for us observe our most significant kapus. Not all, just the more important ones that are religious in nature. And the lowest of foreigner sailors who come here to visit, they eat with our women. We know this, and do not punish them. Neither did your father. I cannot eat with the alii! Why should these visiting common people be permitted to do what your mother and I may not do?"

"All three of us know, or have heard, of the increasing numbers of our people who have secretly violated the various kapus . . . and still live. I have done it myself . . . just to test . . . and came

50

to no harm. The veneration of our Gods and their kapus is most strict—and yet Hewahewa had not caused his ilamukus (constables, executioners) to vigorously enforce them. Why? Did not this relaxation commence after the mai okuu (cholera or bacillary dysentary epidemic of 1804) when there remained but one of every two Hawaiians? The people are precious. When your father died he did not want any human sacrifices to honor him. This was a long-standing custom. Why? Are these occurrences not inter-related?"

"Do we need these kapus to maintain our alii caste system? Are we afraid of our people? Just what were we afraid of back in traditional times which caused these restrictions to be imposed? Or was it just a sneer, or a stamping of the foot upon the makaainana (commoners)?"

"The times have changed so very much. We have a different way of life now, due to these many strangers who come here. They bring many marvelous things and want such quantities of our sandalwood and foods. *They* don't observe the kapus, and come to no harm. *They* have better things than we do, and their way of life is completely different. Do our kapus still appear logical . . . today?"

"I could go on and on," Kaahumanu expostulated somewhat wearily, "but I won't. These things are self-evident of prior practices that do not make sense today. Some kapus are good—don't misunderstand me—for example, those that conserve our different kinds of fish when they get scarce. But the foreigners have rules or what they call laws instead of kapus, and violations do not always end up with death. The same end is achieved. Why could we not do the same?"

"I will not discuss those things directly concerning our religion, that is for Hewahewa to say. I will ask, however, were many of the Gods' kapus not established for arbitrary reasons? How about the one which requires complete silence for certain ceremonies? It is said that this intends to appease the angry Gods. Why should the Gods be always considered angry? Why should it be necessary to muzzle dogs and pigs and shut up chickens? Can we not respect and venerate without going to such an extreme?"

"Liholiho, we cannot force our people to continue practices that they know other people with superior things do not do. This is not pure and true. Our people do not feel they should continue to observe the kapus . . . unless we force them to. The times are very different today. If you are to rule, you must apply logic, and do away with those things that are no longer meaningful."

"Oh Liholiho, I weep for you, for I can see the difficulties you have—of looking at this from the viewpoint you have been taught since childhood—but you *must* look with a fresh approach. Truth *must* be pure. I beg of you, look at us as we are *today!*"

Liholiho had listened, listened intently, for the exploration of logic was one of his favorite pastimes. Yes, Kaahumanu made good points . . . and yet . . . the generations of traditional lore that he had been thoroughly taught and believed in . . . and yet . . . Liholiho knew that the inviolable kapus were being violated secretly, and with no apparent harm. There used to be psychic harm, but this had strangely decreased. Two extremely opposed viewpoints. He sighed, and his brow furrowed with deep thought.

Kaahumanu impulsively reached over and gently touched Liholiho on the cheek. "Aloha," she said softly. Kaahumanu rolled over and grunted as she slowly stood up. "Aloha," she repeated with deep feeling, and then walked away with the fluid motion of a very large woman who was also an accomplished surfer.

There was a long silence. Liholiho and Hewahewa did not look at each other.

After a while Liholiho sighed, and said, "Hm . . ."

About half a minute later Hewahewa also said, "Hm . . ."

Liholiho asked almost absently, "What do you think of the kapus?"[25:220f]

Hewahewa answered after a brief silence, "What do *you* think of the kapus?"[25:220f]

There was another long pause, and Liholiho finally almost muttered, "We have so *many* Gods. A God for everything . . . and we gain our spiritual strength for the present and the future from their total embrace. All things are inter-related, psychically and physically. We venerate the sacred carved figures which represent our many deities from custom and for earthly needs. But the spiritual peace of mind . . ."

"We of the alii know of the Greatest God, Oi-e (Most Excellent, Supreme), which brings order to all—only we know of this—the makaainana (commoners) are denied this most precious and sacred spiritual knowledge. Do you suppose Oi-e is the same God as the one God of the foreigners?"

Hewahewa thought for a long time before he replied, "Perhaps . . . perhaps. I just don't know. And I have thought much about this and discussed this numerous times with my elder kahunas. I just *don't* know if the two are the same. They very well *could* be. My thought has always been, "Akahi walena Akua-nui iloko o ka-lani (there is only one Great God dwelling in the heavens)."[25:220f]

Liholiho carefully considered this for a significant time, and then commented, "The kapus provide our social order, provide our sanctity order, and provide a basis of keeping the alii in their superior place above the makaainana. How things have changed since the foreigners first came when my Father was young! *They* don't observe the kapus. The kapus have been our way of life for generations . . . *maybe* there is more than *one* way of life acceptable to Oi-e."

Hewahewa grunted acknowledgement that he had heard, and darted a quick glance at Liholiho.

Liholiho went on, "You tell me that our people are not responding to our religious observances as they should, and used to." Hewahewa grunted another acknowledgement that he had heard.

Liholiho reflected another long interval and then repeated his earlier question slowly, "What do you think of the kapus?"[25:220f]

Hewahewa replied as before, "What do *you* think of the kapus?"[25:220f]

Liholiho closed his eyes and asked even more softly, "Do you think it well to break them?"[25:220f]

Hewahewa gazed blankly at the distance. After a lengthy pause full of meaning he slowly replied, "That lies with you."[25:220f]

"You are the instrument of the mana (spiritual force) of the Gods."

Liholiho suddenly rolled over onto his back, closed his eyes, and clasped his head—the part of his body which had most intimate rapport with the source of all mana.

"It is as you say," he muttered wearily, "It is as you say . . ."[25:220f]

Hewahewa quietly withdrew, and left Liholiho with his tortured thoughts.

VIII

kohala (whale)

Liholiho had come down the coast from Kawaihae to Kealakekua Bay to visit with the two American moku-o-kohalas (whaleships) which had just anchored there the day before. Liholiho remembered only one other ship of this kind which had visited for provisions, water, firewood (and relaxation)—the English *Duke of Portland*, back when he was 14 years old (1810). His Father had sent an ahuula (feather cloak) and a letter to King George III with Captain Spence. Liholiho was curious to see these whaleships, for he was interested in all sorts of new and different things.

As Liholiho's favorite 40 foot double-canoe entered Kealakekua Bay, Kapihe the hookelewaa (canoe steersman), ordered the schooner-rigged sails down and the twenty paddlers began urging the craft towards the anchored ships. When the sails were furled, Liholiho went to the front end of the five foot wide pola (platform between the two joined hulls) and sat down cross-legged. These two ships certainly weren't built for speed, being so bluff in shape. From what he had learned about ships he presumed that they were very seaworthy, but poor sailors.

Each ship had three masts: the fore and main masts were square-rigged, the aft or mizzenmast was fore-and-aft rigged. Each had a long narrow huelopoki (whaleboat; literally, "tail boat") slung on heavy wooden davits on either side aft of the mainmast. Amidship he could see the brick oven and try-pot he remembered from the earlier whaler he had seen. He motioned for Kapihe to come alongside one of the ships which apparently had visitors, as there were a number of canoes and a western small boat alongside.

As the double-canoe came closer, a Hawaiian happened to look over the bulwark—"Kapu moe! (Prostrate yourself!) . . . Ke Alii Nui! (The Great Chief, King!)" he shouted, and his head disappeared quickly from view. There was a patter of many feet running, and splashes, as the Hawaiians on board hurriedly jumped into the bay in all directions. (They dare not be above Liholiho's head.) The last over were about a dozen women who apparently

55

had been below. Liholiho grinned when he saw that several had not even bothered to take the time to wrap their pa'us (skirts) around themselves.

Two foreigners wearing small, black, peaked captain hats leaned over the quarterdeck bulwark. One waved and shouted, "Hello! Come aboard." Kapihe skillfully directed the double-canoe alongside. At his command the rapidly moving double-canoe was stopped abruptly, just at the right location, by the paddlers thrusting their large oval-bladed paddles straight down and holding them that way with all their considerable strength. It was a picked crew, thought Liholiho with pride. He motioned Jean Rives up the ladder ahead of him.

There were introductions, with Jean Rives assisting when Liholiho's understanding of English fell short. Liholiho was aboard the whaleship *Balena* of New Bedford, Captain Edmund Gardner. The other captain was Elisha Folger, who was visiting from his adjoining ship, the Nantucket registry whaleship *Equator*.[43]

"How long have you been at sea?" asked Liholiho. Captain Gardner, who was tall and lean and had piercing blue eyes, replied, "Well, let's see—it's September 18th, 1819.[20] We left New England in the autumn of '17 so as to round Cape Horn in the Antartic summer, just about two years ago. Two years of slow cruising after whales. Speed and time mean little, it's a full hold of oil that counts."

Liholiho did not comprehend too much of this, and Jean Rives, smiling his long yellowish teeth at everyone, tried to explain in Hawaiian. Liholiho kept his face smooth—he would find out all about this later.

"You catch the kohala (whale)?" Liholiho inquired, and both captains nodded. Liholiho continued, "We see them around here, usually about this time of the year. Sometimes one dies and comes ashore—we especially prize their huge teeth." Both captains looked very interested when they heard this, and Captain Gardner exclaimed, "Elisha, my friend, sounds like sperm whales. If we sight one while the king is aboard, he is mine!"

Captain Elisha Folger nodded and laughed, and said, "You're a hard man, Edmund Gardner, but I'm gamming (visiting) on your ship—so be it." Both captains briefly looked out to sea with narrowed eyes before again paying attention to the royal visitor.

"Where do you hunt the kohala (whale)?" asked the interested Liholiho. Captain Gardner replied, "Let me show you," and squatted down by a spread-out chart that he and Captain Folger had apparently been studying. "You're familiar with this chart?" he asked, and Liholiho nodded (he had had many discussions with others and was beginning to comprehend what a chart depicted).

"Here we are in the middle of the Pacific Ocean, here is the west coast of South America, here are the South Sea islands, here are Australia and New Zealand, and north of them way up here are Japan and China." Captain Gardner pointed out the various locations with a long finger. Liholiho nodded again, and also squatted down by the chart. So did the short, thickset, bearded Captain Folger.

"The first whaling in the Pacific was for right whales at Australia and New Zealand," Captain Gardner began, and was interrupted by Nantucketer Captain Folger, "An English whaler in 1789, *but* the captain and first mate were from *Nantucket!*" Captain Gardner grinned and continued, "The first American whalers rounded Cape Horn in 1791 and found lots of sperm whales off the coast of Chile and further north. This is called the 'on-shore ground'." Captain Folger interrupted again, "*Six* were from Nantucket and only *one* from New Bedford!"

Captain Gardner grinned widely, and pushed Captain Folger so that he fell back onto his stern—"That for you Nantucketers! We'll beat you yet!" Both captains grimaced at each other while Jean Rives sputtered fast Hawaiian trying to explain to Liholiho. Liholiho nodded, and also grinned; he was not quite sure he knew what was amusing.

Captain Gardner continued, "There must be some 60 whaleships out now. We're just picking up again after the heavy toll we lost during the War of 1812. Just this last year my cousin, Captain George Gardner . . ." (Captain Folger interjected, "From *Nantucket!*" and was mock-threatened by the long muscular arm of Captain Gardner) ". . . set out west from Valparaiso and found considerable sperm whales about 1,400 nautical miles out." Captain Folger nodded, and added, "Spect that will be called the 'off-shore ground'."

"Sperm whales are also found among the South Sea islands— we call this 'country whaling'," Captain Gardner went on, "In fact there are abundant sperm whales everywhere in the Pacific, although not at the higher latitudes, north and south—and they are the best kind of whale which brings the best price for their oil, and have spermaceti."

"What is spermaceti and . . ." Liholiho began another question, but was interrupted by an excited shout from a seaman aloft on the foremast who was tarring some rigging:

"BLOWS, THAR SHE BLOWS!"

Kohala (Whale)

Both captains sprang to their feet, and Captain Gardner roared, "Where away?!" All looked in the direction of the pointing seaman. There, just short of the horizon and framed by the bay entrance, was a single small vertical white puff.

"Kohala! (Whale!)" exclaimed Liholiho. "Thar she breachs!" shouted the seaman aloft, and the men on the quarterdeck could see a small black object come out of the water. "Thar she white-waters!" the seaman shouted again, as the whale fell back into the sea, making a white splash which was easily discernible.

"I'll take this one! Clear away and lower the starboard boat!" shouted Captain Gardner to the men who were pouring up from the fo'castle to join those who had stopped working on the deck to stare rigidly at the horizon. "Remember, Elisha, you agreed that this whale is mine—the king brought me luck!"

Captain Folger, who had started shouting for his boat's crew to return him to the *Equator*, stopped and looked rueful—"So I did, so I did," he exclaimed sorrowfully, "Who would have thought of it! New Bedford luck!" Captain Gardner threw back his head and gave an excited wild laugh as he ran to the starboard whaleboat. The two line-tubs were hurriedly placed into the whaleboat and uncovered, the boat-plug tapped home, the water keg checked, and the completeness of the whaleboat's contents quickly verified with practiced competence.

Captain Gardner dropped to the stern of the long, slim, double-ended whaleboat as it was being lowered into the water. He grabbed the 22 foot long steering oar and placed it in the crotch. The harponeer, midship-oarsman, and after-oarsman placed their stout oak 16-18 foot oars between the thole pins; the bow-oarsman and tub-oarsman pushed the whaleboat away from the side of the ship with their 17 foot oars. When clear, they also placed their oars between their thole pins and all began to row in unison, with the cadence being set by the captain. He was standing in the stern, balancing with his long legs as far apart as he could, and leaning on the end of his long steering oar.

"Pull . . . pull . . . put your backs into it . . . it looks like a big bull . . . a pretty addition to your lay (share) . . . pull . . . pull . . . pull!" he inspiringly shouted, as he waved with an eager wolfish grin at Liholiho and Captain Folger, "Pull! . . . pull! . . . pull!"

Liholiho was also excited, and exclaimed to Captain Folger, "Let us go . . ." and in the next breath shouted a torrent of Hawaiian to Kapihe. Liholiho and Captain Folger dropped hurriedly into the double-canoe, whose crew were also excited. Jean Rives climbed down slowly, despite the gibes from the impatient Hawaiians. Liholiho and Captain Folger stood on either

58

side of the foremast, Jean Rives crouched behind Liholiho and clung to the mast with both arms.

The whaleboat's single-banked oars swirled the water and the bow-wave grew. The whaleboat was already far ahead, almost at the entrance of the calm bay, when the double-canoe left the side of the whaleship. "Speedy," grunted Liholiho to Captain Folger. The captain replied with pride, "That's what she was built to be. She's 28 feet long and six feet wide at the widest point, but she has only half-inch cedar planking clinkerbuilt. She's a beauty and will really fly through the water."

Kapihe exhorted the paddlers to their best efforts. Their paddles were heavy, and required much strength. The handles were three feet long, their oval blades 18 inches long and 12 inches wide. One hand grasped the extreme upper end, the other near the blade. Each paddler made: "regular, rapid and effective strokes, all on one side for a while, then, changing at a signal in exact time, all on the other. Each raising his head erect, and lifting one hand high to throw the paddle forward beside the canoe . . . dipping their paddles, and bowing simultaneously and earnestly, swept their paddles back with naked muscular arms and making the brine boil, and giving great speed to their novel and serviceable sea-craft."[7:83]

When clear of the bay, the whaleship hoisted her gaff sail. The mast was set into a hole in the second thwart. The simple rigging was such that it could be raised or lowered with utmost speed. The whaleboat was soon making about eight knots under the brisk tradewind. The rowers ceased rowing. Kapihe ordered the double-canoe's schooner-rigged sails set, and the double-canoe kept pace behind the pale-blue painted whaleboat.

They could see the whale at a distance ahead. He was spouting—the slightly forward curving spout was about 12 feet high and lasted for about three seconds. His huge, jet-black bulk was surging forward, and was slightly awash at times. The powerful sculling horizontal tail propelled the great mass of the whale forward at about four knots.

"I see only one," Captain Folger said, "He's a lone bull, and should be mean. He's a *big* one, almost three times longer than the whaleboat—probably over 80 feet—that's a lot of oil to stow down if Edmund gets him." Captain Folger was counting the number of times the whale slowly spouted, "Edmund had better hurry, for he'll spout about once for every foot of length or minute he was down, and then he'll go down again to feed.[4:76] Then we'll have to wait until he comes up again, and goodness knows how close that will be."

Liholiho asked, "Sometimes you say 'she' and sometimes 'he'.

I do not understand." Captain Folger twinkled, "Well, 'she' is like a ship, and 'he' means male or bull. My eyesight isn't that good to really tell! Usually lone whales are male." Jean Rives attempted to explain in Hawaiian—Liholiho just shrugged, another strange thing.

The whale could now be plainly seen. From time-to-time the ponderous surging whale would come awash and spout. Excitement rose in Liholiho, and he wished that he was in the whaleboat. So did each of the crew of the double-canoe.

"Look," Captain Folger said quietly, "Edmund's lowering his sail and mast, the men are beginning to row using thole mats to muffle the sounds of their oars. Keep quiet, for a whale has good hearing." Liholiho motioned to Kapihe; the double-canoe sails came down. The crew began to paddle quietly, each man looking eagerly ahead to see what was going on.

A few minutes later Captain Folger almost whispered, "Ah see . . . they're going on the whale . . . perfect position . . . they're approaching from the rear and from the right side . . . now, stand up! . . . look . . . the harponeer has peaked his oar and is up in the bow! That Narragansett Indian is a wonder . . . he's braced and has his iron . . . Lay the boat on, and . . . *strike!*"

Captain Folger was almost beside himself with the excitement of the perilous hunt. Both he and Liholiho watched eagerly. The whaleboat was suddenly steered by Captain Gardner so that it actually bumped onto the whale behind the right fluke.

"There's the first harpoon! And the second one!" Captain Folger almost screamed, "*Well stuck!* Buried to the hitches! Now, *stern all!*"

The whaleboat backed away from the huge bulk of the whale, who was startled into furious commotion. His flukes churned the water. His head raised and his long, narrow jaw opened wide. He rolled from side to side, smacking the sea with his tremendous flukes. He stood on his head and flailed his enormous deep-notched tail from side to side. There was so much whitewater that Liholiho was fearful for the whaleboat. He was delighted to see it still backing away from the danger.

"He's fighting at both ends!" Captain Folger bellowed. The captain was almost jumping up and down with excitement, "He's a mean one!"

The whale suddenly disappeared, and Liholiho could see considerable activity in the whaleboat. Captain Folger explained, much too rapidly, that the oars were being peaked so as to clear any rough water and yet be readily available; the angle of the oar looms helped guide the whaleline down the center of the whaleboat. The three-quarter inch hemp line, which was stowed in Flemish coils in the line-tubs, was singing and smoking out forward across the bow; and how dangerous it was. Water was being thrown on the rapidly moving line where it passed over wood to prevent burning by friction. The men were on the outboard sides of the whaleboat to avoid contact with the fast moving line. A nasty rope burn would be the least that might occur if they came into contact with the line . . .

"They're fast!" shouted Captain Folger.

Suddenly the whaleboat appeared quiet for a few moments. The line was slack in the water. The harponeer rapidly scrambled aft and took the steering oar from the captain (the first thing he checked was to be sure that the emergency knife was in its proper place so he could cut the line if the whaleboat's safety absolutely depended upon it). The captain quickly moved forward to the bow (the first thing he checked was to be sure that the emergency axe was in its proper place). The end of the slack line in the whaleboat was snubbed around the small logger-head by the harponeer, now boatsteerer. The captain re-guided the line through the bow-chock.

The line in front of the whaleboat slowly rose glistening wet, and the whaleboat's bow sank down in the water as the whaleboat began to be towed by the whale. Faster and faster. Faster yet. "A Nantucket sleigh ride!" chortled Captain Folger, as they could see the whale, far ahead, plunging through the sea with his enormous square head coming completely out of the water at times.

Kapihe urged his paddlers to follow the whaleboat, but they were soon far behind. Captain Folger chuckled, "Might as well save their backs—set your sails, you won't catch up with them for a while. They must be doing all of 15 knots." Liholiho translated this as an order to Kapihe.

The whaleboat rapidly drew ahead, vigorously towed by the 80 ton[4:76] to 120 ton[44:335] whale. Captain Folger explained to Liholiho that the fluke harpoons were not intended to kill the whale, but were to fasten onto the whale. The whale's great exertions in trying to get away from his hurt, and the drag of the line and the towed whaleboat, would tire him out in time. When the whale was tired and slowed, the line in the whaleboat would be hauled in. When the whaleboat was hauled close to the whale, it would move in for the kill. This was the really dangerous time, for the whale would be maddened and desperate and would realize who his assailant was. It wouldn't take much of a blow from that huge beast to smash the whaleboat.

The towed whaleboat was now far away, still speeding in the

seas. "Look," said Captain Folger, "The whale is beginning to turn. He'll gradually turn in a circle, and then in smaller circles, or my name's not Elisha Folger. I bet they're beginning to haul in line."

The double-canoe cut the circle and began to close on the whaleboat, and soon Liholiho could see what the men were doing. The captain and the oarsmen were hauling in the line; the line had been unsnubbed so that there was just one loop around the loggerhead. The tub-oarsman was *carefully* re-coiling the recovered line back into the line-tubs. The standing boatsteerer was, of course, very occupied with his long steering-oar.

The whaleboat was gradually brought closer and closer to the tired wounded whale—three times the whaleboat's length and many many times its weight. "There she mills around!" exclaimed the captain, as the whale surged rapidly around in a close circle, "Let her be until she runs again. Daren't have any slack in the line . . ."

The whale began to move ahead again, much slower now, and the whaleboat closed rapidly as the line was hauled in. "See," almost whispered Captain Folger, "The bow-oarsman has taken the line from the bow-chock and is hauling in from his position so the whaleboat is towed almost parallel to the whale. Gotta get past that huge lethal tail." Liholiho was rigid with apprehension and anticipation.

Cautiously the whaleboat crept forward until it was almost at the side of the still slowing whale. Captain Gardner stood up and braced himself. He raised the lance from the crotch—six feet of heavy handle and six feet of iron tipped with a razor-sharp spear-headed blade. The big moment was at hand. He quickly glanced at the boatsteerer. When the huge whale was rising, and the wave was favorable, the boatsteerer suddenly swung his long steering oar and the whaleboat swerved in to almost touch the whale just behind the buried harpoons.

Captain Gardner placed the keen point of the lance against the side of the whale—and shoved it in as far as it would go with all of his strength. The iron went in to the haft! He quickly withdrew it. When the lance was free and his arms were above and behind him, he violently jerked his head back and shouted, "STERN ALL!"

The alert oarsmen made quick, violent backing pushes with their long oars. They had just backed away far enough so that— when the tremendous whale suddenly rolled from side to side, thrashing his huge flukes, raising his head and chomping his 18 foot lower jaw armed with the row of some 30 large gleaming teeth— they were in the outsurge of whitewater, and safe for the moment.

The whale fled again madly, plunging, lashing the water with his powerful flukes and tail. The line again sang and smoked out of the whaleboat. There was fast action to orient the whaleboat in the right direction so that the line streamed true from the bow.

"Look!" screamed Captain Folger and he clapped Liholiho heartily on the back (it was the first time anyone had ever done this to Liholiho!), "His chimney's afire!" The startled Liholiho looked blank, and his eyes followed Captain Folger's extended arm pointing to the whale. He could see that the spout had become reddish.

"A *good* lance!" exclaimed Captain Folger, who was more controlled now, "Lucky, it must have gotten to the lungs right off. That'll save a lot more close dangerous lance work. And this is a big one that is really a handful! Ah . . . he's slowing down!"

They could see the men in the whaleboat once again hauling in the line which had become slack. The double-canoe was able to come closer. The whale began to list to one side and plunge through the water in a small circle. The spouting was more frequent, and crimson in color now. The sea became stained with the whale's blood. All of a sudden there was a terrific commotion of the huge flukes and tail threshing about. This slowly subsided.

"Fin up!" shouted Captain Folger triumphantly. The captain was jumping up and down. "He's a *big* one . . . he'll make a hundred barrels!"

There was much light-hearted chatter as the two boats converged on the almost dead whale, whose bulk was slightly moving and twitching. The whale was on its side, with one large slightly-moving fluke pointing skyward like a huge flag or sail. The double-canoe came to the wind. The whaleboat's crew were ragged with physical fatigue; the double-canoe's crew were ragged with excitement fatigue.

"Are you sure that Narragansett Indian harponeer isn't from Nantucket?" quipped Captain Folger, and enjoyed the kidding the tall, dark Indian got at this sally, "Want to join my ship?" The impassive Indian leaning wearily on the steering oar smiled slightly and shook his head.

"What now?" asked Liholiho. Captain Gardner slowly replied, "Since you brought me luck, could you bring me some more and go back to my ship and tell the first mate to bring her out here? For we've got lots of work with this big fellow."

Captain Gardner stood tall looking with pride at the huge black mass heaving awash in the sea. Suddenly he clambered rapidly aft and clapped the harponeer on the back. "We are New Bedford men!" he shouted with pride and glee. His whaleboat crew set up a cheer. Captain Folger smiled and nodded; he but waved his hand in reply.

"Any of your people want to join my crew?" shouted Captain Gardner to the king as Kapihe started the double-canoe towards the distant Kealakekua Bay. Liholiho smiled and waved a reply. He noticed that there was considerable chatter among the double-canoe's crew, for they were still excited about the chase and the kill.

On the way back Liholiho reflected, "It takes a lot of na'au (guts) to do this. And they *have* na'au!"

Liholiho equated himself with the ships' leaders—"Captain Folger was familiar with me, and Captain Gardner was familiar with the dark seaman who threw the harpoons and then steered the whaleboat. Could I do this? Not with my people! And I admire and respect these brave hunters of the huge kohala (whale) . . . hm . . ."

NOTE: The first whale taken in Hawaiian waters yielded 110 barrels of oil.[43] Many Hawaiians did sign aboard whalers in the future and did well, for they were at home with the sea. Whaling in the Pacific increased dramatically during the next few years. There were not only some whales in the vicinity of the Hawaiian Islands during the "winter' months but, even more important, the islands were a convenient place to stop enroute to and from the various good whaling grounds. In the year 1824, 104 whaleships touched at Honolulu and Lahaina.[40:78] In later years there were even more.

IX

OVERTHROW OF
the kapus

The semi-annual season of kau was almost over—the season of new leaves and growth, and when the makani moae (tradewinds) cooled the long warm days. It was now the lunar month of ikuwa. The makahiki in honor of the great God Lono was in progress—the four month period of the Hawaiian year devoted to festival, sports, and the gathering of annual offerings and taxes.

Normal religious ceremonies of the people were suspended. Pork was kapu as it could not first be consecrated to the Gods; coconuts and fish were also kapu.[28:19] The kahuna-pules (religious priests) continued their venerations of the Gods. So did Liholiho, as ruler he was the titular head of the Hawaiian religion, kapus, and way of life.

It was the night of akua, following the kapu night of hua, when the moon was first fully round.* The night was cool, and half over. The moon spread its ghostly light over the frowning Puukohala Heiau at Kawaihae. Liholiho and Kahuna-nui (Head Priest) Hewahewa were alone on the upper terrace. A small shadowy group of white kihei (mantle)-clad heiau priests were assembled on the lower terrace. The large sacred carved figures atop the heiau walls seemed to glare approval in the shimmering light.

This was the prescribed time for the private ceremony of breaking the king's ka niu a kelii nui (a beautifully carved and highly polished coconut dish containing choice small personal belongings). [33:142] The ritual required the pule aha, a prayer during which there must be absolute silence for ceremonial perfection.

Both Liholiho and Kahuna-nui Hewahewa looked around, and listened carefully for any sound, before they entered the almost-dark small thatched house entitled waiea. This was the most sacred part of the temple. It contained the sacred symbolic cord which

*October 3, 1819 presumed.

bound the mana (spiritual force) of the heavens, home of the Gods, to the earth's surface.

Kahuna-nui Hewahewa began the long aha prayer which was an appeal on behalf of Liholiho to propitiate the major Hawaiian God Ku, the deity most favored by the alii. Liholiho stood opposite the head priest and held the coconut dish in front of him with both hands. He listened intently—half of his attention on the priest's prayer, and the other half of his attention for any other sound from any source. The thatch was uki sedge, and quite overdue to be replaced. The tradewind stirred its fine dust in the thatched house; Liholiho desperately restrained several sneezes by swallowing rapidly. The aha prayer droned on and on.

At the close of the pule aha, Liholiho raised his arms and smashed the coconut dish to the ground with all of his strength. It shattered (properly). He squatted down and groped for as many pieces as he could find. He rose, held the broken pieces high in both hands, and exclaimed loudly so the Gods could hear, "O Ku! Here are my choicest possessions which I have given you. Keep and preserve me, and safeguard the government . . ."

Before he could say the final word "amama" (literally, offer in sacrifice) . . . there was a *sound*. Both Liholiho and Hewahewa froze in their positions.

A rooster crowed!

And it sounded nearby!

"What . . . ? How . . . ?" Liholiho sputtered, "All are under kapu to keep silence—animals and chickens are supposed to be shut up so they won't make any noise! How could anyone have let a rooster out at this late hour? The rooster must have thought that the moonlight was daylight!"

Liholiho looked agitatedly at Kahuna-nui Hewahewa, whom he could barely see, and who was regarding him sternly.

"There is no aha (ceremonial perfection)," Kahuna-nui Hewahewa said seriously.

"Let us do it again," Liholiho implored desperately, "For you know without this perfection our lore tells us that the people will not have confidence in the stability of government."

Kahuna-nui Hewahewa shook his head with the dignity of his priestly office, "No, Kalani, you have already broken the ka niu a kelii nui (coconut dish), and there is not any time available to prepare another."

"Tomorrow night?" asked Liholiho apprehensively.

The high priest slowly shook his head again, "No, you know

that this ceremony can only be performed on this night of akua." He repeated, "There is no aha."

Liholiho continued to expostulate . . . but stopped. He knew that Hewahewa was right. He slumped, and was not aware when Hewahewa left the small thatched house. Liholiho soon weakly walked outside and looked around the heiau (temple). It was silent and deserted. The only sound was that of the sigh of the tradewind. He slowly and carefully looked at the forty sacred carved figures on the stone walls, one by one. They all seemed to frown in the moonlight, and did not return his gaze. Liholiho dejectedly sat down and looked at nothing. It was almost dawn before he rose and stumbled out of the high-walled entrance of Puukohala Heiau and wearily woke his retainers to return to his residence compound.

A month passed by—it was now the month of welehu, and the kapu of hua had come again. It was the evening of mohalu, when the moon was still egg-shaped and not quite round.* It was the prescribed time of the makahiki when the makaainana (commoners) broke their ceremonial coconut dishes to propitiate the Gods. Liholiho had been intoxicated most of the time during this past disturbing month. He was half-intoxicated and irritable now.

Liholiho's favorite double-canoe led the other three canoes of his followers to the landing near Maliu Point at Honokohau, just four miles north of Kailua. The kahuna-pules (religious priests) met the king at the canoe landing and escorted him with flaming torches up the ramp to the tiered wall of waterworn slabs surrounding the Puuoina Heiau. As he glanced inland he could dimly see the holua (toboggan) slide on which he had enjoyed himself in years gone by.

The king was escorted on the flagstone path inside the north wall to the 16 x 24 foot thatched house on the east terrace. Liholiho could barely see, and almost feel, a large group of people on the west terrace across the roughly paved depression. They who would ceremoniously break their coconut dishes to propitiate the Gods. He was amazed at the number of people—it appeared there were many more than those who lived at Honokohau. He rationalized, I suppose it is because I am here for the first time as Ke Alii Nui (The Great Chief, King).

The hours passed, and the moon rose high in the heavens. Liholiho remained alone in the thatched house meditating, with a sip now and then from a small bottle of rum that he had just

---

*October 29, 1819 presumed

happened to bring along with him. He could hear the murmur of voices and sounds on the west terrace. Those who had assembled for the ceremony appeared to be gossiping profusely. He suspected that some had rum also, which they shouldn't have.

Just before midnight the murmuring suddenly stilled, and Liholiho was warned that the priests were approaching. This ceremony also involved the pule aha, the prayer which required complete and utter silence for perfection. Liholiho stood inside the thatched hut with the leading kahuna-pule (religious priest) of the heiau. The other priests of the heiau stood outside.

The kahuna-pule started the aha prayer, and Liholiho listened intently, slightly swaying from side to side. He heard a sound—someone had coughed. He motioned to the kahuna-pule, who stopped, and soon started again from the beginning. There was another sound from the west terrace. Again the kahuna-pule stopped, and again recommenced the pule aha.

After this had happened six times Liholiho was almost frantic. There could be no aha (pure ceremony) for the Gods! He began to rage at the priest, "There is *no* aha! There is *no* aha! The people are impolite and disturbed! Something must be wrong with your service!"

The kahuna-pule, who was old and respected, protested in obvious dismay. Liholiho was now furious. He stamped his foot and exclaimed, "Not we but the God shall be destitute, for he will not give us the aha by which he should be entitled to offerings!"[9:149]

Liholiho stormed out of the thatched hut and began to malign the assembled people on the west terrace. He could see the faceless throng in the moonlight. "Irreligious! Ungodly! You cannot expect peace and happiness during the makahiki and the coming year . . ."

Liholiho shouted on, and the west terrace was rapidly emptied of people endeavoring to escape the wrath of his strident voice.

Liholiho was as angry as he had ever been before. All at once he stopped, and declared, "If this be so, so be it. Be it upon *your* heads, for *you* will be the losers."

He stomped back to the thatched house, ordered the kahuna-pule to leave, and sat down. He glowered in quiet rage. The rum bottle was within reach.

About an hour later a messenger crawled to the door of the thatched house and announced himself hesitatingly and fearfully. When the now cooled-off Liholiho asked what his message was, the messenger replied, "I am sent to you by your guardian (Kaahumanu) to request that when you return to Kailua you will return with your God enveloped in ti leaf." [9:149-150] (This meant a request to cover the God so his guidance no longer need be followed—to remove the kapu.) Liholiho bowed his head in deep thought, and remained that way long after the messenger had crawled away.

Finally he rose, and made his way slowly from the deserted heiau to the canoes. In some strange way the canoes were ready and loaded with his silent people. He asked but one question of his aipuupuu (steward) Manuia as he climbed into his double-canoe, "Have we sufficient rum?" Upon being assured this was so, Liholiho motioned to Kapihe, the hookelewaa (canoe steersman), to depart saying, "Let us go onto the bosom of the mother kai (sea)."

The canoes slowly set out to sea in the moonlight. Liholiho went to the small shelter on the pola (platform between the two hulls), lay on his back, and brooded at the many stars in the heavens.

What was wrong with the Gods and the people? Was this an omen, a most important omen?

Kapihe kept the canoes standing off and on several miles from shore the next day, hua. A minimum crew was kept on the double-canoe, the majority of the paddlers had swum to the other canoes and patiently existed in crowded conditions awaiting their master's will.

Liholiho was in a rum-induced stupor most of the time to dull his tortured thoughts. He ate and drank alone in the shelter. His queens ate and drank outside on the pola (platform between the two hulls) in order to preserve the ai kapu (segregated eating between the sexes). One can dimly discern that at one period of this sojourn Liholiho became at odds with his favorite queen (and half-sister) Kamamalu. In any event, at one stage of the debauch, let us say the night of hua, he devoted his attention to his young Queen Kinau (Kamamalu's younger sister).

"Oh, Kinau," Liholiho said indistinctly, "Come into the shelter and let me rest my head on your bosom—I am so weary with myself." Kinau, also some intoxicated, crawled into the small shelter and curled up behind Liholiho. He gratefully eased his head back and cradled it between her breasts, cool in the evening tradewind. "Hmm . . ." Liholiho muttered with satisfaction, and he turned his head rapidly from side to side with masculine relish, "This I like!"

Kinau stroked his long black hair, there was some desultory conversation and giggles, and mild lovemaking between regal husband and royal wife. After a while Liholiho said, "I am thirsty, Kinau, leave me so I can drink some water." Instead of leaving the shelter, Kinau hugged Liholiho tight and rocked back and forth. "Oh, my Liholiho, I am so comfortable, and it is so pleasant. Let me give you some water as if you were my keiki (child)."

She took a mouthful of water from a nearby bowl and nuzzled Liholiho's mouth, letting water pass between her lips. This amused Liholiho, who lay back with his eyes closed. He soon muttered, "More, more." Kinau again filled her mouth with water, but this time let it pour down in a small stream into his open mouth. [9:150] When she reached for the bowl again, Liholiho suddenly sat bolt upright . . . and said clearly with sudden soberness:

"AI NOA! (Free eating between the sexes!).''

Kinau tumbled back to a scared prone position, suddenly realizing what she had done. She tensed away from Liholiho's wide staring bloodshot eyes. *"Ai noa!"* almost breathed Liholiho. He had a look of horror on his face.

Liholiho quickly composed himself, sat erect with a stern fatalistic look on his face, and placed his arms tight against his body. He awaited the Gods' fatal action which he expected for having broken the kapu. He waited. He waited . . . and waited. The double-canoe was quiet, except for the gentle laps of the waves on the slowly heaving hulls. He waited . . . and nothing happened. Nothing.

Liholiho turned his head very cautiously and looked at frightened Kinau. He picked up the bowl of water, very slowly, and took a large cool gulp—and then slowly handed the bowl to Kinau. Liholiho made an expressive command with his head, and Kinau took an apprehensive slight sip. Liholiho and Kinau looked deep into each other's eyes. The wrath of the Gods for violating the ai kapu did not descend and destroy them both.

Nothing happened. Both took another and deeper drink of water, and still nothing happened. Kinau scrambled to refill the bowl. Both drank again, staring seriously at each other. There was no wrath of the Gods!

Liholiho slowly relaxed . . . and very casually said, "I am hungry. I want rum. I want to smoke. Fetch the rest of my wives." When they all crowded into the small shelter, some wet with the sudden swim from other canoes, Liholiho offered them some dog meat,* which had been cooked in an imu (underground oven) ashore.

Liholiho and Kinau led the way. Both began to eat. The other queens nibbled very slowly, with scared eyes. They knew that

---

*The Hawaiians considered pigs and dogs as equal meat animals.

others had secretly broken the ai kapu with apparent impunity, but this was vastly different. Liholiho was the kahu (guardian) of the kapus! There was no harm. There was *no* harm. Soon all began to chatter, and they waxed merry. They ate and drank rum together, and smoked from the same tobacco pipe.[2] This *did* appear to be most enjoyable . . .

The king sat back and considered. "My psychical acumen is not bothered by this sacrilege, I the keeper of the kapus and the way of life! I am free of fear of the many Gods. The violation of this most important kapu does not hurt me. But can I and should I communicate this to the people? Is Kaahumanu right when she states the people want this? I must test . . ."

"Lama! Lama! (Rum! Rum!)" Liholiho shouted into the moonlit night. "Lama for all my people. Let us eat and drink together." Manuia, the steward, hurriedly broke out food and bottles for all. Those asleep were awakened, and soon revelry was rampant. Rampant until excesses caused most to seek sodden sleep. Liholiho remained awake, and watched everything. "There is no harm. They too are free of the wrath of the Gods." He muttered over and over and over again, "Ua pau ke kii i Hawaii nei (Hawaii's Gods are no more)." Liholiho finally went to sleep amidst his crowded queens.

It was the afternoon of the next day, akua, when the moon would be completely round that night for the first time this month.* This was the day of the lunar month held most special by the alii. The revelry had thoroughly revived aboard the king's canoes when a double-canoe from nearby Kailua came swiftly alongside Liholiho's double-canoe. The old Chief Eeka (whom Liholiho was very fond of) came aboard and had a very private conversation with Liholiho. When both rose, Liholiho announced that he was going to Kailua with Chief Eeka to join the other alii in an 'aha'aina (feast), and for Kapihe to follow with the king's canoes. Chief Eeka's double-canoe was soon far ahead, as the king's canoes were being paddled in a very ragged manner.

Liholiho was greeted at the shore by Kuhina-nui (Regent) Kaahumanu, his mother Keopuolani, Kahuna-nui (Head Priest) Hewahewa, Prime Minister Kalanimoku, the counsellors, and other high chiefs. He was escorted to a large halau (open-sided thatched structure) some 30 by 100 feet in size.[39:38] Two series of tables had been set up after the European fashion, one for chiefs and the other for chiefesses.[21] Liholiho greeted the foreigners who had also been

---

*November 1, 1819 presumed.

invited—among them he welcomed Captains Blair and Clark from Boston, whom he had known for a long time.[35]

He insisted that Olohana (John Young) join him on his left and Prime Minister Kalanimoku on his right at the head of the chiefs' table. The tables had been covered with ti leaves and flowers, and practically groaned with the immense weight of all kinds of food not kapu during this period of time. Of course the chiefesses did not have some of the kinds of food provided for the chiefs.

When the large number of chiefs and chiefesses sat down, separately, on the benches and before they began to eat, Kahuna-nui Hewahewa rose. He raised both arms high and pronounced, *"One and all*, may we eat in peace and in our hearts give thanks." Before Hewahewa sat down he placed his hand on Liholiho's shoulder. Liholiho and Hewahewa looked at each other earnestly. There was peace between them.

All began to eat with gusto. Liholiho soon rose and walked around the tables several times, greeting various of the chiefs and chiefesses. Suddenly he hesitated . . . and seated himself at a vacant place (just by chance) available between his high lineage mother, Keopuolani, and Kuhina-nui Kaahumanu. Liholiho began to eat "most voraciously, but evidently much perturbed".[21] Keopuolani and Kaahumanu calmly continued eating.

There was a sudden stunned silence!

All stopped and stared, some with horror, and most with their mouths open in astonishment. The makaainana (commoners) who were serving, froze in whatever positions they were in, and looked with mingled curiosity and fear. This had not happened for generations (openly), free-eating between the Hawaiian sexes during a normal period of time.

After a minute or so—which seemed like an hour or so—Liholiho stood up. He stood with set face, tall, erect, imperious. Nothing happened to him! There was no harm! All rose and exclaimed to each other, "Ai noa! (The eating kapu is broken!)." A few chiefs and chiefesses were quiet and apprehensive, a few others went the extreme, "The kapus are at an end, and the Gods are a lie!"[2] Soon many took up this shout.

Liholiho walked slowly to Kahuna-nui Hewahewa who had risen to his feet. Kaahumanu and Keopuolani followed. Kuhina-nui Kaahumanu stood at Liholiho's side with her fists on her hips and tensely watched the crowd. Liholiho and Hewahewa earnestly looked deep into each other's eyes.

"The Gods and the heiaus (temples) cannot survive the death

of the kapu," said Hewahewa clearly and distinctly so that almost all could hear in the sudden hush.

"Then let them perish with it!" Liholiho shouted, "The Gods have not hurt me for breaking the ai kapu (forbidden eating between the sexes). There will be no harm to the people."

"Ae! (Yes!)" said Kaahumanu grimly in agreement.

Hewahewa bowed and turned, and slowly walked to the nearby heiau. Some of his priestly followers trailed along. With his own hand, Hewahewa seized a torch and set fire to the sacred thatched structure in the heiau.[2] "While the flames were raging, the idols were thrown down, stripped of the cloth hung over them, and cast into the fire."[35]

"Ua pau ke kii i Hawaii nei (Hawaii's Gods are no more)," Liholiho muttered as he swallowed some rum which he didn't even taste. He glanced around at the excited multitude. His mother, Keopuolani, looked at him proudly and sadly—she bowed her head in respect. The large Kuhina-nui Kaahumanu was triumphant. Prime Minister Kalanimoku seemed composed, and was closely looking at the expressions and reactions of the chiefs. Liholiho's cousin, Kekuaokalani, stalked out with a few followers, and Liholiho's scalp tingled.

Liholiho walked outside of the open-sided thatched structure so he could see the fire better. A group of excited makaainana (commoners) saw him coming, and they prostrated themselves. Liholiho looked at them, prone in their required respect for his lineage, and abruptly shouted, "Rise, and stand like men, strong in your own stature. My kapu moe (prostrating requirement) is no more. And it is the same for all other alii."

There was a great murmur from those within hearing. They passed the pronouncement to those at a distance. The awestruck prone makaainana slowly rose, and stood in front of their ruler—for the first time.

Prime Minister Kalanimoku sent messengers (who just happened to be standing by) to all of the districts of the island of Hawaii, and to the other islands in swift canoes, to announce ai noa (free eating) and that the kapus had been overthrown and were no more. This news reached the foreigners at Honolulu on the island of Oahu two days later, November 6, 1819.[34]

Kahuna-nui Hewahewa sent his priestly messengers (who just happened to be standing by) to the religious structures in all the districts on all the islands with instructions to destroy the heiaus (temples) and images. The Gods were overthrown! Only Pakalani in Waipio Valley, with its Hale-o-Liloa which contained royal bones, and Ka-iki-Alealea at Honaunau, with its similar Hale-o-Keawe, were spared. Hewahewa was aware that at some places this order would not be followed, and he rightly anticipated difficulties.*

Kaahumanu's raised voice was heard, "Let us have pork, it is no longer kapu! Let the tables have equal food! Let each sit where each wishes! Let us feast as we never have feasted before!" The excited chiefs and chiefesses returned to the feast, and did just that.

"Ua pau ke kii i Hawaii nei! (Hawaii's Gods are no more!)" was heard in every direction. This indeed was a momentous feast in honor of a now very momentous day. It lasted all night and well into the next day.

Male and female Hawaiians, alii and makaainana alike, all over the islands ate together freely without fear of death for the first times in their lives.

The kapus were no more, the pillars of the old Hawaiian way of life. And there was nothing to replace them. Of more significance, the Hawaiian religion was no more, and there was no spiritual guidance to replace it.

---

*The priests were granted the continuing use of lands which had supported the heiaus. This assisted in avoiding a priest-inspired insurrection.

X

Battle of kuamoo

It was hilo, the first day of the month of makalii and the first day of the Hawaiian new year.* There had been great rejoicing the day before when the makalii (pleiades) could again be seen in the early evening on the eastern horizon as the kilohokus (astronomers) had predicted. The new moon was faintly visible today. These two occurrences cued this day as the beginning of the new year.

The weather was cool, and there was a light rain late that afternoon at Kailua. The council was assembled under the faintly rustling thatch of a Hawaiian house. Those present wore either western clothes or kiheis (mantles) for comfort. A number of kukui-nut oil stone lamps provided a warm odorous light.

Kalanimoku was speaking, "I asked for this council to report to you about the trouble in Hamakua district. As you know, we had heard that some were vigorously advocating the ways of Old to the point of insurrection. I sent Chief Lonoakahi and some men to investigate. They met the trouble-making leader, Chief Kainapu, enroute at Mahiki (a land division of Waimea). Kainapu killed Lonoakahi and two of his men. There is no question now that this deed means war."

There was excited comment. When it subsided, Kalanimoku continued calmly. "It is not good policy to carry on the war in that quarter; for Kekuaokalani, the source of war, is at Kaawaloa. To that place let our force be directed. The fray at Hamakua is a leaf of the tree. I would lay the axe at the root, that being destroyed, the leaves will, of course, wither."[23]

There was a pause, while all reflected. Kuhina-nui Kaahuma-nu said quietly, "I asked my younger sister, Piia, to visit Kekuaokalani at Kaawaloa (Kealakekua Bay). He is her foster-son. Piia, what can you report?"

The large corpulent Piia (who had been the sixth wife of Ke Alii Nui Kamehameha) was a little nervous, as she was addressing

---

*November 17, 1819 presumed.

the council for the first time. "Kekuaokalani is observing the kapus and worshipping our old Hawaiian Gods. I visited with him yesterday, the day of muku, when the kapu was freed at the end of the makahiki.* There are many men there. I begged him to return to Kailua and discuss things with us. He was stubborn, and wouldn't open his mind. Kekuaokalani is terribly bitter about the destruction of the heiaus and images—and ai noa (free eating)."

"The kahunas (priests) Kuaiwa of the Order of Kauhi and Holoialena of the Order of Nahulu are there and strongly advocating the ways of Old. They say that "the ungodly chiefs of old who lost their lands never sinned like this!"[27:226] They are urging Kekuaokalani to take over the Rule . . . by force. I think the only reason he has not taken any action yet is that he has been observing the traditional ceremonies which mark the close of the makahiki. I am fearful!"

All assembled glanced at Liholiho. He sat impassively, but felt the chill of the day even more.

"Who are the chiefs with him?" asked Kaahumanu curiously.

"I saw Wahahee, Kuakamauna, Peapea, Naheana, Manono the son of Kanaukapu, and Keawehaku," replied Piia, as she counted them off on her fat fingers.

"I thought as much," muttered Kalanimoku, "I say let us attack them now and be done with this before it grows so big we will have real trouble handling it."

A chief excitedly chimed in, "All I need is forty men, and I'll bring Kekuaokalani to Kailua as a prisoner within three days!"

Hewahewa shook his head, and soberly said, "Not with forty numbers of forty men! Kekuaokalani, his kahunas and his chiefs and men, are too strong. No, this calls for much greater consideration than a mere forty men. To overcome the belief of generations will take much effort. But I agree with Kalanimoku's earlier statement. The rallying point of return to the old ways *is* Kekuaokalani. To him we must devote our attention."

All considered soberly. The silence was broken by Liholiho, "I have talked many times with Kekuaokalani and I know his belief is the strongest of the strong. He deeply feels the responsibility of Kukailimoku (the war god), and his consequent veneration. If Piia could not sway him to open his mind, I fear no one could."

"Yet," interjected Kaahumanu gravely, "Yet we must try. I

*The four month period of the Hawaiian year in honor of the great God Lono. It was devoted to festival, sports, and the gathering of annual offerings and taxes.

am not afraid of war, for I fought at Kamehameha's side many times. War should be considered the last resort. The vagaries of warfare should not determine the future. It is better to try and change a mind than to endeavor to impose a will. I say let us try once more."

There was silence, and Kaahumanu read the silence as consent. She glanced rapidly around and continued, "Hoapili, Kekuaokalani is your sister's son. Will you try?" The doughty Hoapili nodded grimly, and qualified, "I cannot offer you much optimism, for I too know Kekuaokalani's strong beliefs."

Kaahumanu nodded and looked around again, "Naihe, you are the chief of Kealakekua. Will you accompany Hoapili, for two may find a way where one cannot?" Naihe nodded acquiescence, as he tossed his hands up in a futile gesture. All understood that he too was not optimistic.

"Good," Kaahumanu sighed, "Let us make this attempt."

"Ae (Yes)," said Liholiho firmly, for he did not want to be left out of the decision.

After the council ended, Kalanimoku thoughtfully mentioned to Liholiho and Kaahumanu, "I think I had better alert our old regiments—the Keawe (the "Lifeguard"), the I (the "Best"), the Ahu (the "Strong"), the Mahi (the "Mass"), the Palena (the "Partitioner"), the Luahine (the "Old Women"), and the Paia (the "Wall")." All three nodded the wisdom of this move.

Kalanimoku considered deeply. He knew that the regiments were but in name only, as they had only had fragmentary training during the past 23 years—since the last actual warfare. Ah well, Kekuaokalani is not any better off, and I believe that he will draw upon fewer men . . .

The next morning as Hoapili and Naihe made ready at the beach for the thirteen mile canoe trip down the coast from Kailua to Kealakekua Bay, the Sacred Queen Mother Keopuolani joined them. She quietly insisted on also going. Was not Hoapili her man, and what kind of wife would allow her husband to go into danger without her? Was she not of the highest alii caste and had much at stake? Didn't she have kinship ties with both Kekuaokalani and his wife Manono? And wasn't Liholiho her son, and what kind of mother wouldn't support and assist her son?

The canoe left the shore with three ambassadors as passengers.

There were affectionate greetings when the canoe landed at Kawaaloa, Kealakekua Bay. Kekuaokalani (properly) escorted Sacred Queen Mother Keopuolani to High Chief Naihe's residence compound, and insisted that she rest. (Keopuolani noticed that her prostrating kapu was observed by all in view.)

Hoapili and Naihe accompanied Kekuaokalani to his hale mua (men's eating house) and were offered refreshments. High Chief Kekuaokalani was his usual dignified stern self, and a perfect and gracious host. There was some desultory preliminary conversation, and Naihe gave Kekuaokalani the most recent news of the happenings elsewhere, to include the insurrection of Chief Kainapu and the killing of Chief Lonoakahi. Kekuaokalani did not seem surprised.

Hoapili knew it was time for business. He knew of only one approach, the blunt, and he addressed Kekuaokalani, "Attend; I am sent to you on business; look at me, you are my sister's son, I am come for you; let us go to Kailua to the king, for the common people are fighting and they lay the blame of it upon you; you and the allegation has an appearance of truth, inasmuch as you reside by yourself at a distance from the court. Let us return to Kailua and reside with Liholiho, that the charge of this rebellion may not rest upon you;—at least visit the king and have a talk with him;—whether you shall break the ancient tabu or not, that is quite at your option."[23]

High Chief Kekuaokalani thought for a moment with downcast eyes as he toyed with his coconut bowl. He finally looked at Hoapili squarely, and said soberly, "Very well, I will go, but don't be in a hurry, I must confer first with my wife, then I will go, but understand I shall not eat in violation of the old system."[23]

Hoapili was quite surprised at this quick acquiescence, and his jaw almost dropped. He recovered quickly, and expressed pleasure at the amicable conclusion to his business. After a bit more general conversation, Hoapili and Naihe returned to Naihe's residence compound.

When Hoapili and Naihe told Keopuolani the results of the discussion, she was thoughtful. She slowly and carefully said, "He is an uku fish, a fish of Kahoolawe; he should be drawn in as soon as he is hooked (He uku maoli ia he i'a no Kaho'olawe). (!) He has consented to go to Kailua, but he has refused to practice free eating, and he is going to talk with Manono and go with us tomorrow. I am not sure of it. Perhaps yes, and perhaps no."[27:226-227]

The three carefully considered all they knew about Kekuaokalani, and their wary conclusions were uneasy. They soon heard criers calling the people to make ready to go to Kailua the next morning and join in demolishing the old institutions. [23] They looked at each other . . . was it true? And yet . . . (If they had only known, Kekuaokalani's chief advisors were urging him to kill Hoapili and Keopuolani, and perhaps Naihe too. Kekuaokalani would not consent.)

Hoapili, Keopuolani and Naihe joined each other at the entrance of the residence compound before dawn the next morning, having been awakened by the sounds of many people. They saw Kekuaokalani's men assembling in groups by torchlight—each man was carrying either a musket or a spear. High Chief Kekuaokalani came to Naihe's compound; he wore an ahuula (feather cloak) and a mahiole (feather helmet), and carried a musket.

"Is this the style in which we are going?"[23] inquired Hoapili. The answer was seriously affirmative.

Hoapili continued, "You will accompany us in the canoes?"[23] The reply was, "I and my company will go inland, where are men to prepare and ovens to bake food, else we shall die of hunger."[23]

Hoapili rejoined, "Be not solicitous about your men, accompany me yourself; let the others go by land; you are the one for whom I came."[23]

As Kekuaokalani turned away he stated with a gleam in his eye, "I will not go by sea, I will lead my men."

Keopuolani quickly whispered to Hoapili, "Attend, brother, cut the cord of friendship, for Kekuaokalani has become our enemy."[23]

Naihe casually mentioned that, as chief of Kealakekua, he was concerned that his people had sufficient to eat. And many of his people were with Kekuaokalani. So he had better stay and oversee the gathering of foodstuffs. Both Hoapili and Keopuolani regarded him casually and thoughtfully. Naihe urged Hoapili to take the canoe and go to Keauhou and await the coming of Kekuaokalani by land. Keopuolani would have none of this, and Hoapili and Keopuolani hurried to the beach and entered their canoe. The crew was ready, having assembled with alarm. The paddlers were urged on to Kailua to the point of exhaustion.

All was hustle at Kailua the next morning. Men, dressed in Hawaiian or partial western attire, were scurrying around busily engaged in equipping themselves for war. Some of the younger men were boastful, the older men who had experienced warfare were grim and deliberate. An occasional musket shot could be heard, as the more martial made sure that their scarcely-used firearms would still work. Others, armed with spears and slingstones, practiced their use—for the first time in many moons. Files of men could be seen hurrying along the trails to Kailua. A number of canoes loaded with armed men were approaching the shore and landing. The mobilization of the militia was in final progress. The growing tempo of excitement was infectious.

Kalanimoku stood in front of the thatched house where the war council had just finished. He was mentally exhausted for the moment. The council had been difficult. The war plan had been comparatively easy—but everyone wanted to be the pukaua (war leader). It had been difficult to persuade everyone that this was the right of his position. He glanced towards the shore where a belligerent Kaahumanu was superintending the preparation of turning nine vessels into war vessels. Swivel guns were being placed on the polas (platforms between the two hulls) of the largest double-canoes and on several small western vessels.

The strategy was simple. Kalanimoku would lead the regiments along the shore until they met Kekuaokalani's force. Kaahumanu would lead the war vessels along the coast and support the land action with cannon and musket fire.

Kalanimoku acknowledged Liholiho with a bow when the excited king strode rapidly to Kalanimoku's right side. It was to be Liholiho's first battle! He wore a blue English naval captain's uniform, and had difficulty in keeping his hand from the hilt of the slung sword that Captain Freycinet had given him. The king was breathing a bit more rapidly than usual, and his eyes darted around observing everything with great interest. It was hard to stand still.

Kalanimoku adjudged that the time was ripe—he nodded to an attendant conch shell blower to give the signal. At the spine-tingling mournful sound, the scurrying men began to gather into regimental groups at the vigorous urgings of their leaders. What a difference from the army of the old days under Kamehameha! There were only a hundred men or so in each regiment. When they had assembled, Kalanimoku caused another signal of the conch. The seven regimental groups moved towards Kalanimoku and Liholiho. Some women accompanied their men. The small Keawe Regiment, composed of alii (chiefs), all armed with muskets, took their rightful place in back of Liholiho and Kalanimoku. Their mission was to be the lifeguard of the pukaua (war leader) and the king.

Liholiho stood as erect as he could while Kalanimoku briefed the men on the war plan and tactics to be used. He concluded with,

"Go quietly, be strong, be soldiers, and drink the bitter waters, O my little brothers! There are lands ahead, honor, wealth. Do not turn back, whether death or life lies ahead."[27:227-228]

Kalanimoku then ordered the movement of the army to Keauhou, some six miles down the coast. He knew that this march could be the only pre-battle training, and he made the most of it. There were frequent orders and changes of position in the order of march. Various regiments would be sent to various places on the flanks to investigate non-existent things and engage non-existent enemies. The men were weary when they camped that night at Keauhou.

Kalanimoku was pleased to see that they were more orderly when the march commenced again early the following morning . . . the day of battle.*

Kaikeoewa, the seven foot tall high chief who had attended Liholiho at his accession, led the huna-lewa (vanguard). He made first contact with Kekuaokalani's force at Lekeleke. Kaikeoewa was wounded in the leg by a lucky musket shot in this small skirmish. Holualoa was also wounded. As was customary in Hawaiian warfare, when a leader fell or was seriously wounded, his side withdrew. Kaikeoewa fell back as orderly as possible with his untrained men to Kalanimoku's main force, which by now had advanced to Kuamoo.

Kalanimoku narrowly contemplated what was to be the battleground. The terrain was rough lava with some sparse shrubs and grass here and there. The ground was almost level near the shoreline, but rose rapidly inland. Kalanimoku smiled grimly as he rapidly estimated that Kekuaokalani had fewer men than he had.

The pukaua (war leader) briskly gave orders to form the makawalu order of battle. Most of the men were stationed in a line from the sea to where the land began to rise steeply. Fewer men extended this line further up the mountainside. He motioned for Hoapili, and rapidly gave him instructions to take two of the regiments and start climbing—and outflank Kekuaokalani.Liholiho was almost beside himself with excitement as Kalanimoku advised him of the reasons for troop dispositions.

Kalanimoku noticed that Kukailimoku was being brandished at his men. He could hear the blood-curdling screams of the war god's carrier. He was completely aware that this would frighten his men, despite the Gods having been recently overthrown. He kept a

*November 21, 1819 presumed. One reference indicates the battle may have occurred a month later.[50]

steady relay of messengers on runs with minor orders. One could get very superstitious when one was alone.

The two forces closed—there were yells and screams of rage, muskets were fired with their attendant white puffs of smoke, slingstones whistled in all directions, and small groups of men dashed from one cover to another endeavoring to gain advantageous positions. The musket fire was quite inaccurate, the maneuvering extensive. Liholiho's face was now powder stained; he had acquired a musket and was firing it with determination.

Gradually, very gradually, Kekuaokalani's men were forced back—and towards the shoreline due to pressure from Hoapili's flanking force. Kalanimoku had a clear superiority of muskets too. Soon Kaahumanu's offshore swivel guns and muskets went into action. This caused uneasiness among Kekuaokalani's men, as they were not only receiving flanking fire from two directions but were being strongly pressed on their front. They withdrew slowly and made a stand behind a stone wall running inland atop a slight rise.

Kekuaokalani was everywhere, exhorting his men. He had been slightly wounded early in the battle, now almost ten hours in duration. He fell from weakness. His wife, Manono, helped him to his feet. He sat on a fragment of lava, still exhorting his men and firing his musket. Kekuaokalani was conspicuous in his ahuula (feather cloak) and mahiole (feather helmet), and Kalanimoku's men within range concentrated their fire on him.

Kekuaokalani received a musket ball in his left breast. He covered his face with his ahuula, and slipped to the ground, dead. Manono called for quarter, as Kalanimoku and his men advanced. She was hit in her left temple by another musket ball, and fell lifeless onto the body of her late husband.

Kekuaokalani's force rapidly disintegrated into a mass of fleeing individual warriors when their leader died. Some did not stop until they reached the puuhonua (place of refuge) at Honaunau. Others hid in the bush or in caves when they could run no longer. Still others found canoes and set off for the island of Maui. Kahuna Kuaiwa and Wahahee were captured, killed, and their bodies dragged along the path to Kailua.

Kalanimoku finally got word to his pursuing warriors that an amnesty had been declared. (Liholiho later pardoned those who had sided with Kekuaokalani.) Kalanimoku had ten men killed in battle, some fifty of his opponents were also killed. There were many latent deaths among those wounded. The bodies on the battlefield were covered with rock cairns.

Kalanimoku made sure that the war god, Kukailimoku, was secured and safely hidden.

Hoapili was dispatched by canoe to Kawaihae with a number of men. He marched inland against Chief Kainapu of Hamakua, who was discovered still at Waimea. Chief Kainapu was killed, as well as a number of his followers.

The test of the "New" versus the "Old" had been met, and the "New" had won decisively. Ua pau ke kii i Hawaii nei! (Hawaii's Gods are no more!) Hewahewa and Kaahumanu redoubled their efforts to destroy the images and heiaus (temples). Those who chose to worship the Hawaiian Gods did so in secret places.

Worship of the old Hawaiian Gods and religion died out . . . gradually . . . very gradually.

XI

to propagate
the gospel

The 85 foot 241 ton brig *Thaddeus* from New England went on the other tack as she rounded Upolu Point, Hawaii at 4 PM March 30, 1820. When truly in the lee of the high mountains of the island of Hawaii, the breeze failed, the sails flapped and hung limp, and the ship lost way.

"That does it," exclaimed Captain Blanchard, "We'll have to wait for a breeze. First Officer Hunnewell, take a couple of those young Hawaiian missionary helpers and go ashore and see what news there is."

The 23 passengers lining the port rail glanced briefly at the captain. First Officer Hunnewell ordered a ship's boat and crew, and motioned to two of the passengers, Thomas Hopu and John Honolii, to join him. Thomas Hopu was especially excited, as Kohala was his home district. He hadn't seen it for a dozen years.

The passengers watched the small boat being rowed to the abrupt island shoreline—the land rose sharply and increasingly verdant to be hidden in the low bank of clouds. Seven men, seven women, and five children were from New England. This was to be their new home. The four other passengers were young Hawaiians returning home. The drab appearance of their somber clothing reflected the long voyage, 159 days around Cape Horn from Boston, with only salt water for infrequent washing.

The two stern American Protestant Calvinist missionaries stood side by side, tall intensive Rev. Hiram Bingham (age 30) and tall athletic Rev. Asa Thurston (age 32). Their "stove pipe" hats made them seem even taller. They had graduated together from the Theological Seminary at Andover, Mass., the previous year. Both had been ordained at Goshen September 29, 1819. They had been married one day apart, October 11 & 12, 1819, less than two weeks before the *Thaddeus* had sailed from Boston. (The Prudential Committee of the American Board of Commissioners for Foreign Missions had wisely insisted, and helped arrange finding suitable helpmates, so that only married couples would be in this pioneer company of missionaries to the Sandwich (Hawaiian) Islands.)

Rev. Bingham, whose strong personality had caused the mantle of leadership to fall upon his shoulders, was audibly repeating a part of their Instructions (he knew them all by heart, as did most of the company)[24:27]

> Your mission is a mission of mercy, and your work is to be wholly a labor of love. Your views are not to be limited to a low or narrow scale; but you are to open your hearts wide, and set your mark high. You are to aim at nothing short of covering these islands with fruitful fields and pleasant dwellings, and schools and churches: of raising up the whole people to an elevated state of christian civilization; of bringing, or preparing the means of bringing, thousands and millions of the present and succeeding generations to the mansions of eternal blessedness.

The clergymen's wives were by their sides. Sybil Bingham was three years younger than her husband, and it was apparent that she was with child. Lucy Thurston was 24 years old, eight years younger than her husband. She peeked up at him from her poke bonnet and barely resisted taking his hand. She *knew* that he was thinking of his favorite part of the Instructions they had received prior to embarking[24:21]

> Hitherto, though christians, you have been, like other christians, laboring for yourselves or your families, henceforth you are to labor for Christ; and all the fruits of your labors are to be held as irrevocably consecrated to him, for the purposes of his mercy towards the dwellers in the midst of the seas.

LO I AM WITH YOU ALWAYS . . .

Lucy Thurston glanced at the assistant missionaries. The oldest of the group was Daniel Chamberlain (age 38) who was a farmer. He was holding Daniel Jr., (age 6). Dexter (age 13), Nathan (age 11) and Mary (age 9) stood eagerly by his side. They *had* received good disciplined training from their War of 1812 captain father! His wife, Jerusha Chamberlain, was holding baby Nancy (age 2) in her arms. How they had been concerned for their children's safety on this long voyage!

Dr. Thomas Holman and his wife Lucia (both age 26) stood quietly together, holding hands, and a little apart from the group. Lucy Thurston looked at them and couldn't help herself; she inaudibly repeated a scripture quote in the Instructions pertaining to Subordination to Rightful Direction:[24:24]

> "Yea, all of you be subject one to another and be clothed
> with humility: for God resisteth the proud, and giveth grace
> to the humble."

She could have bitten her tongue, and quickly thought, THIS IS MY COMMANDMENT, THAT YE LOVE ONE ANOTHER, AS I HAVE LOVED YOU.

Next was Lucia's brother, Samuel Ruggles (age 25), a teacher. His wife Nancy was four years older than he, and was with child. Then came Samuel Whitney (age 27), a teacher and mechanic, and his wife Mercy, also apparently with child. Lucy Thurston couldn't help thinking . . . except for the Chamberlains, all of us were married within a month of sailing from Boston . . . and the accommodations were *so* cramped and close together in this ship . . .

The last of the group of New Englanders was the spare and stooped Elisha Loomis (age 20), the printer. His wife Maria was several years older than he, and stood uncomfortably as she was six months with child.

The remaining young Hawaiian helper of the pioneer company, William Kanui, chattered excitedly in Hawaiian with the only passenger not a member of the missionary party, George Humehume* from the island of Kauai. How Thomas Hopu and William Kanui had recounted their adventures on privateers during the War of 1812, and George Humehume his hazards aboard the *Guerriere* fighting at Algiers! And how extremely valuable they all had been in teaching the Hawaiian language to the missionaries!

It was dusk when they saw the ship's boat being rowed rapidly back to the *Thaddeus*. First Officer Hunnewell was obviously excited, as he was standing up and waving. When just within hearing distance, he cupped his hands and shouted slowly and distinctly, "Kamehameha is dead . . . his son Liholiho is king . . . there has been war, but now there is peace . . . the kapus are no more . . . the Hawaiian Gods are destroyed . . . and the temples are demolished!"

The pioneer company of missionaries looked at each other open-eyed and open-mouthed in astonishment.

DIVINE PROVIDENCE!

*Also known as George P. (for Prince) Tamoree.

Rev. Bingham fell to his knees and began to pray. All followed suit. The brig's crew stood silent, and some fell to their knees also and joined in the prayers. It *must* have been Divine Providence!

The prayers had just ceased when they heard the sound of approaching people paddling canoes. They lined the rail again, eager for their first flimpse of Hawaii islanders. Some blanched and turned away when they saw the occupants of the several small outrigger canoes . . . then resolutely turned back and continued calmly looking. Several waved their hands in greeting. The children were rapidly sent below; Lucy Thurston volunteered to shepherd them. She hurried to an open cabin window to see more.

The Hawaiians were *so naked*! The men but wore a narrow girdle around their waists which covered their private parts. The women wore bits of bark cloth wrapped around their waists . . . *only* covering from the hips to the knees. Some were tattooed. Their hair was so long and appeared unkept. Yet they were friendly, smiling, and chattered animatedly.

One canoe slid along the side of the brig to where Lucy Thurston was peering out of the cabin window. A Hawaiian gave her a banana (she couldn't remember later whether the Hawaiian was a man or a woman). Lucy returned the gift with a biscuit. The Hawaiians said, "Wahine maikai (good woman)." Lucy gave them more biscuits, and repeated the word "wahine (woman)" which was part of her limited Hawaiian vocabulary. All smiled at each other. Lucy looked deep into the friendly Hawaiian eyes, and suddenly felt at ease. They *were* God's children . . .

The light breezes had barely moved the brig to abreast of Kawaihae by the next morning. The anchor was dropped, and Mr. Ruggles, Thomas Hopu and George Humehume were sent ashore to invite the resident chief to visit the *Thaddeus*. A number of canoes came offshore to trade with the ship. The fresh fruits were especially enjoyed.

Around noon of the next day, a large double-canoe was paddled by 18 men offshore to the brig. The passengers were shielded from the sun by a huge Chinese umbrella, their ranks were indicated by tall waving kahilis (feather cylinders atop tall staffs). Kalanimoku led his wife Likelike and the huge dowager queens Kalakua and Namahana aboard. Kalanimoku was "decently clad", much to the pleasure of the missionaries: a white dimity roundabout, a black silk vest, yellow nankeen pants, shoes, white cotton hose, plaid cravat, and fur hat. The large dowager queens and Likelike wore "dresses" over ten thicknesses of pa'us (skirts), which made them look even more enormous. There were many "alohas" and much shaking of hands. Much was made of the Chamberlain children.

The chiefesses soon stretched out comfortably on the deck (mattresses were brought for them). Retainers, who had come in other canoes, brought them calabashes of poi and large bowls of raw fish. The corpulent chiefesses used their fingers to eat, which the missionaries knew they would, but were still amazed at their first sight of eating without utensils.

The dinner bell rang, and all crowded into the cabin for the late afternoon meal. Namahana felt hot, and took off her unaccustomed outergarment, simply retaining her thick pa'u (skirt), and felt more comfortable. The missionaries were quite nonplussed, and tried to ignore the exposure. Lucy Thurston thought that "she looked as self-possessed and easy as though sitting in the shades of Eden."[51:31]

The conclusion of conversation with Kalanimoku was that their staying in the Hawaiian Islands was up to King Liholiho. He was at Kailua, down the coast, and Kalanimoku would be pleased to accompany them there the following day. The distinguished guests returned to shore about sunset.

That night, as the moon rose, Revs. Hiram Bingham and Asa Thurston climbed to the main-top and sang the hymn that they had sung at their ordination and on the day of their embarkation from Boston. Hiram's bass and Asa's tenor blended beautifully.

> *Head of the Church triumphant,*
> *We joyfully adore thee:*
> *Till thou appear,*
> *Thy members here,*
> *Shall sing like those in glory:*

The following day was the Sabbath, April 2, 1820. Captain Blanchard and Rev. Bingham went ashore and visited Puukohala Heiau, the site of "heathen idol worship". They returned to the brig in time for services.

The *Thaddeus* weighed anchor that evening and set off under still light breezes for Kailua with their distinguished guests and a deck-load of retainers. Time meant little to the Hawaiians and they enjoyed the slow progress of the ship. Rev. Bingham was almost impatient as the brig crept towards their destination. Dowager

Queen Kalakua decided to see what the missionary women could do for her "temporal benefit". She gave them a bolt of white cambric and blandly stated that she wanted a dress like theirs. It was the Sabbath, and work was put off until the following day.

Scissors and needles were plied with vigor in almost a sewing circle on Monday as all the missionary "sisters" assisted in making the huge 1819-style garment. By that evening it was completed—a long straight dress gathered to a very short bodice.* Kalakua was a sensation the next day upon landing at Kailua wearing her new dress and a lace cap and a neckerchief. She set a new fashion!

The *Thaddeus* anchored at Kailua April 4, 1820, 164 days from Boston. The pioneer company of missionaries were not aware that the next eight days would be extremely frustrating, for it took that long to secure permission to land as permanent residents.

April 4, 1820. Captain Blanchard, Rev. Bingham, Rev. Thurston and Thomas Hopu went ashore. Rev. Hiram Bingham recorded his first impressions:[7:86]

> As we proceeded to the shore, the multitudinous, shouting, and almost naked natives, of every age, sex and rank, swimming, floating on surf-boards, sailing in canoes, sitting, lounging, standing, running like sheep, dancing, or laboring on shore, attracted our earnest attention, and exhibited the appalling darkness of the land, which we had come to enlighten."

They met the large High Chief Kuakini and visited with him at his residence complex. They called upon old John Young, who was surprised and glad to see the missionaries. They met King Liholiho as he was returning from sea-bathing. Rev. Bingham told the king that their sole purpose in coming to Hawaii was to offer the gospel of eternal life and proposed to teach the written word of the God of Heaven. Liholiho was hesitant to consent—he had just abolished the Hawaiian religion; if he permitted a new religion, would it's kahunas (priests) and followers oppose his will? However, he would think upon it, and confer with his advisors.

These initial courtesy calls did not seem very productive, and

---

*The missionary Mother Hubbard, adapted today in Hawaii as muumuu. Lucy Thurston wrote that the "length of the skirt accorded with Brigham Young's rule to his Mormon damsels—have it come down to the tops of the shoes. But in the queen's case, where the shoes were wanting, the bare feet cropped out very prominently."[51:32-33]

it was difficult to be patient. There was a lengthy prayer meeting that eve on the *Thaddeus*.

April 5, 1820. The same party went ashore again in the morning, this time bearing gifts. King Liholiho was found at informal (and scanty) ease with his queens. He was presented an "elegant copy" of the bible furnished by the American Bible Society. Liholiho appeared pleased as he leafed through some pages. He did not know how to read. Bibles were also presented to the queens. The king was given a good brass "spy-glass", and he was delighted with it. It was difficult to turn the conversation to business, as the king was rushing around peering at the distances and exclaiming about what he was able to see.

Other chiefs joined the king, and soon there was quite a group. Rev. Bingham met the ex-high priest of the former Hawaiian religion, Hewahewa, and was not at all impressed with him. However, Hewahewa was neutral in the following discussions. A number of questions were posed to the missionaries:

> Your custom is to have one wife. If we receive and patronize you, will we be permitted only one wife under your religion? This is not our custom. The diplomatic answer was that one wife was the accepted number for christians. The king had quite a jovial conversation with his five queens.

> Would not our friends, the British, object to the settlement of American missionaries rather than British missionaries? Rev. Bingham alleged that American missionaries were approved of by British missionaries, for did they not worship the same God? And besides, as was true of the British missionaries, the American missionaries had no intention of interfering with the governmental affairs of the Hawaiian Kingdom nor concern themselves with trade.

> Jean Rives advises us that the religion of France is the true religion of the foreigners, and yours is not the same. Answer: the same God is worshipped in different ways.

> Who are your Gods? Answer: the great Jehovah, his son Jesus Christ and the Holy Spirit. There was considerable discussion among the Hawaiians. Question: are they not the same as Kane, Maui and Kanaloa of our old religion?

Rev. Bingham was almost beside himself with frustration. He was beginning to suspect the extent of the Hawaiian vocabulary and interpretation capabilities of the young Thomas Hopu. How could he *communicate* ideas and teachings if he could not be thoroughly understood? Fortunately, John Young appeared, and offered a fluent flow of interpretations.

There was another earnest and lengthy prayer meeting that eve on the *Thaddeus*.

April 6, 1820. Another inconclusive and frustrating day of presenting arguments for permission to settle in the Hawaiian Islands.

Later that afternoon the royal family visited the *Thaddeus* by invitation. King Liholiho wore a malo (loin cloth), green silk kihei (mantle), a string of large beads and a feather wreath on his head. He was thus introduced to the first white women he had ever seen.* His queens wore pa'us (skirts) and kiheis. All dined in the cabin, with the king at the head of the table. There was considerable concern among the Hawaiians at the closed-eye blessing of the food. Was this anaana (praying to death)? The explanation was lengthy and partially understood. Liholiho was finally satisfied when he equated it with the old Hawaiian practice of consecration of pork in the heiau (temple) before eating it.

Following dinner, all adjourned to the quarterdeck. The missionaries and some of the crew sang hymns to the accompaniment of a bass-viol played by George Humehume. The royal visitors appeared impressed not only with the singing but also with the apparent goodness and sincerity of those who desired to live in their islands. They were most impressed with the bass-viol. They were almost as impressed with the Chamberlain children, who were fondled almost to the point of their rebellion.

April 7, 1820. Several of the "brethren and sisters" went ashore and visited with the king, queens, chiefs and chiefesses. The missionary wives were great curiosities to the hundreds of Hawaiians who crowded around. How white they were! What bright-colored eyes! How many clothes they wore! What pinched-in and skinny bodies they had! Their bonnets which jutted forward earned them the nickname of ai-oeoe (longnecks). The missionaries were known by this sobriquet for many years.

When they called on the Sacred Queen Mother Keopuolani the lack of interpretive skills was again apparent. Thomas Hopu did his best, but that was not good enough:[27:247] "These white people are kahunas of the most high God who have come to tell us of the One who made heaven and earth," and added, "Hereafter will

---

*Liholiho may have met Rose Freycinet (August 1819) and Peter Dobell's "Russian subject" wife (late 1819).

come the great day (la) when all will be judged before God.''

Hawaiian words have many shades and meanings. The listeners equated "la" with the sun, and were concerned that the message was that the sun would grow bigger. Some became terrified that the sun was about to increase in size and destroy the islands with its heat. Others considered that Thomas Hopu was telling "tall tales" to Keopuolani. He was known to the Hawaiians as ma'oi (impudent) everafter.

There were sober discussions in the cabin of the *Thaddeus* that night about their new homeland. The plants and foliage were *so* different. The food the Hawaiians ate was so strange (dogs and raw fish, *ugh!*). The houses (!) were so odd. How destitute of the comforts of civilized life . . . The people were so different, and wore so *few* clothes. Yet they were so friendly. Much more friendly than some of the white men they saw. Some of the few white men were actually antagonistic. The Demon Rum appeared to have grasped some of the people, the king too! No one seemed to have any privacy. How difficult it would be *initially* to have a normal deportment in the face of all the curiosity. And how they wished they could *speak* and *understand* the Hawaiian language so that they could *converse intelligently* . . .

April 8, 1820. Rev. Bingham again persisted with King Liholiho. He discussed mission location, and stated that Honolulu would be the best place as it was now the largest trading center of the islands. There were many western christians there who also needed spiritual guidance. Liholiho was averse to this. All white men wanted to live at Honolulu, and he thought that Americans would like to possess that island. As king, shouldn't he have any new religion with him so he could keep an eye on it? If the missionaries were accepted, they should be with him at Kailua. But didn't the king sometimes move from place to place? Yes, and the missionaries could move with him. There was a long dissertation about what a church was and the need for a permanent facility. Liholiho considered, and reaffirmed that, if accepted, he wanted the missionaries with him at Kailua.

A counter suggestion was offered. How about part of the mission to be with the king at Kailua and the other part at Honolulu? (Rev. Bingham did not mention at this time that the missionaries were also considering using George Humehume as entré to the island of Kauai. George's father was King Kaumualii of that island, his mother was a makaainana (commoner). The king said he was dubious, but said that he would think upon it.

On the way back to the *Thaddeus* that afternoon, Captain

Blanchard urged that the missionaries disembark at Kailua so he could be about his business.* Rev. Bingham disagreed, firm in his convictions.

There was another lengthy prayer meeting that eve on the *Thaddeus*.

April 9, 1820. This was the Sabbath. No missionaries went ashore, and the day was devoted to the Lord.

April 10, 1820. All the missionaries went ashore to endeavor favorable reactions from individual chiefs and chiefesses for the mission to be admitted into the Hawaiian Islands. Rev. Bingham reiterated to the king his counter proposal for part of the mission to be at Kailua and the other part at Honolulu. Liholiho said that he would have to discuss this with Kuhina-nui (Regent) Kaahumanu, who was out fishing. Fortunately for the missionaries, she returned after midday with her brother, Keeaumoku. A council was set for late that afternoon.

The council was delayed at the stated hour as all, except the missionaries, enjoyed a "heathen" hula dance. At sunset the council got down to business.

Rev. Bingham made a carefully worded formal presentation, interpreted by Thomas Hopu, which recapitulated the reasons for their coming to Hawaii and the useful arts which they could teach the Hawaiians. He reiterated his former arguments and rebutted former objections. The pros and cons of mission location were presented in detail.

When the discussion began, Rev. Bingham became much impressed with the fast and piercing questions of the large imperious Kuhina-nui Kaahumanu. He recognized that she had dominant influence. Much was made by Kalanimoku of their goodness of intent by bringing their wives and children, and that some of the women were hapai (pregnant).

The old white-haired John Young was last to speak: [27:246-47]

> These kahunas worship the same God as those of our country of whom Vancouver said to Kamehameha, 'When I go back to Great Britain let me ask King George to send you kahunas.' Let the chiefs try them out by permitting them to remain in Hawaii for a year; then, if you discover that they are not doing right, let the chiefs send them away.

The discussion ceased, and the missionaries rose to leave so

---

*Appendix 5 contains Captain Blanchard's instructions in the passage contract.

that the council could deliberate without their presence. As they departed with "alohas", John Young advised them that they would be fortunate if the council would decide within six months!

The prayer meeting aboard the *Thaddeus* that night was especially serious.

April 11, 1820. "Mr. Bingham being somewhat exhausted by the long continued negotiation, and seriously indisposed today, Mr. Thurston and Dr. Holman went on shore to hear the decision."[36:120] The king announced that the missionaries would be permitted to stay for one year on a trial basis. If at the end of this one year the king was not satisfied with them, they would leave. The location of the missionaries would be at the pleasure of the king. He wanted Dr. Holman, one preacher, and two of the Hawaiian helpers to stay at Kailua. The remainder could go to Honolulu.

Needless to say, the missionaries were very pleased that at long last they had permission to enter and stay in the Hawaiian Islands. They thought a year was a very short probation period to prove the worth of God's Mission.

When they returned triumphantly to the *Thaddeus*, there was a sober meeting of the missionary "brethren and sisters". A ballot determined that Rev. Thurston would remain at Kailua with Dr. Holman. Thomas Hopu and William Kanui would also remain. The rest of the pioneer company would go on to Honolulu on the island of Oahu, some 145 nautical miles of open sea away . . . as the Hawaiian crow flies. A day and a half to two days to Oahu if there were good tradewinds, and much more time when the ship would have to beat to windward from Oahu to Hawaii.

April 12, 1820. The common stores of the pioneer company were divided and a proper portion assigned to the Thurstons and Holmans for the initial mission at Kailua. These goods were sent ashore under the protection of the Hawaiian helpers.

Rev. and Mrs. Thurston and Dr. and Mrs. Holman bade a brave farewell to the remainder of the pioneer company after a final tea aboard the *Thaddeus*. Rev. Bingham accompanied them in the late afternoon through the crowds of curious Hawaiians to a thatched house in the middle of Kailua village (some 3,000 people) which had been provided by the king for their use.

It was three and a half feet high at the foot of the rafters, rectangular in shape and about a dozen feet long. There were no ceiling, windows, floor or furniture—just a bare room with a small opening to enter and a windhole at the peak to let out smoke from any fire. It was crowded with their boxed possessions. (They were later to discover that it was also crowded with a sizable population of fleas.) The two couples began to arrange the dark interior for privacy and common use. The king had thoughtfully posted a sentinel outside of their house to safeguard their property.

Rev. Bingham said goodbye to King Liholiho, who indicated that he was ready to learn how to read.

The *Thaddeus* hoisted anchor just before sunset and set sail for Honolulu. The Thurstons and the Holmans stood on the lonely strange shore and waved and watched the brig until she was out of sight in the dusk. They could just see each other in the gathering night as they slowly walked back to their first Hawaiian residence. They walked side by side, each couple holding hands, and listening to the unfamiliar sounds of a Hawaiian village about to go to sleep.

The tradewind sighed, and seemed to quote:

> . . . henceforth you are to labor for Christ; and all the fruits of your labors are to be held as irrevocably consecrated to him, for the purposes of his mercy towards the dwellers in the midst of the seas.

All four looked up at the bright starred heavens when a gust of the tradewind seemed to trumpet—
LO I AM WITH YOU ALWAYS!

XII

pRoBation

The Thurstons and Holmans cleaned house vigorously. They cleared and swept the house and laid down a new grass floor. Atop this they placed gratefully received gifts of lauhala mats. They cut several small windows in the low thatch walls for light and ventilation and hung curtains. Queen Kamamalu kindly lent them two Chinese-made bedsteads. These they trimmed with curtains for privacy at night in their small quarters. The king gave them a round mahogany table. They rearranged their possessions, nailed up shelves for small much-used articles, and made racks for their clothes.

They set up a stove at a safe distance from their house, and made arrangements for brush wood to be brought from several miles away. The king had kindly arranged that his steward kept them supplied with cooked fish, taro and sweet potatoes. Fresh water was brought in calabashes from a good source four miles away. Washing of clothes turned out to be quite a problem. The missionary men built a portable open-roofed enclosure for outhouse privacy. The people were *so* curious. It was rare not to find up to a hundred Hawaiians squatting or lying around watching their activities for the first several weeks. The queens called on them several times a day just to make sure that they were getting along alright. The queens couldn't understand why they didn't have domestic retainers.

Dr. Holman was soon at professional work:[17:41]

I was called upon by the King to render medical aid to one of his wives and a number of his attendants and servants with all of whom, by the blessing of God, I had very good success, although some of them were dangerously ill. The native physicians were much opposed to my practice, telling my patients that I should kill them, and it is to be suspected that had I not been successful in my first setting out, the consequences might have proved unhappy for me.

97

Payment for these medical services was in the form of foodstuffs—pork, taro, sweet potatoes, fish, etc. These were placed in the common stores of the mission and shared equally between the Thurstons and Holmans.

After three days of this new life Mrs. Holman stated emphatically that she was not going to accept this degree of self-denial from civilization. Dr. & Mrs. Holman left the mission three months later. (They went the "long way" home via Canton and the Cape of Good Hope. Mrs. Holman achieved the distinction of being the first American woman to go around the world.)

Such strange things happened. There was a great feast April 29, 1820 in honor of the late Ke Alii Nui Kamehameha, at which the delicacy was several hundred baked dogs. The missionaries were invited to sit at the king's table (he wore a brilliant military uniform for the occasion). Queen Kamamalu was very friendly with Lucy Thurston, and wanted to borrow a dress to wear at this affair. It would have taken two of Lucy's dresses to make one for the six foot 200 pound Kamamalu! So Kamamalu dressed in the height of Hawaiian fashion. Ten thicknesses of beautifully dyed kapa (bark cloth), 30 inches wide by some 25 feet long, were carefully placed down lengthwise on mats. Kamamalu lay down on one end and rolled over and over until the kapa was wrapped entirely around her as a pa'u (skirt). Seventy thicknesses of skirt! She had to be laughingly assisted to her feet. She also wore a wreath of rare yellow feathers on her head and a maile lei around her neck.

Rev. Thurston preached before the king and his queens as soon as he could. He was thoroughly conscious of his, and Thomas Hopu's Hawaiian vocabulary inadequacies, and kept his words simple. "I have a message from God unto thee . . ."[51:42] When the prayer (pule) was offered, *all* knelt before the One God.

King Liholiho started to learn to read and write (heluhelu and palapala). But there were so many other demands on his time, he so enjoyed relaxing with his friends (and rum bottle), etc. He insisted, however, that his six and a half year old younger brother, Kauikeaouli, his favorites, John Ii and James Kahuhu, and a few others attend classes regularly. Within three months they were reading simple lessons in Webster's spelling book. The king was delighted at their progress. He himself was soon able to read a little in the New Testament.

These were not the only students. The missionaries diligently set about enlarging their Hawaiian vocabularies. They had discovered that each word could sometimes have many meanings, the sense of the word dependent upon how it was used. They also discovered that the alii (chiefs and chiefesses) had a more extensive vocabulary than the makaainana (commoners).

Queen Kamamalu soon arranged and insisted that the missionaries move to a better house closer to hers. It had two doors! They were two and a half and three and a half feet high, but nevertheless, two doors. There were of course no closures other than planks, and no locks.

Lucy Thurston was alone most of the time after the Holmans left Kailua. Her clergyman husband was busy many long hours spreading the Lord's Word. The Hawaiians welcomed the missionaries with hospitality, but Lucy Thurston had some apprehensive incidents with intoxicated Hawaiians. There was one especially frightening incident.

One day she was teaching Kauikeaouli, Ii and Kahuhu when a partially intoxicated dirty and evil looking old Hawaiian entered her house. The Hawaiian retainers, who were lolling around at the sides of the house, shrank away. They exclaimed that he was a bad priest of the old religion. They scrambled away under his baleful look. Lucy's students ran for help.

The ex-priest took off his malo (loin cloth) and began to pursue Lucy Thurston around the room. "He threw himself upon the bed and seemed to enjoy the luxury of rolling from side to side upon its white covering."[51:49] He continued to pursue Lucy "with increased eagerness." In and out, around the furniture and boxes, dodging here and there—when finally entrapped in a corner, Lucy grabbed a "substantial" stick and struck her pursuer and escaped to the outside of the house. He followed. She held up her long skirts and ran as she had never run before—through the quickly gathering crowd of Hawaiians, and towards where she knew her husband was.

He had been advised of the trouble, and was running to meet her. They returned to their house where Lucy finally burst into tears. Within minutes the house became filled with solicitous queens, students, retainers, etc. The ex-priest returned. The Hawaiians again shrank away. The athletic Rev. Asa Thurston mastered his tremendous wrath—the interloper was "walked out off the premises with a muscular strength that no common man could resist."[51:50]* King Liholiho was determined to have the troublemaker put to death, but Rev. Thurston dissuaded him.

The small mission at Kailua grew rapidly in stature and respect. The kahuna-pule (religious priest) Thurston was so sincere in telling about the One God and the way of life of *good* christians.

---

*Rev. Bingham infers use of a cane. [7:125]

Did he not follow his own teachings and use forebearance when dealing with that evil old ex-priest? He was not afraid of him! And also when one of the foreigners wanted to fight him and make him leave Hawaii? When Dr. Holman was here, didn't he cure and relieve suffering that the Hawaiian doctors could not help? These missionaries are industrious, and are trying so earnestly to learn Hawaiian. And they are trying to do good to all the people, alii and makaainana alike. Rev. Thurston was always ready to lend a helping hand for any big task. Lucy Thurston is so *different* than Hawaiian women, but so nice! She is teaching the strange art of reading and writing to the king's younger brother and the others that the king designated. It is indeed strange that foreigner women do the cooking! These missionary people work hard, do not get intoxicated like the other foreigners and cause trouble. They are good people!

The *Thaddeus* took 36 hours to sail from Kailua to Honolulu. The missionaries were eagerly looking at their new home as the sun rose April 14, 1820. Rev. Bingham recorded that the island of Oahu:[7:92]

> . . . presented successively its pointed mountains, covered with trees and shrubbery, its well-marked, extinguished craters near its shore, its grass covered hills, and more fertile valleys, its dingy thatched villages, its cocoanut groves, its fort and harbor, and its swarthy inhabitants in throngs—the primary objects of our attention and concern.

Anchor was dropped in the roadstead abreast of Honolulu village. Rev. Bingham and several of the missionary assistants went ashore to pay their respects to Governor Boki at Kekuanohu ("Thorny Back", Honolulu Fort). They hoped that King Liholiho had not forgotten to advise the governor that they could reside in Honolulu (on probation). Francisco de Paula Marin,* the official interpreter, advised that Governor Boki was visiting another part of the island. Messengers were sent to advise Boki of their arrival. The missionaries paid their respects to Kekuanaoa, the "second in command". The official calls being over, the missionaries curiously walked on the winding dusty paths through the village of some 3-4,000 people—which was to be their new home. They climbed Puowaina (Punchbowl) and viewed the countryside with interest before returning to the *Thaddeus* that evening.

---

*Marin was an early foreign resident of many talents. He is most noted today for his horticultural imports.

Governor Boki returned to Honolulu two days later ". . . so much under the debasing and distracting influence of strong drink as to be unfit for business, except that of a speedy reformation, to which our business would call him."[7:94] The following day he gave indifferent permission to land. Appropriate orders were issued in "Hawaiian time" several days later.

The *Thaddeus* was towed by Hawaiian canoes from the roadstead through the narrow channel into Honolulu Harbor on the 18th, and dropped anchor. Rev. Bingham estimated that the harbor was sufficiently large "to admit 150 sail, of the capacity of 100 to 700 tons". The missionaries disembarked April 19, 1820.

Governor Boki was not then, nor later, very hospitable. The American resident traders, Messrs. Winship, Lewis and Navarro, offered them three small Hawaiian thatched huts, which the missionaries gratefully accepted. Storage space was also provided for their possessions and supplies. The traders and other foreign residents initially provided them with greatly appreciated fresh foods.

The missionary women were as great curiosities in Honolulu as they had been in Kailua. Much was made of the Chamberlain children. The fifteen New Englanders had a crowded and restless first night in their new home—the Watch at Honolulu Fort some 500 feet away rang a large ship's bell once an hour and shouted the Hawaiian version of "All's Well".

As happened at Kailua, the first order of business was housekeeping. Then to the Lord's Work, which had brought the missionaries to the Hawaiian Islands. The first public service in Honolulu was held April 23, 1820 with the theme:[7:97] Fear not, for behold I bring you good tidings of great joy, which shall be to all people. Lo I am with you always.

Samuel Whitney and Samuel Ruggles accompanied George Humehume to the island of Kauai May 2, 1820 on the *Thaddeus*. King Kaumualii welcomed his son with open arms, and included the missionaries in his welcome. He provisioned the *Thaddeus*, and promised Captain Blanchard some $1,000. worth of sandalwood in gratitude for bringing his son home. Messrs. Whitney and Ruggles were laden with gifts when they returned to Honolulu two months later. The Whitney and Ruggles families established a mission station at Waimea, Kauai shortly thereafter. Nathan Chamberlain, age 11, went with them to assist the missionary effort.

Maria Loomis' time for childbirth had come. There was no

resident doctor in Honolulu, and Dr. Holman was then at Lahaina, Maui. Dr. Holman was not available to come to Honolulu for personal reasons, and the missionaries were considerably disturbed. Fortunately, the British whaleship *L'Aigle*, Captain Valentine Starbuck, arrived at the roadstead and had a physician on board (most unusual for a whaler). Dr. Williams delivered the first white child born in the Hawaiian Islands July 16, 1820—Levi Sartwell Loomis.

Missionary efforts took precedence over family concern. Elisha Loomis left a fortnight later for Kawaihae, Hawaii. There he taught English, reading and writing, to Prime Minister Kalanimoku, his wife Likelike, and a group of favored youths.

The missionaries became busily dispersed. Daniel Chamberlain, age 7, went to assist the Thurstons at Kailua, Hawaii. Each small mission station was basically equipped with the bible, Watt's catechism, and Webster's spelling book. The missionary wives were not only in great demand as teachers, but also as seamstresses. There were many requests from the chiefs and chiefesses for making shirts and dresses. The Hawaiian missionary helpers were of great assistance in the beginning of Hawaiian literacy. And the missionaries began to speak Hawaiian with some fluency—and began to be able to *communicate*!

Liholiho and Kaahumanu became restless and commenced moving around their kingdom in the Hawaiian traditional manner. Their court was large, and there were many retainers. They stayed in a district as long as food was reasonably available. They went to Lahaina, Maui in early August 1820, thence to Hilo, Hawaii, and back to Kailua.

Preoccupation with foreigners who resided in the islands without permission was a chronic problem. Jean Rives was sent to Honolulu in August 1820 to expel those who did not "belong" to either Liholiho or Kaahumanu or Kalanimoku. This met with limited success.

A council was held September 10, 1820. The view was presented that most of the trading activity, and troubles therefrom, was at Honolulu rather than at Kailua. Honolulu would be the best place in the kingdom for the king and regent to reside. Liholiho and Kaahumanu finally agreed. They started off, but made a lengthy stay on the island of Maui enroute.

Liholiho wanted Rev. & Mrs. Thurston to accompany him. They followed the king several weeks later in a small brig. Lucy

Thurston recorded of the voyage from the island of Hawaii to the adjoining island of Maui that[51:52]

> Four hundred seventy five souls were on that brig, and with the exception of a few individuals, all were then above deck. Several hundred calabashes, containing poi, fish, water &c., provisions for the passage, occupied not a little room, while a large number of dogs with here and there a nest of puppies, served to fill up the crevices. The officers were obliged to keep watch most of the time, and to proceed from place to place on the sides of the vessel. We were treated with a great deal of kindness, being presented with fruit, vegetables, fresh meat, &c. My hands, fingers, nails, and every part of dress, were examined and felt of with the utmost minuteness. They were all good, *very* good.

The morning following the Thurstons arrival at Lahaina, the already partially intoxicated king impetuously commandeered the brig to take him around to the windward side of the island of Maui. The Thurstons' almost irreplacable clothes were in the hold, and when recovered several months later, were soaking wet and almost ruined. The Thurstons stayed on Maui for a month and finally arrived in Honolulu December 21, 1820 for a heartfelt pre-Christmas reunion with the "brethren and sisters".

The frugal New England background missionaries became aghast when they found out about the "extravagant" chiefs' purchases from the traders. Ships of questionable use and "useless" things were obtained for *very* high prices. Payments were made in sandalwood, or mostly promises of sandalwood, the prime Hawaiian trading commodity. Exorbitant! Wasteful! It had such an impact upon the people, for they had to laboriously gather the sandalwood!

The chiefs had engaged in an "orgy" of buying western vessels for promises of sandalwood following the death of Ke Alii Nui Kamehameha in May 1819. As examples, Liholiho purchased the new sloop *Kirouea* in late-1819 and Kalanimoku purchased the brig *Neo* in mid-1820. Liholiho acquired the 83 foot 191 ton hermaphrodite brig *Cleopatra's Barge* November 16, 1820. This luxurious yacht was bought for promissary payment of 6,000 piculs of sandalwood ($50-90,000. dependent upon the market in Canton). The vessel was renamed *Haaheo o Hawaii* (Pride of Hawaii).

The *Thaddeus* and a schooner were bought from Captain

103

Blanchard (for his owners) in early 1821 for the promise of 8,000 piculs of sandalwood.[8:62] First Officer James Hunnewell remained in the islands to collect payment (final balance was paid off seven years later). The "credit" of King Kaumualii of Kauai was strained when he bought "a very inferior Brig & Cargo", and the cargo of a second ship at about the same time. There were some ten ships purchased by the chiefs in 1821 for promised sandalwood. The paper profit to the traders was considerable, the collection of promised sandalwood difficult.

The makaainana (commoners) were ordered to the mountains to cut immense amounts of sandalwood, now getting difficult to find in quantity. Those who did not follow this order to the mountains had their houses burned down. Sandalwood trading was no longer a managed royal monopoly—each chief secured as much as he could get. All sandalwood was cut down, to include new growth. The men were in the mountains so much now that their agriculture and aquiculture suffered considerably. Living for the people became difficult.

Some 30,000 piculs of sandalwood were shipped to Canton, China in 1821.[8:64] Promissory debts of sandalwood were said to have exceeded 22,000 piculs at the close of 1821.[8:68] The Hawaiian sandalwood trade began to decline rapidly.*

These considerable purchases of ships, and a growing awareness that the Hawaiians were paying "outrageous" prices for goods and ships, greatly disturbed the thrifty missionaries. They did not interfere with the affairs of the chiefs, but when asked by individual chiefs, were free in their opinions about this exploitation.

Competition was keen among the traders, and sales methods were often unscrupulous. Prices charged were what the traffic would bear. Some ship captains were in the practice of leaving seamen in the islands who were insubordinate or not good working sailors—to get rid of them and to save payment of their wages. Many of these became destitute. A number of Hawaiians signed-on ships at far less than the going wages for seamen.

There became a growing coolness and antagonism between some of the traders and the missionaries as the chiefs began heeding missionary advice and became more cautious in their purchases.

---

*Fortunately for Hawaiian commerce, the decline of sandalwood trading coincided with the beginning of whaleship servicing. A rich sperm whaling ground was discovered off the coast of Japan, some 40 days whaleship sail west of the Hawaiian Islands. Whalers began to refit and re-provision at Honolulu and other Hawaiian ports in rapidly increasing numbers.

Even more annoying to these traders, residents and visitors who "hung their consciences on Cape Horn when they entered the Pacific", the missionaries made it *very* clear that they did not approve of those who lived with Hawaiian women, unmarried.

Why, the missionaries even disapproved of Hawaiian women swimming out to greet arriving ships that had been at sea for a long time! What were the islands coming to?!

Liholiho arrived at Honolulu the evening of February 3, 1821. His presence had been expected for some time, and was well prepared for. There were many salutes from Honolulu Fort and the battery atop Punchbowl when the brig *Haaheo o Hawaii* was sighted approaching the roadstead off Honolulu Harbor. These salutes were answered by the brig. The Hawaiians were most excited at the nighttime flashes of the cannons and the reverberations of the loud booms from the valleys.

The king landed the following morning. Revelry and feasting immediately began. Rev. Bingham and Rev. Thurston waited until evening (it being the Sabbath) to visit King Liholiho at his residence complex adjacent to Honolulu Fort. Rev. Bingham recorded that they ". . . found him in a mood not sufficiently companionable to speak to us. We were struck, however, with the ingenuity of Kamamalu, his favorite wife, who, in the dilemma, unexpectedly lifted the nerveless hand of her lord, that he might receive the salutation of his missionaries. . ."[7:126]

Kalanimoku's wife, Likelike, gave birth to a son in Honolulu shortly thereafter. This event was made startlingly well known by the firing of several hundred pounds of gunpowder from a number of cannon which had been dragged to the place of birth. Likelike came down with a "burning fever". Her companions carried her to and from the shore for four nights and immersed her in the sea to cool her off. This didn't help. Her brother-in-law Boki, the governor of the island of Oahu, was at her side when she died. He commenced wailing. This was taken up by all others within hearing, and the missionaries had their first observations of respect paid upon the death of a personage. Hair was cut off on the sides of heads, semi-circular scars were burned on exposed skins for living memories, riotous parties began, etc. The body "disappeared".

The missionaries were aghast. They entreated Kalanimoku to have a funeral service on the Sabbath. He consented. At the termination of the service his only question was, had his departed wife really gone to heaven?

The missionaries called on King Liholiho to stop the revelry on the Sabbath. They were informed that this mourning was Hawaiian custom, and all normal observances were temporarily suspended. They also asked Liholiho to attend Sabbath services, but he said he was going to return to Lahaina for a while. He asked the missionaries to pray to Jehovah to give him a good wind—and pointed out the direction he wanted it from.

Liholiho, Kaahumanu and the court finally came to Honolulu to reside more or less permanently in March 1821. Much of the time Liholiho was intoxicated, which vexed the missionaries terribly.*

Two ships of a Russian exploring expedition visited Honolulu April 2-18, 1821, the *Otkutic*, Commodore Michael Vasilieff, and the *Blagonamerenniy*, Captain Schishmareff. Rev. Bingham reported of their visit, commencing April 4, 1821, that:[37:112]

> The Russian officers came on shore and were introduced to the king. But as he had no place on shore, where he could politely ask them to sit down, or give them comfortable seats, he took them to the elegant dining-room of the Cleopatra's Barge, where they were well accommodated, and politely served with a glass of wine, when [whereupon] they rose, and drank to his Majesty's health. They were welcomed on board, also with a salute of 8 or 10 guns. When they had made known their business, obtained permission to receive supplies, to make astronomical surveys, to survey the harbor and examine the country; I had the pleasure of conducting them to the missionary establishment, and of introducing them to the brethren and sisters of the mission family. We were all happy to see so many of the subjects of Alexander at our house, as friends and neighbors. They were generally dressed in the uniform of their Navy officers, with their side arms girded on. A priest of the Greek Church, 73 years old, in a large black cloak, having a cross suspended from his neck; two physicians, a naturalist, and an astronomer, attended the Commodore. Two of the gentlemen (Lieutenants) speak English with some facility; some speak Latin, some Spanish, and all Russian. The Commodore inquired with interest

---

*As examples, Marin's diary recorded under the date March 12, 1821, "This day the King is not very drunk" and May 3, 1821, "The King sober".[34]

whether we were supported by the American Government; how long we had been here; and how long we intended to stay. He appeared satisfied with our answers, pleased with our enterprise, and said all nations would approve of it.

April 6—According to previous request, they visited our school, and favored us with their company at tea. They appeared to be pleased with the state of the school, and with the improvement of the pupils, the marks of genius they exhibited, and with our general prospects. The Commodore spoke of the superiority of our system over the Catholics at California, as we were attempting the promote learning, as well as Christianity. The papists there, he says, make slaves of those, whom they attempt to proselyte.

April 8. We had divine service at our house, preaching from the text, "We glory in tribulations also," followed by Melton-Mowbrey.* One of the Russian officers, who was present, finding that Mrs. B. was unwell, kindly offered to bring one of their physicians; who soon came and gave his advice. We notice this kind providence, which sends us such seasonable advice; and would acknowledge the blessing attending it.

April 9. The king and queen dined on board the Commodore's ship, sleeping an hour before dinner in the cabin. As I had gone on board to obtain the medicine prepared for Mrs. B. I was requested to dine, and to ask a blessing at table. The Commodore said to the king, "We acknowledge God as the giver of our food." We hope the interview enjoyed by the king, with these gentlemen, will be useful to him.

April 12. The family dined on board the Commodore's ship, agreeably to a polite invitation previously given;—and received much kind attention. They were shown many interesting curiosities, collected from different tribes and nations; as well as the accommodations of the ship.

Beside the Russian seamen, we were gratified to see two Kamtschadales, and one Siberian, who were said to have become excellent sailors, with little practice.

April 14. We were invited on board the other ship. Both ships are well fitted out for the purpose of discovery. All the sea Captains in port, dined today,—a sumptuous dinner of 8 or 10 courses; one dish of soup put up in London 1819; also

*A missionary favorite piece of music.

milk put up at the same time and place, and preserved good, for coffee. These were curiosities. They enlivened the natives for several successive evenings with the exhibition of fireworks.

April 16. At their request, I gave the Commodore a written communication, respecting the state of this nation, and committed to his care a letter addressed to the Governor of Kamtschatka, and, with the approbation, a copy of the Memoirs of Obookiah, for Prince Galitzin. They sailed on the 18th.*

From what we have seen of these gentlemen, they appear to be well educated; attached to the Emperor, whose full length portrait accompanies them wherever they go. They appear exceedingly happy in each other's society, fond of cheerful conversation, and kindly disposed toward all men, especially to us, the American Missionaries.

The missionaries celebrated the first anniversary of their landing at Honolulu and establishing the Honolulu mission on April 19, 1821. The day was devoted to thanksgiving, prayer, an examination of the small beginning schools, and a review of progress. The king invited them to a public dinner that evening.

The following day Liholiho and several of his chiefs visited the missionaries, and:[7:132]

> . . . on being assured anew of our unvarying intention to do him good, and not evil, to elevate the nation, and promote their prosperity and salvation, he confirmed the original permission granted us, to remain and labor as missionaries, approved of our erecting a permanent house for our accommodation, and requested us to aid him in building a palace three stories high; the upper story of which, he said, should be devoted to the worship of Jehovah.

The king gave the missionaries a hog and 90 pieces of kapa (bark cloth). Kaahumanu, Kalanimoku and Kalakua gave them a liberal amount of usable supplies. The large imperious Kuhina-nui Kaahumanu looked Rev. Bingham square in the eyes and asked him to pray for the king.

The probation was over! The Lord's Work could and did progress at an even faster and faster pace.

*Commodore Vasilieff visited again in December 1821.

XIII

kaumualii

The council was reclining at ease at Pakaka "Palace," the largest structure in King Liholiho's thatched residence complex aside the brooding walls of Honolulu Fort at the mouth of Honolulu Harbor. It was late afternoon of one of the first few days of July 1821. The council members were relaxed. Their normal restlessness was at ease, as they had just completed a long, leisurely trip around the island of Oahu.

Kalanimoku finished telling the council how hard it was to collect taxes from the makaainana (commoners), for they were so much in the mountains collecting sandalwood that their husbandry had been neglected. Most of the council just shrugged—so what was new? Taxes were always difficult to collect. Kuhina-nui Kaahuma-nu looked thoughtful, but did not comment.

The next and final item on the agenda was a request from Rev. Hiram Bingham. He awaited without, and was invited to address the council. Although Rev. Bingham was rapidly learning Hawaiian, he deemed it advisable to ask long-time resident Francisco de Paula Marin to interpret for him to assure correctness of meaning.

"King Kaumaulii of the island of Kauai is planning to visit Tahiti in his recently purchased brig *Becket*. He has invited two of the missionaries to accompany him. British missionaries of the London Missionary Society have been in Tahiti for over 24 years. We would like to gain the benefit of their wisdom and knowledge. We know that Hawaiians and Tahitians are the same stock of people, and have similar customs and traditions. We are particularly interested to discover what Tahitian language they have put in writing, for we wish to do the same for the Hawaiian language. To be able to read (heluhelu) and write (palapala) is a mark of a great and civilized people. This we want to do for you."

The chiefs listened intently. Tahiti, the Mother Country of alii lore! Kaahumanu, Liholiho and Kalanimoku spoke in favor of allowing two missionaries to join King Kaumualii on the (envied) trip. (Rev. Bingham had shrewdly consulted with these three beforehand.) The chiefs nodded concurrence, and Rev. Bingham left the council with a mahalo (thanks) and an aloha (goodbye).

Liholiho asked a question in the ensuing quiet, "What sort of man is Kaumualii? I don't remember much about his short visit here with my father eleven years ago. I was but a boy of 14."

Kalanimoku replied thoughtfully, "That is the first and last time I have seen him also. But I remember him well." He reflected, "Kaumualii is a large good-looking man, and has the ideal presence of an alii. He must be a little over 40 years of age now, a few years younger than Kaahumanu. He is very intelligent, gracious, and much loved by his people."

Kalanimoku continued, "I remember well what your father said to him when they met:[32] 'I am not going to take away your authority nor any part of your lands; go home and retain your power. But this is my wish, that my chiefs may visit your island and that you will receive them graciously.' Since that time Kaumualii has sent annual tribute to us, as you know. In a private conversation between Ke Alii Nui Kamehameha and King Kaumualii, which I attended, it was agreed that you, Liholiho, would be Kaumualii's heir-designate."

"Hmmm . . ." said Liholiho softly, "I would like to visit the island of Kauai and see Kaumualii again."

This met with considerable opposition. Kaumualii was an unknown factor to most of the counsellors, and they did not trust the unknown. Maybe Liholiho could go to Kauai sometime, but only with many ships and men. Had not George Humehume recently sent a letter to Liholiho addressed with the limited title of "King of the Windward Islands"? This appeared belittling, and implied scanty sovereign overlordship. This was quite different than Kamehameha had established. Perhaps there was danger.

Liholiho did not belabor the point, but his lips closed in a very stubborn way. The council meeting terminated shortly thereafter.

It was not ten minutes later that Liholiho received a message from his mother, Keopuolani: "Be not apprehensive about visiting Kauai, for the men of Kauai are your men also. Kaumualii is a good honorable alii." Now how had Keopuolani discovered the negative advice of the council so soon? Liholiho never ceased to be amazed at his mother!

Rev. Bingham and Mr. Ruggles embarked on the *Tarter*, Captain Turner, for Kauai July 8, 1821, to finalize arrangements for the trip to Tahiti. Prior to their departure, Kuhina-nui Kaahumanu visited Rev. Bingham. Marin interpreted a gracious salutation to be presented to King Pomare of Tahiti. An ahuula (feather cloak) and some beautifully dyed kapa (bark cloth) were to be taken as gifts from the Hawaiian rulers.

The large motherly Dowager Queen Kalakua impetuously joined the two missionaries at the last minute and achieved the distinction of being the first member of the royal family to visit the island of Kauai. Kaahumanu (her sister) and Kalanimoku showed their respect and interest by seeing them off. The brig took twenty hours to reach Waimea, Kauai, where their reception was most cordial and hospitable. (Liholiho was quite irritated when he was advised that Kalakua had gone to Kauai.)

Rev. Bingham and Mr. Ruggles did not go to Tahiti.

Mr. John C. Jones, Agent of the United States for Commerce and Seamen in Hawaii (and also Honolulu representative of the Boston firm of Marshall and Wildes), came to Kauai several weeks later and dissuaded the missionaries. Rev. Bingham summed Mr. Jones arguments:[7:137]

> The objections urged against it by the traders were, that it would be injurious to bring speculators from the Society to the Sandwich Islands;—that the honor to the American people (so young, and so recently independent), of sending out first, and establishing so large and important mission, at these islands, would be diminished if we should now apply to the English missionaries for aid, for it would be said in England, we could not succeed without their help;—that it would not be well for the mission to be laid under so great an obligation to Kaumualii as the favor contemplated would impose;—and finally, that there was such a total dissimilarity between the two languages, that the procuring of books and translations would be of little or no use.

The course of events overtook King Kaumualii—he did not go to Tahiti either.

It was July 21, 1821, the day after Mr. Jones had dissuaded Rev. Bingham from going to Tahiti. King Liholiho, High Chief Boki (governor of Oahu), Counsellor Naihe and his wife Kapiolani, John Ii, and attendants to total thirty in the party, set out from Honolulu for Ewa in a small Hawaiian-built sloop. The rum bottle had passed freely among the leading passengers with its usual result.

Liholiho sprawled back with his elbows over the side of the

low freeboard boat. He enjoyed the grand weather and the brisk tradewind which made the sloop heel and slide swiftly through the sea. When the helmsman started to put in for the mouth of what is now called Pearl Harbor, King Liholiho motioned to continue on out past Kalaeloa (Barbers Point). Liholiho grew silent, brooded at the close living sea, and did not participate in the light fun conversation. His sipping from the rum bottle became more frequent.

When truly off Kalaeloa, he suddenly sat up straight and muttered, "Let us go." His companions had not heard what he had said, and glanced at him respectfully and inquiringly. "Let us go," the king repeated clearly, and then commanded *"Let Us Go!"*

"Let us go where?" Boki inquired with a smile.

"To Kauai," answered Liholiho firmly.

"But this boat is too small for Kaieiewaho (the outside high waves) Channel between here and Kauai, and the weather is freshening. Besides, we have no water or provisions. None of us have been there and we're not sure what direction to sail or how far away it is."*

"So . . . Let Us Go! Enough is enough!" growled the partially intoxicated Liholiho as he rose to his feet. He moved forward to the mast and held his right arm forward with his fingers extended upward. "Helmsman, this is your compass. Steer past Waianae and Kaena Point, and then follow the direction of my manamana pili (third or ring finger). *That* will take us to Kauai!"

Liholiho would allow no protest, and the small boat sailed on as he directed. The occupants were silent, and they were sure that they were sailing to their watery graves. On and on they sailed. When the sloop got past the lee of the island of Oahu the seas became rougher and rougher. Soon the heavily occupied small boat was taking in water. All except Liholiho and the helmsman began to bail.

Liholiho sat in the bow with his back against the mast and contemplated the horizon with eager eyes. The helmsman kept well to windward of Liholiho's direction as he didn't want to miss the island of Kauai, or get to leeward and have to try and beat to windward.

Just before the skies grew dark when the sun went down, the cloud cover over the island of Kauai gave them their first exact direction. The helmsman held to his course by reference to the stars seen infrequently through the fast moving clouds. The seas were

---

*The island of Kauai is 72.4 statute miles of open sea northwest of Oahu.

almost regular, but grew in size as they continued well into the wide channel between the islands.

The sloop was almost swamped by a rogue wave and a contrary gust of the tradewind. All bailed frantically, except for Liholiho and the helmsman.

"E hoi kakou—o make! (Let us return lest we perish!)"

"Aole! (No!)," replied Liholiho thickly but firmly, "Imua! (Forward!). If the boat turns around I will swim to Kauai myself."

The hours were long with continuous bailing. The sloop almost swamped twice more. Finally they could dimly see the bulk of the island under their lee bow in the pre-dawn light. There was increased difficulty as the helmsman altered their course westward. The following seas caused even more water to enter the overcrowded sloop. Several sat at the stern, in an effort to stop the incoming water with their bodies. The weary occupants bailed even more frantically. Indeed fearsome Kaieiewaho (The outside high waves)!

The seas abated somewhat when they got in the partial lee of the island of Kauai. As tired as they were, they glanced curiously at the splendor of the island in the early dawn light. The helmsman headed towards a bay which turned out to be Waimea Bay.

An early morning Kauai fisherman came close to this strange vessel. He sped back to shore when he was apprised of who the principal occupant was. Shortly after he reached the shore, another and larger outrigger paddled by four men set out to meet the sloop. As the two craft came close together, the tall malo-clad Hawaiian passenger in the rear of the outrigger stood up and balanced erectly. Liholiho immediately felt sure that he was Kaumualii. He was.

King Kaumualii agilely sprang into the sloop when the two boats closed, glanced sharply around at the exhausted occupants, and slowly walked forward to face the standing Liholiho by the mast. Both looked at each other steadily.

"Aloha," said the soft-spoken and dignified Kaumualii with a smile.

"Aloha," Liholiho replied serenely with a smile.

They "joined noses" with alii affection.

Kaumualii escorted Liholiho ashore, and ordered the cannons fired and the bell rung at Hipo Fort.*All the Hawaiians within hearing ran to Waimea Bay. When they discovered who the distinguished visitor was, they crowded around at a respectful

---

*When the Russians built this fort in 1816, they named it Fort Elizabeth.

distance, most curious to see the son of the famed (and dreaded on Kauai) Ke Alii Nui Kamehameha. Liholiho regarded them carefully, and felt at ease. The throng exclaimed approval as they observed Liholiho's dignified bearing, and the obvious deference of their King Kaumualii.

The Kauai king appropriated a large newly-constructed Hawaiian residence complex on the mana-side (west) of Waimea Bay for the unexpected sovereign visitor and his party. Refreshments were hurridly provided. The two kings courteously chatted for a while as Liholiho's exhausted followers thankfully fell into safe and needed sleep. Liholiho admired the beautiful finely-plaited Niihau mats, and requested Kaumualii to send word to Oahu that he was safely on the island of Kauai. Kaumualii immediately ordered his newly acquired brig *Becket* to do this, and left Liholiho so he could rest. Sleep was difficult for Liholiho—he was so excited. He eventually did, woke in the late afternoon, and enjoyed a great feast with Kaumualii and the Kauai chiefs and chiefesses. The immense Dowager Queen Kalakua was present, and greeted Liholiho with a roguish grin.

Liliha, High Chief Boki's wife, arrived at Hanapepe the next night, having followed her husband across the rough channel in an outrigger canoe with a small sail and four paddlers.

The next evening, July 24, 1821, tributary King Kaumualii assembled his chiefs to hold council with King Liholiho. They met at Kaumualii's "palace," the largest structure of his residence complex at Papaenaena adjacent to the frowning stone walls of Fort Hipo. Kaumualii opened the council, and emotionally addressed Liholiho:[32]

> King Liholiho, hear! While your father, Kamehameha, lived, I acknowledged him to be my king. He is now dead; you are his rightful successor, and you are my king. I have plenty of muskets and ammunition and many subjects at my command: these, with the vessels I have bought, with my fort and its guns, and with my islands, are yours. All are yours. Do with them as you please, and make anyone governor that you like.

Naihe, Liholiho's counsellor present, then briefly addressed the council. He stated that it was understood by Liholiho's counsellors that Kaumualii had agreed to hold the island of Kauai and its fief smaller islands under Ke Alii Nui Kamehameha, and under his successor, who was Liholiho.

There was a silence, which Liholiho deliberately prolonged.

Finally he quietly and modestly replied:[32]

> Kaumualii, I have not come to take your island from you. I
> am not going to put any governor over it; keep it yourself.
> Take care of it as you have done; and do with your vessels
> and all your possessions as you please.

The assembled Kauai chiefs exclaimed loudly in appreciation. The council terminated, and another feast was begun. Both
Liholiho and Kaumualii soon became very jovial with the assistance
of convenient rum bottles. Kaumualii became so jovial and
hospitable that he offered Liholiho his wife, Kekaihaakulou.
Liholiho deliberated quickly for a moment, took a quick glance at
the statuesque queen standing nearby with demure downcast eyes,
and agreed with appreciation.

Later, after the feast, he gave his prior fifth wife,
Kekauluohi, to his aikane (friend) Kanaina.*

Liholiho's brig *Haaheo o Hawaii* arrived from Oahu the
following day bringing Liholiho's other wives, Kaahumanu, Hoapili
and Keopuolani, Keeaumoku and his wife, and retinues.

Kaumualii was impressed with Kuhina-nui Kaahumanu's
imperious bearing, obvious power, and physical stature.** Kaahumanu's first speculative glances at the tall and stately Kaumualii
became glances of cordial and slightly calculating interest.

When Kuhina-nui Kaahumanu was apprised of the results of
the Kauai council meeting, she just grunted, and glanced sharply at
a nonchalant Liholiho. When she discovered that Liholiho had a
new wife, and had "given away" his prior fifth wife, her niece
Kekauluohi, she was perturbed. Wasn't this disrespectful to her
niece Kekauluohi? And also disrespectful to her other nieces who
were also Liholiho's wives? And who was this new wife, even
though she had been Kaumualii's wife? And why was it that she had
not been consulted beforehand?†

The genealogists were called to relate Kekaihaakulou's
ancestry. It turned out that her lineage traced to Kaahumanu's home

---

*Issue of this couple was William Lunalilo, who later became the first king
of the Hawaiian Kingdom to be determined by popular election.

**Large female size was greatly admired as the ultimate of affluential
Hawaiian alii beauty.

†An additional reason for Kaahumanu's ire was that Kanaina was an alii of
comparatively low lineage.

island of Maui. Moreover, Kaahumanu and Kekaihaakulou were kin, as they shared ancestry from Hawea, Kaneikaheilani, and Kawelo, son of Mahuna-alii. Sacred Queen Mother Keopuolani quietly indicated her approval. Kaahumanu became mollified and reconciled.

Kaumualii appropriated houses for his distinguished guests. He ordered large new houses quickly constructed for Kuhina-nui Kaahumanu—adjacent to his residence complex at Papaenanea. He offered to show his visitors the island of Kauai. All agreed with interest, and they started off on what turned out to be a forty two day grand tour of the islands.

Kaahumanu was with the grand tour from time to time. She was mostly at Papaenaena, conducting the affairs of the Hawaiian Kingdom by means of a constant relay of messenger vessels. She sometimes consulted with Liholiho.

Kaumualii was very gracious and generous. When Kaahumanu expressed an interest in acquiring some expert Niihau mat plaiters for her household, the order was immediately issued. When Hoapili expressed an interest in some timber for his ship *Hooikaika*, it was immediately provided. Kaumualii was the height of Hawaiian alii hospitality. He could not do enough for his distinguished visitors.

The grand tour returned to Waimea September 6, 1821, having depleted the foodstuffs of each portion of the island of Kauai that they had visited.

Kaahumanu, Kaumualii, Liholiho and Kaumualii's son, Keliiahonui, sprawled at ease at Papaenaena watching the sun go down beyond the fief island of Niihau the evening of September 16, 1821.

Liholiho sighed, "Kaumualii, this is a marvelous visit to your island. It is beautiful, and you have fine chiefs and hard-working people."

"Your island, your island," Kaumualii corrected courteously and absently. He was entranced with the glorious sunset. (Liholiho and Kaahumanu glanced at each other briefly.)

"How I would like to reciprocate your gracious hospitality. I don't think it possible to equal it." Liholiho casually said as he plucked a stalk of pili grass and began to nibble the end, "Each island is the same, yet different. The people of each island are the same, yet slightly different. The meles (chants) and traditions of lore have fine differences which are intriguing to discover."

Kaumualii stirred slightly, and absently replied, "Yes, I have always been very interested in the other islands, and have often thought that I would like to see them, but the burden of my responsibility has kept me here."

(Kaahumanu darted a quick glance at Liholiho.) She rolled over so that she was directly facing Kaumualii, and softly said, "My friend, time fleets, and this day will never be here again. One should do what one wants to do . . . is curious to see . . . today."

The tributary Kauai king sighed. "Yes, I know, but responsibility cannot be avoided, even for one's personal desires."

There was a silence, Liholiho casually pursued the subject. "So very true, yet reflect upon this. You are concerned with your island. Kaahumanu and I are concerned with six other islands. You are concerned with your people. Kaahumanu and I are concerned with more than ten persons for every one person on your island. Yet we have visited with you on your island for over a moon, and still have accomplished *our* responsibilities."

Kaumualii quickly replied, "Yes, I appreciate the honor of your visit, and I appreciate the many larger things that you are concerned with."

The sunset faded, and night began. Kaahumanu slightly rolled from side to side and almost whispered, "My friend Kaumualii, there are a number of beautiful places I would like to *personally* show you—on the other islands . . ."

Kaumualii looked at Kaahumanu squarely, and slowly replied with a bow of his head, "I appreciate the honor . . ."

Liholiho turned to Kaumualii's son, Keliiahonui, and queried, "Wouldn't you like to see the rest of the islands we Hawaiians live on? For we are one people."

"Yes, yes," eagerly replied Keliiahonui. He turned to his father, "We *are* one people, father. I would dearly love to see the other islands and people."

Liholiho quickly added, "I came to your island of Kauai because the spirit moved me. Come, Kaumualii, let the spirit move you—let us go and have fun."

Kaahumanu added with enthusiasm, "Yes, Kaumualii my friend, come with us, and let us return your gracious hospitality for a while. Life is so short—let us enjoy it while we may."

There was a pause. Liholiho, Kaahumanu, and Keliiahonui engagingly looked at Kaumualii with hopeful smiles. (Kaahumanu thought she read the pensive Kaumualii's thoughts, and darted a quick glance at Liholiho.)

Liholiho rose to his feet and held out his hand to Kaumualii. He smiled, "Let us go . . . so we can reciprocate your hospitality."

Kaumualii looked at his sovereign soberly for a long moment. He accepted the outstretched hand and rose to his feet. "So be it," he murmured, "the spirit moves me. Let us go." Kaumualii sighed as he looked at his eager son who was obviously very happy about the decision.

The tributary Kauai king wanted to advise his chiefs that he would be going to the other islands. Liholiho chided him, using his own trip to Kauai as example. Kaahumanu reminded Kaumualii that she had run the affairs of the other islands while she was on Kauai, and so could Kaumualii if he was on another island. Kaumualii allowed himself to be swept along with the enthusiasm of impetuous adventure which the others expressed so vigorously.

Each of the four ordered their private attendants to gather minimum belongings and attend them immediately aboard Liholiho's brig *Haaheo o Hawaii*. The brig sailed at 9PM for Waianae, Oahu.

It just so happened that this ship was followed by another of Liholiho's vessels with the windward chiefs and chiefesses and their retinues. All except High Chief Keeaumoku and some selected retainers.

When Kaumualii and Keliiahonui were discovered gone the following morning, the Waimea Chief Haupu turned to High Chief Keeaumoku for information.

"Yes," said Keeaumoku blandly, "they have gone on a grand tour of the other islands to reciprocate King Kaumualii's hospitality here on Kauai. I was advised to remain and be their agent here. Agent . . . not governor."

Lucy Thurston recorded on Oahu October 9, 1821:[51:64]

> That night Kaahumanu associated with the king in the government of Hawaii, Maui, Oahu &c., and Kaumualii, tributary king of Kauai, reclined side by side on a low platform, eight feet square, consisting of between twenty and thirty beautiful mats of the finest texture. Then a black kapa (native cloth) was spread over them. The significance of it was, it pronounced the royal pair to be husband and wife. An important political union was likewise peacefully effected, connecting the windward and leeward islands under one crown.

> Kaahumanu also married Kaumualii's son, Keliiahonui.

Kuhina-nui Kaahumanu, with her husbands in her court, remained on Oahu and conducted the affairs of the Hawaiian Kingdom. Liholiho went on an extended visit to the island of Hawaii.

XIV

heluhelu and palapala
(reading and writing)

Among the instructions to the first company of American Protestant missionaries was a section on Benevolence Towards the Objects of Your Mission. Included in this section was the following:[24]

> To obtain an adequate knowledge of the language of the people; to make them acquainted with letters; to give them the Bible with skill to read it . . ."

Seven missionaries and their wives were thus given the task of providing literacy to a nation of some 135,000 Hawaiians located on eight islands in the middle of the vast Pacific Ocean.

When these missionaries arrived in Hawaii they had a rudimentary knowledge of the spoken Hawaiian language. The Hawaiian language was unwritten—they had acquired this knowledge by rote from their young Hawaiian missionary helpers, John Honolii, Thomas Hopu and William Kanui. They soon discovered after reaching Hawaii that the vocabularies of their helpers were distressingly limited. They soon also found that the foreign residents in Hawaii generally knew only enough Hawaiian to conduct their business affairs. When the Hawaiians found that these new residents were sincerely interested in learning their language well, they were most helpful; especially the learned Hawaiians who appreciated scholarship.

The small group of missionaries diligently applied themselves to thoroughly learn the language. No small task, as they were always going from the known to the unknown. They *must* be able to communicate fluently if they were to present God's Word properly, and have it received affirmatively.

The Hawaiian language was different than the English, Latin and Greek these 1820 American missionaries were acquainted with. Rev. Bingham summed the basic characteristic of spoken Hawaiian as:[7:152]

> To one unacquainted with the language it would be impossible to distinguish the words in a spoken sentence, for

119

in the mouth of a native, a sentence appeared like an ancient Hebrew or Greek manuscript—all one word. It was found that every word and every syllable in the language ends with a vowel; the final vowel of the word or syllable, however, is often made so nearly to coalesce or combine with the sound of the succeeding vowel, as to form a diphthongal sound, apparently uniting two distinct words. There are, on the other hand, abrupt separations or short and sudden breaks between two vowels in the same word. The language, moreover, is crowded with a class of particles unknown in the languages with which we had any acquaintance. There were also frequent reduplications of the same vowel, so rapid, that by most foreigners the two were taken for one.

There was a lack of uniformity in the way the Hawaiians spoke their language on the different islands. For example: the word kapa (bark cloth), as spoken on the island of Hawaii, sounded more like tapa when spoken by Kauai islanders. Some Hawaiian word sounds could be represented by different English letters (e.g. l and r, k and t).

There must have been discussion after discussion on the sounds and meanings of words between each missionary and individual Hawaiians, and between the missionaries. Discussions with Hawaiians must have ranged from those with limited vocabularies to learned men with extensive vocabularies. The missionaries slowly began to learn the language.*

The ultimate in rapid and lasting communication is the written language. The missionaries came prepared to provide the Hawaiians their language in writing—they brought a printer, press and printing supplies. They had a strong inkling of the difficulties they would be faced with—accounts of the early voyagers to Hawaii did have some Hawaiian words and names, but the spelling differed from author to author. Kamehameha, as an example, was severally spelled as Cameamea, Comoamoa, Maiha Maiha, Tamahame, Tamaahmaah, Tammeanea, etc.

---

*One suspects that the missionaries were exposed to some esoteric words and meanings, and that a number were discarded as not being meaningful to the majority of Hawaiians or the futherance of christianity. One further suspects that the missionaries were not exposed to a number of Hawaiian words or meanings, being beyond their social comprehension. One can theorize with some rationale that the extent of the Hawaiian language was sophisticated.

How does one go about reducing a strange spoken language to writing for the first time?

Rev. Bingham furnished their approach to the problem:[7:152-153]

> To make the spelling and reading of the language easy to the people, and convenient to all who use it, was a matter of great importance, almost indispensable to our success in raising the nation. It was, therefore, a part of our task to secure to the people a perfect alphabet, literal or syllabic, of all the sounds which were then in use, and which would need soon to come into use in the progress of the nation. Those who had attempted to write the names of places and persons in the islands, had materially failed, even in the most plain and common. No foreigner or native, at the islands, could illustrate or explain the peculiarities and intricacies of the language. Though we obtained a few words and phrases from W. Mosley [a resident for some years] and others, we found the dialect in use by the foreigners often materially misled us, so that none could be trusted as to accuracy; and it required time to detect and unlearn errors. In the oft recurring names of the principal island, the largest village, and of the king of the leeward islands, "Owhyhee," "Hanaroorah," and "Tamoree,"* scarcely the sound of a single syllable was correctly expressed, either in writing or speaking, by voyagers or foreign residents. Had we, therefore, followed the orthography of voyagers, or in adopting an alphabet, made a single vowel stand for as many sounds as in English, and several different vowels for the same sound, and given the consonants the ambiguity of our *c*, *s*, *t*, *ch*, *gh*, &c., it would have been extremely difficult, if not impracticable to induce the nation to become readers, in the course of a whole generation, even if we had been furnished with ample funds to sustain in boarding-schools, all who would devote their time and labor to study.

The adaptation of the English alphabet to Hawaiian words was of primary concern. The familiar five vowels were given constant pronunciations (continual sounds) to avoid double vowels. Twelve consonants were established for the first alphabet, and were pronounced as in English: *b*, *d*, *h*, *k*, *l*, *m*, *n*, *p*, *r*, *t*, *v* and *w*. There was

*Hawaii, Honolulu and Kaumualii.

a supplemental list of *f*, *g*, *s* and *γ*, which were used for spelling foreign words.

The missionaries determined that when Hawaiian word sounds were accurately written, the following general rules would apply:*

Every word is spelled precisely as it is pronounced.

Every word and syllable ends with a vowel.

A vowel must be between two consonants.

There could be couplings of vowels (diphthongs) in which each letter retains its original monosound.

The missionaries were acquainted with the methodology of John Pickering, then well-known for reducing Indian languages to writing. They followed his vowel plan, but did not apply his compound consonants. They determined that:[7:155]

> To preserve the identity of a foreign name embracing a compound consonant which cannot well be omitted, we take the more important or practicable part of the power— as *p*, for *ph* or *phi*; *t*, for *th* or *theta*; *k*, for *ch* and *chi*, &c., when two consonants joined in a foreign word, need both be preserved, we interpose the vowel *e*, and after a final consonant add usually the vowel *a*—as Bosetona for Boston.

Most western "things" did not have Hawaiian words for them. The most obvious solution was to make them phonetic load words (e.g. puke for book, lutanela for lieutenant, etc.). Biblical names were of course most important—Jehovah became Iehova, Sabbath became Kapaki or Sabati, Matthew became Makaio or Mataio, Zion became Kiona or Ziona, etc.

The American Protestant missionaries to Hawaii were most pleased January 1, 1822, to discover that their approach to reducing the Hawaiian language to writing paralleled that adopted for another branch of the Polynesian race—that of the English missionaries for the Tahitians of the Society Islands:[38]

> We received, also, two copies of the *New Zealand Grammar and Vocabulary of the Society Islands*, and were happy to see at once such a striking resemblance between the language of

---

*Hindsight tells us that the missionaries could have been more precise in providing better identification of long or short sounds and glottal stops. However, they did a magnificent job.

the Sandwich (Hawaiian) and Society Islands. This work will afford us considerable aid in settling the orthography of this language. We are confirmed by it, in some measure, in the choice we had made of five vowels, viz. *a* as *father*, *e* as in *hate*, *i* as *ee* in *feet*, *o* as in *pole*, *u* as *oo* in *boot*, and *ai* for the sound of the English *i*. These five vowels, with twelve consonants (*b, d, h, k, l, m, n, p, r, t, v, w*), will be sufficient to express with little variation, all the sounds in the language, which we have yet been able to analyze. Indeed, seven consonants, with five vowels, might very well serve for the notation of the language. The *b*, *d*, *r*, *t* and *v*, might be omitted; for, though their sounds are heard, and it is believed they would be of use, their places might be supplied by using the *p* invariably for *b* and *p*, the *l* for *d*, *l* and *r*, the *k* for *k* and *t*, and the *w* for *w* and *v*. The interchange of such letters, the unsettled, doubtful, varying, and widely diverse pronunciation among the people, we find to be no small embarrassment in fixing the spelling of the language. This, together with the diversity of spelling used by voyagers, in their accounts of these islands already published, must be our apology to our patrons and the public, for the want of that decided uniformity, so desirable in spelling names, which has appeared in the communications from the mission.*

The first instruction in reading and writing was in English, and to the chiefs, their families and selected retainers. This commenced in 1820 when the missionaries arrived. It was apparent that the leaders of this feudal Hawaiian society must be won over first, if the mission was to be successful.

It took almost two years of tremendous effort for the missionaries to attain the semblance of anywhere near fluency in the Hawaiian language. The clergymen still could not preach complete sermons unassisted by interpreters. The missionaries were anxious to provide written communications in the Hawaiian language—it took this long to acquire the knowledge to be able to reduce Hawaiian to writing.

The first printing was commenced in the Hawaiian Islands

---

*The English alphabet applied to the Hawaiian language was reduced by missionary committee action in 1826 to the present five vowels and seven consonants *a, e, i, o, u; h, k, l, m, n, p and w*). Perhaps over-simplification, but deemed practicable at the time.

January 7, 1822[5]*—Lesson I of Pi-a-pa, which became 500 copies of a four inch by six inch eight page primer containing the alphabet, some spelling lessons, and selections for reading, in Hawaiian. High Chief Keeaumoku struck off the first impression, Elisha Loomis (the printer) the second, and James Hunnewell the third.

Three days later King Liholiho came to the Honolulu Mission to see the new printing. Mr. Loomis printed the king's name "in large elegant capitals" in two forms, Rihoriho and Liholiho. The king was asked to determine whether "R" or "L" should be used in spelling his name. After some discussion on letter sounds, the king decided "R" was more correct than "L".[5] So there was more research by the missionaries in trying to apply English letters to the Hawaiian language. (They later determined that "L" was more correct!)

The Hawaiian primer was immediately put to use teaching selected Hawaiian youngsters and adults eager to learn how to heluhelu (read) and palapala (write) their own language. Powerful Hawaiian chiefs and chiefesses provided the all-important motivations. Learning how to read Hawaiian was much easier than learning to read English. Progress was rapid. The Honolulu Mission "school" initially averaged 40 students at a time, the Kauai Mission "school" 25 students.[7:160] As students would reach the limits of instruction then available, they would spread out to teach small groups elsewhere before returning for further instruction.

It has been estimated that within two years of the first printing (1822) 2,000 Hawaiians could read and write their own language.[1:188]

AUTHOR'S NOTE: The beginning mission schools in the Hawaiian language and the scattered individual teachers evolved to Mission Station School and satellite Common Schools. The number of Station and Common Schools increased after the first missionaries were reinforced. Higher level schools were started (ie: Lahainaluna in 1831) to train Hawaiian teachers. School enrollments soared from some 2,000 in 1824 to 37,000 in 1826, 45,000 in 1829, and 52,000 in 1831 (some 40% of the population).[52] Literacy before marriage was required on the island of Maui in 1835; this was the law of the land on this island for 15 years and for nine years on the other islands.[45:194]

It has been estimated that one-third of Hawaii's people were literate by 1830,[47:12] and three-quarters of the over age 16 population in 1853.[45:12] Based on the large number of students versus the estimated population, one

*During the significant following eight years, the Mission Press printed 28 works averaging 33 pages in 387,000 copies.[52] The bible was translated into Hawaiian, a monumental task which took 14 years, 1824–1839.[8:155]

can roughly interpolate on the low side that the Hawaiians were at least two-thirds literate in the bench mark year 1840.

Comparisons of literacy rates between nations are difficult as criteria (of illiteracy rates) and data collection systems vary. Literacy in the United States in the same bench mark year 1840 has been crudely estimated to have been 78% of the over age 20 population.[22:206] This was probably overstated, as the data was secured from census queries.

One can say with some rationale that in 20 years, from 1820 to 1840, the Hawaiians became almost as literate as the population of the United States.

This can be attributed to the efforts of a total of *184 American Protestant missionaries*. Paul Sullivan well-concluded:[47:89]

"The Missionary impact on Hawaiian education was enormous and lasting.
In meeting a monumental task those men and women built a monument to
themselves—a monument in the minds of men."

The Hawaiian Kingdom assumed responsibility for educating their people in 1840, and the missionaries ceased their total teaching efforts. Pressures began to mount for maximum emphasis on teaching English rather than Hawaiian in the schools. Arguments were presented that English was the language of commerce, only a few of the foreigner businessmen knew adequate Hawaiian, the Hawaiian Kingdom leaders knew English, and it was becoming the language for conducting government affairs. This can partially be attributed to the number of influential foreigners in high government positions.

The missionaries resisted this trend as:[26:79] "It was a maxim with the Mission that in order to preserve the nation, they must preserve its speech."

The Hawaiian population declined from some 130,000 people in 1823 to some 90,000 in 1890—of which over half were non-Hawaiians.[45:74] The Hawaiian language ceased to be of importance in the last quarter of the 19th Century. Little Hawaiian was taught in the schools during King Kalakaua's reign (1874-1891).

Few can speak, read or write, Hawaiian today.

XV

PROGRESS

There was much sickness among the Hawaiians.*

The rulers were not immune—Kuhina-nui Kaahumanu became seriously ill in December 1821. Commodore Vasilieff's Russian exploring expedition had again visited Hawaii, and two of their physicians attended her. The missionaries were, of course, very conscious of the powerful feudal rulers of the Hawaiian Kingdom. Rev. Bingham visited Kaahumanu "repeatedly" during her affliction. He knelt by her eight foot square bed of thirty beautiful mats and prayed for her recovery. He "implored the health-giving mercies of God upon her body and soul." Kaahumanu recovered, and appreciated the solicitude and comfort of the Christian kahuna-pule's (religious priest's) concern. "There was from this period a marked difference in her demeanor towards the missionaries, which became more and more striking, till we were allowed to acknowledge her as a disciple of the Divine Master."[7:149]

Two months later King Liholiho became ill at Waikiki, and came close to death. The king was surrounded by his weeping

---

*The Hawaiians had lived in isolation from other peoples for centuries. They had little or no resistance (herd immunity) to such diseases as influenza, mumps, tuberculosis, measles, smallpox, cholera, plague, etc. Intruded diseases caused a catastrophic and demoralizing depopulation. The estimated Hawaiian population at the time of Captain James Cook's discovery, 1778, was 300,000 people. An epidemic entitled mai okuu by the Hawaiians (cholera or bacillary dysentary?) reputedly halved the population in 1804. The population was again halved by 1853, due in significant measure to measles and whooping cough epidemics in 1848, an influenza epidemic in 1849, and a smallpox epidemic in 1853. The low point of Hawaii's total population was in 1872—56,897 people, of which 5,366 were non-Hawaiians.[45:74] Thereafter the population grew, due to the immigration of other racial background peoples to Hawaii. Western and Asian contacts certainly had a fatal impact upon the Hawaiians. The population decreased to one-quarter of its estimated former size in three generations, and to one-sixth in four generations.

wives, Kaahumanu, his mother Keopuolani, and other high chiefs and chiefesses. Multitudes of Hawaiians gathered outside his residence compound and wailed in apprehension. Rev. Bingham visited the king frequently, prescribed and provided medicine, prayed by his bedside, and stayed with him through at least one critical night. Rev. Bingham recorded:[7:159] "No wonder they should have been alarmed by the singular symptoms, in rapid succession—great redness of skin, rigidity of muscles, convulsion, difficulty of respiration, emission of blood from the mouth, etc.—*the result doubtless of his excesses*" (emphasis added).* King Liholiho recovered in several weeks. Shortly thereafter, he and a number of the high chiefs attended Sabbath services. The king became more concerned for the welfare and progress of the small mission. His personal acceptance of Christianity, however, progressed very slowly.

King Liholiho received an exciting message in early April 1822 from High Chief Kuakini, governor of the island of Hawaii. The report routinely advised of the arrival of a vessel at Kawaihae March 29, 1822, the small sloop *Mermaid*, Captain Kent, from the Society Islands. The sloop had left for Kealakekua Bay where there were eleven whalers at anchor. The passengers were of great interest. There were three English missionaries, one of whom had been at Huahine, Society Islands, for six years and spoke Tahitian.** There were two Tahitian alii and their wives, who were christians! They had five Tahitian makaainana (commoner) servants with them. These passengers were circuitously enroute to the Marquesas Islands to establish a mission there.

And, of even more import, Captain Kent was expecting to be joined by a schooner which was a gift from the British king to the Hawaiian king! This was the vessel that Captain Vancouver had promised Ke Alii Nui Kamehameha back in 1794, and Governor Macquarie of New South Wales (Australia) had written in 1816 that he had been instructed to build and deliver to Kamehameha.

The *Prince Regent*, Captain Brown, a 70 ton copper-bottomed schooner built at Port Jackson and mounting six guns, arrived off Honolulu April 9, 1822, (while Captain Kent of the *Mermaid* was awaiting her at the Kona district of the island of Hawaii). The

*Could this illness have been a severe case of influenza?

**Tahitian and Hawaiian may be considered to be two dialects of the general Polynesian language. Hawaiians and Tahitians could communicate with each other if the talking was slow and not too complicated.

schooner was towed into Honolulu Harbor and Liholiho boarded her on April 11, 1822. There was a 21 gun salute from the *Prince Regent*, which was answered by 30 guns from shore. King Liholiho admired the smart small schooner, which was to be given to him as a royal gift. A fast messenger was sent to inform Captain Kent of the *Prince Regent's* arrival.

The sloop *Mermaid* arrived at Honolulu and was towed by a number of Hawaiian canoes into the harbor April 16, 1822. Twenty-four ships were then at anchor in Honolulu Harbor, mostly American whalers.

Captain Kent landed with his passengers and called officially upon King Liholiho at his Pakaka "Palace," a large thatched Hawaiian house by the canoe landing adjacent to Honolulu Fort. The king had assembled his wives and a number of available chiefs and retinues. Liholiho was dressed in European style, wearing a "shirt, jacket, waistcoat, and pantaloons." A long fan of white feathers was continually waved over his head, as there were numerous flies. One of the queens adjacent to King Liholiho held the royal spittoon, covered with a handkerchief. It was duly used from time to time. The leading Hawaiians sat on a large lauhala mat for the audience; the numerous retainers squatted in the background. A tobacco pipe was passed around, and wine was served.

The captain presented his credentials from Port Jackson, and officially informed the king of the *Prince Regent* gift. Liholiho was very pleased. The principal passengers were introduced: Rev. Daniel Tyerman and Mr. George Bennet of the London Missionary Society, who were visiting their missions in the Pacific; Rev. William Ellis, who had been stationed in the Society Islands for six years; the Tahitian "native teachers," Auna and Matatore, and their wives.

Tyerman and Bennet recorded of Liholiho's queens:[39:392-393]

> His five queens are women of no ordinary magnitude; two of them must be, at least, six feet high each, and of a comely bulk in proportion. Their dresses were silken girdles, of divers colours, thrown round the body, with necklaces of flowers, and wreaths of fern leaves on their heads. Each of these great ladies was disfigured by the voluntary loss of two or three front teeth, in memory of the death of the late king.*

*They went on, "We have hardly seen a mouth since we landed in Hawaii, which has not been thus barbariously dismantled of some part of its most useful as well as ornamental furniture."

The English missionaries were received by the American missionaries as brethren, and accepted the invitation to reside at the Honolulu mission. The captains of the two vessels were offered quarters in Liholiho's residence complex, port and pilotage fees were not charged, and the *Mermaid* was provisioned free.

It just so happened that one of Kuhina-nui Kaahumanu's trusted retainers was a Tahitian, and it was discovered that he was a "long lost " brother of the Tahitian alii Auna's wife. They were granted quarters in Kaahumanu's residence complex.

Auna was impressive. He was of high Tahitian alii rank and had previously also been a kahuna (priest) who had venerated the Tahitian God Hiro (God of thieves). He had great dignity, was of commanding stature and presence, and was very intelligent. Matatore was also well-equipped to be a "native teacher", as he was described as ". . . a pious, intelligent, and remarkable ingenious man in any kind of work to which he turned his hand". [39:354]

The Tahitians' wives were also impressive in their own way. They kept very busy, rather than luxuriating in idleness, and constantly reproached the Hawaiian women for lack of modesty and scanty clothing.

The Hawaiian alii were intrigued with the Tahitian alii, Auna and Matatore. Was not Tahiti the source of their revered forebears some 27 or so generations ago? There were many extensive and serious conversations with the learned Tahitians. One may be sure that these "native teachers" thoroughly covered the advantages of present-day living in the Society Islands under Christian beliefs and principles.

Auna conducted "family prayers" in Kaahumanu's household, morning and evening. The Tahitian wives spoke at great length to the leading Hawaiian women of the wonderful changes to the life of Society Islands women due to new standards of religion (which they could now participate in rather than the old religion where their participation was excluded), manners, politics, dress, deportment, etc. Auna devoted particular attention to King Liholiho, when not engaged in talking to Kuhina-nui Kaahumanu.

Captain Kent, on behalf of his Britannic Majesty, formally presented the *Prince Regent* to King Liholiho at noon on May 1, 1822.* When Captain Kent was about to lower the British colors, the king said, "No, no; I shall always hoist the English flag." [39:436] Following the brief ceremony which included many cannon salutes, the captain provided an English dinner for a company of twenty-five—a sit-

---

*Liholiho enjoyed this addition to his fleet of some ten vessels for only several months; the *Prince Regent* was wrecked on the east coast of Oahu.

down dinner at a large mahogany table with table cloth, forks, knives, and spoons. The Hawaiians used these eating tools with "dexterity."

Rev. Ellis was greatly appreciated by the American missionaries. He preached in Tahitian to the Tahitian visitors, and they sang hymns in Tahitian. The Hawaiians flocked around to listen with interest to the Tahitian language and to observe the behaviour of the small congregation. King Liholiho, his queens, and the chiefs often attended. They sat or reclined on the floor with attendants waving fly whisks. Very often attendants would lie down, cover themselves with cloth, and thus provide convenient pillows.

Rev. Ellis, in due course, began to substitute the Hawaiian "k" sound for the Tahitian "t" sound, and the words became more intelligible to the Hawaiians. He "composed" several hymns in Hawaiian, which met with immediate success and were rapidly learned. The Hawaiians enjoyed the range of singing, which was so different than the monotone of their chants. Rev. Ellis was soon preaching several times a week. He was also of great assistance in the reduction of the Hawaiian language to writing.

The combined American and English missionaries had long interviews with King Liholiho—urging him to publicly adopt Christianity. Liholiho amiably agreed that this was a good idea, and "professed a wish" that he and his people could become Christians. *But*, he didn't feel that his principal chiefs were completely ready for it. It would require more time and more knowledge before they would agree to such an important decision.

Liholiho often changed the subject during these discussions. It was hard to keep him entirely on the subject of Christianity. Rev. Tyerman and Mr. Bennet were shrewd men, and they detected shrewdness in King Liholiho:[39:462-462]

> He . . . turned the discourse upon strangers visiting these islands, and described with much humour and no mean knowledge of human nature, the principal foreigners whom he had known, telling both the good and evil which they had done among the natives.

Kaahumanu took her husbands, Kaumualii and Keliiahonui, and a large retinue on the promised grand tour of the windward islands for two months, leaving Oahu on May 1822.* Wherever they

---

*The American and English missionaries made a "grand tour" of their own; they looked around Oahu May 14-21, 1822.

went there were many gifts (e.g. June 3, 1822: 12 baked dogs, 60 live ones, 590 pieces of cloth (kapa), 35 calabashes of poi, and two large canoes.[39:484]). Whereever they went there was great feasting and dancing. In Kailua, Hawaii:[39:484] "Forty-one men danced in four rows; behind them were thirty-one musicians beating time on the sticks, besides five great drums."

The Tahitian alii "native teacher," Auna, accompanied Kaahumanu. Due to his and prior missionary efforts, or for political reasons, or a combination of both, Kuhina-nui Kaahumanu ordered the sacred carved figures of the old Hawaiian religion brought to her. The poison God, Kalaipahoa, and nine smaller images were collected and burned June 4, 1822. Twenty days later, eight more images were burned. One hundred and two images were burned at Kailua, Hawaii on June 26, 1822! Yet . . . one can be sure that many were still hidden away.

Rev. Bingham recorded somewhat wistfully:[7:162]

> In her new war with idolatry, she gave a new demonstra-
> tion of her energy, which, if it should ever be sanctified and
> brought under the sway of the love of Christ, seemed likely
> to make her a burning and shining light among her people.

Captain Kent advantageously chartered the *Mermaid* to Captain Davis for a voyage to Fanning Island, some 1,000 nautical miles south of Honolulu. The purpose of this voyage was to secure béche de mer (sea cucumber)—when dried and preserved it was much in demand in the Chinese market. The captain set sail May 22, 1822, and the departure of the English missionaries for the Marquesas Islands was delayed. As their passage was gratis, they bore this change to their zealous plans with as much Christian patience as possible. Captain Kent returned to Honolulu two months later, July 29, 1822.

The Hawaiian rulers and chiefs wanted Rev. Ellis, Auna, and Matatore to remain with them in the Hawaiian Islands. The American missionaries wanted them to stay too. Rev. Tyerman and Mr. Bennet were representatives of the London Missionary Society, and gave their consent for them to stay, subject to Rev. Ellis returning to the Society Islands first for his wife.

Rev. Tyerman and Mr. Bennet wrote a letter to the American Board of Commissioners for Foreign Missions August 9, 1822, advising that they ". . . were induced to give our consent to Mr. Ellis's joining your Mission, but still remain in connexion with the London Missionary Society, and to be supported by it."[39:408] They stated their basic considerations as: Rev. Ellis had a knowledge of the language, there was great need among the

Hawaiians for Christianity, and that Rev. Ellis' experience in the Society Islands should be shared with the American missionaries in Hawaii.

Thomas Hopu, one of the Hawaiian missionary helpers, and a Hawaiian girl renamed Delia were married August 11, 1822. The first Christian marriage in the Hawaiian Islands was before a large solemn congregation. Rev. Bingham performed the ceremony, and Rev. Ellis preached a sermon. Thomas Hopu had written a letter the previous month to Rev. Bingham requesting permission to preach the gospel. In this he was seconded by the English missionaries, who utilized this practice to good advantage elsewhere in the Pacific. The American clergymen did not agree or consent, as their religious standards did not then provide for "lay" missionary preachers: [7:166]

> Our views of the importance of consistency and weight of character in an ambassador of Christ, of knowledge and skill in the evangalist to wield the Sword of the Spirit, in the circumstances of our mission, at that time, and the abundant and favorable opportunities for the labors of well-disposed laymen, several of whom, then in the mission, were better qualified to be preachers than Hopu, led us to decline giving him a formal license. He labored on as a layman.

A council was held August 13, 1822, to which the missionaries were invited. It appears that there were two significant items of business. The first pleased the missionaries immensely, as it resulted in criers announcing that drinking intoxicating spirits was forbidden. This kapu extended to even Liholiho. (Liholiho's and others' compliances were less than satisfactory.) The pronouncement was impossible to enforce.

The second item was the composition of a letter to King George IV thanking him for the *Prince Regent*. One suspects that King Liholiho did not compose the letter himself, but was assisted by the English missionaries: [39:480-481]

Oahu, Sandwich Islands, Aug. 21, 1822.*

May it please your Majesty,

In answer to your Majesty's letter from Governor Macquarrie, I beg to return your Majesty my most grateful thanks for your handsome present of the schooner, Prince Regent, which I received at the hands of Mr. J. R. Kent.

*This letter was dated to coincide with the planned departure of Captain Kent, who was asked to start it on the long uncertain trip to England.

I avail myself of this opportunity of acquainting your Majesty of the death of my father, Tamehameha, who departed this life, the 8th of May, 1819, much lamented by his subjects; and, having appointed me his successor, I have enjoyed a happy reign ever since that period; and I assure your Majesty it is my sincere wish to be thought as worthy your attention as my father had the happiness to be, during the visit of Captain Vancouver. The whole of these islands having been conquered by my father, I have succeeded to the government of them, and beg leave to place them all under the protection of your most excellent Majesty; wishing to observe peace with all nations, and to be thought worthy the confidence I place in your Majesty's wisdom and judgement.

The former idolatrous system has been abolished in these islands, as we wish the Protestant religion of your Majesty's dominions to be practiced here. I hope your Majesty may deem it fit to answer this as soon as convenient; and your Majesty's counsel and advice will be most thankfully received by your Majesty's most obedient and devoted servant,

TAMEHAMEHA II
King of the Sandwich Islands

When the council meeting was over, Kaahumanu left with her husbands, Kaumualii and Keliiahonui, to go back to the island of Kauai on a continuation of their grand tour of the Hawaiian Islands. Four overloaded vessels, two brigs and two schooners transported some 1,200 people, most of whom had barely standing room. The windward islanders were indeed anxious to see the island of Kauai. Kaahumanu sent the following letter back to Liholiho's favorite queen, Kamamalu, which indicates the Hawaiian desire to read and write:[7:172]

This is my communication to you: tell the puu A-i o-eo-e (posse of Long necks) to send some more books down here. Many are the people—few are the books. I want elua lau (800) Hawaiian books to be sent hither. We are much pleased to learn the palapala. By and by, perhaps, we shall be akamai, skilled or wise. Give my love to Mr. and Mrs. Bingham, and the whole company of Long necks.

While on the island of Kauai, Kaahumanu probably heard the old chants about Kauai and the adjacent islands. Among them could well have been a reference to the island of Nihoa:[13:10]

Wanalia was the man
And Hanalaa was the woman;
Of them were born Niihau, a land, an island.
There were three children of them
Born in the same day;
Niihau, Kaula, ending with Nihoa.
The mother then conceived no more.
No other island appeared afterwards.

None of the people on Kauai knew where the island of Nihoa was. Kaahumanu and Kaumualii, with the usual large retinue, sailed on several ships under the command of Captain Sumner to re-discover the long-lost island. They did; it was 120 miles northwest of Niihau (250 miles from Honolulu).* The small uninhabited island was "annexed" to the Hawaiian Kingdom.

The *Mermaid* departed Honolulu for the Society Islands August 22, 1822. It was uncomfortable for the English missionaries and the Matatores to be passengers, as Matatore's wife had either "defected" or had been seduced by the captain at some time during the visit to Honolulu.[7:161] This embarrassed the English missionaries no end. There was no other ship available which was going in the direction they wanted, so they had no choice. The planned mission to the Marquesas Islands was abandoned. Auna and his wife remained in the Hawaiian Islands for a year before returning to the Society Islands.**

The *Mermaid's* departure was well-attended. As the ship was leaving the harbor, Queen Kamamalu, who had missed the shore farewells, came out in an outrigger with one paddler besides herself. When she came within "a bowshot," she dived from the canoe, swam to the *Mermaid*, and climbed the side to the deck for her tearful farewell. When she had done this with sincere affection, she dived back into the water, swam back to her outrigger canoe, and returned to shore.

---

*The British ship *Iphigena*, Captain Douglas, had sighted this island March 19, 1789. The bark *Columbia*, Captain Jennings, also sighted it April 17, 1817.

**Rev. William Ellis returned to Hawaii February 5, 1823, bringing his wife and two "native teachers," Taua and his family, and Taa Motu, "a female." Rev. Ellis remained for a year and a half, and left for England in September 1824 due to the ill-health of his wife.

XVI

anniversary

King Liholiho observed the fourth anniversary of Ke Alii Nui Kamehameha's death and his accession as king with a fortnight of holiday festival. There was a grand ahaaina (feast) at Waikiki the third day, April 26, 1823. A hundred foot table was piled high with all kinds of food available. Two hundred leading Hawaiians and foreigners were invited. All sat on benches; a novelty to the Hawaiians who were used to sitting or reclining on the ground. Everyone wore western-style black clothing, as the king had directed.

When the banquet was concluded, four hundred white-clad Hawaiians representing the eight districts of the island of Oahu brought their taxes in kind, which resulted in a huge mound of tribute for their king.

The ship *Thames*, Captain Clasby, came to anchor in the roadstead off Honolulu Harbor the following day, April 27, 1823. One hundred fifty eight days and 18,000 miles around Cape Horn from New Haven, Connecticut. The day was appropriately the Sabbath, as on board was the second company of American missionaries. There were three missionaries (clergymen) and their wives; four male assistant missionaries, three of whom had wives; one female assistant missionary, a teacher who was a negress*; and four young Hawaiian missionary helpers from the Cornwall mission school, three Hawaiians and one Tahitian.

The three missionaries, Revs. Artemas Bishop, William Richards and Charles S. Stewart, were impatient to see their new home. They went ashore with the captain and two of the Hawaiian

---

*Betsy Stockton may not have technically been an assistant missionary as, by agreement, she assisted Rev. Stewart's family as well as being a teacher. She was born in Princeton, N. J. (in slavery) in 1798 and was "freed" in 1818. She educated herself in the library of her owner/employer, Rev. Ashbel Green, President of Princeton College.

missionary helpers to act as interpreters. The 24 year old Rev. Stewart was a remarkable man—aside from being a good sincere missionary he was also a gifted writer.* Some of his first colorful eyewitness descriptions follow:[46:75-81,91-95,106]

> Perceiving a low stone quay on a point under the fort, and near a cluster of native buildings, we were about to land on it, when a party of islanders exclaimed, "*kabu! kabu!*" [kapu! kapu!] and informed our interpreters, William and Richard, that the largest of the houses was the residence of the king, and he had prohibited any one from landing at that place. William replied, "New missionaries have arrived," when they ran to the *palace*; and a fine looking young female in a European dress of pink satin, with a wreath of yellow flowers on the head, made her appearance. It was Kamehamalu [Kamamalu], the favorite queen of Liholiho. She expressed her regret that the quay was *kabu*; and politely requested us to row to a spot on the beach nearer the town, to which she pointed, and where she would meet us.

> By this time she was joined by a gentleman whom we afterwards found to be Mr. Jones, the American consul; and taking his arm, they proceeded together to the place appointed. On landing, we were introduced to her Hawaiian majesty by this gentleman. She received us very cordially; and after bidding us welcome to the islands, consigned us to the care of Mr. Jones, and returned to the point. The queen appears about twenty or twenty-two years of age; and though well formed, is tall and masculine in figure. Her countenance is open and intelligent, with fine black eyes and hair; but her features are too broad and flat for beauty; and her complexion that of a dark mulatto, the general color of the islanders.

> Thronged by a crowd of chattering and noisy natives, who expressed their pleasure at our arrival, by hooting and dancing, and running along our path, we proceeded immediately with these gentlemen [Rev. Ellis and Mr. Loomis] to the mission-houses, situated on the plain, half a

---

*Rev. Stewart graduated from Princeton College in 1815; attended law school, and studied at the New York College of Physicians and Surgeons (now Columbia); attended the Princeton Theological Seminary in 1821, and was ordained in 1821. He married five months before sailing for the Hawaiian Islands. A son, Charles Seaforth, was born on the *Thames* sixteen days before arriving at Honolulu.

mile from the village: here we were introduced to the rest of the family, consisting of the Rev. Mr. Thurston and Mrs. Thurston, Mrs. Bingham, Mrs. Ellis, and Mrs. Loomis.* Mr. Bingham was absent at Waikiki, three miles distant, attending religious service with a large party of chiefs, at a temporary residence at that place.

At eleven o'clock, Mr. Thurston preached in English at the mission chapel, to an audience of about one hundred foreigners—sixty of whom were captains, officers, and seamen, from the ships in port. The hour could not be otherwise than deeply interesting to us: the chapel in which we worshipped was the first ever erected on the ruins of idolatry in this land; and though of the simplest and rudest construction, being entirely in the native style, it was on this account beautiful and lovely in our eyes.

On returning to the mission house, we had the pleasure of meeting the Rev. Mr. Bingham. The report of our arrival had reached Waikiki, and one of the queens of Liholiho had been sent with him as a messenger from the chiefs there, to request a visit from us at their afternoon worship; and after dinner, we accordingly proceeded to that place.

The queen, in a dress of white cambric, rode in a light wagon, drawn by a troop of natives, who hurried it along with great rapidity; and was followed by a train of attendants, one with a spit-box, another with an umbrella, some with fans of cocoanut leaf, &c. &c. Among the rest, one bore two *feathered staffs*, six or eight feet in length, with handles of ivory and tortoise-shell; these were carried as badges of rank. We ourselves made the excursion on foot; first over the large open plain to the east, which is entirely without trees or cultivation; and then through successive groves of the cocoanut and plantations of the banana. We found the chiefs encamped in slight bamboo bowers under a grove of cocoanuts by the seaside, and near the bay of Waikiki.

The party consisted of *Keopuolani*, the queen dowager, and mother of the present king; the prince *Kauikeaouli*, her son, a lad nine or ten years of age; the princess *Nahienaena*, his sister, two years younger; *Kaahumanu*, the favorite queen of Kamehameha, and her present husband, *Kaumualii*, king of Kauai and Niihau; his son *Kealiiahonui*; and *Kalaimoku*, or *Mr.*

*The Chamberlain family had returned to America.

Pitt, as he is usually called, prime minister both to the former and present king, with two or three hundred of their favorite attendants and followers. The chiefs were all under one *lanai*, or rude bower, the floor being spread with several thicknesses of mats, on which some were seated, a la turc; others lounging, and some lying down, with their heads resting on round pillows of silk velvet, damask, and morocco. Behind, or near each one, a servant sat or kneeled, fanning his master or mistress with a fan made of the leaves of the cocoanut, and holding in the other a small round bowl of dark polished wood, filled with the leaves of an aromatic vine for a *spittoon*. Another servant sat or stood near each chief with a *kahile* [kahili] or feathered staff, which he constantly waved, to keep off the flies. They were all dressed in European costume, and each had a small spelling book and slate on his mat with him. They greeted us with much kindness of expression and manner; and seemed interested in the improvements they are making, and in the religious services of the day. They wrote their own names on their slates, for us to read, and secure the right pronunciation; and requested us to leave ours with them, for the same purpose. They repeatedly shook hands with us, reiterating their joy at our arrival, saying, they were glad too, that we had come on the *la kabu*, the Sabbath-day; appearing to view this circumstance as a propitious omen.

Two days later . . .

It was signified early after our entrance into the harbor today, that some of our number would be expected by the king to wait upon him soon at his residence. Four or five of the gentlemen, including myself, therefore landed immediately; and were introduced to his majesty and most of his court. Liholiho was much indisposed, being just on the recovery from his late debauch. He was stretched on a couch of silk velvet, and naked, except a strip of chintz thrown loosely round his waist. Several servants were fanning him, and one of his queens giving him a cup of tea. He looked exceedingly stupid; and so much the worse for his excess, as to be a brutish object, as he tossed his arms and legs about in all the restlessness of a fit of nausea. He was too ill to do more than signify his pleasure at our arrival; and to request the whole company to call upon him and the chiefs, on their way from the ship to the mission house.

Accordingly, at eleven o'clock, we all went on shore for the purpose of a formal presentation to the government. The *palace* stands on a stone quay, within a few feet of the water. It is a large and fine house for one of the kind; perhaps fifty feet long, thirty broad, eight feet high at the sides, and thirty at the peak of the roof. The exterior is entirely composed of a thatch of grass; and in its whole appearance is strikingly like the Dutch barns seen in many parts of our country. There are two large doors, one at each end, and several windows without glass, but furnished with Venetian shutters on each side of the house. This is the only native building in which I have observed windows. The interior, making one apartment only, is neat, well finished, and elegant for the Sandwich Islands. All the timbers, the side posts, a row of pillars supporting the ridge-pole through the whole length of the house and the rafters, are straight and substantial, and all beautifully hewn. The cinet or braid formed from the shreds of the husk of the cocoanut, by which the whole are fastened together, exhibits both skill and taste in its manufacture and arrangement. The furniture is rich, consisting besides handsome mats with which the ground is everywhere covered, of three or four large chandeliers of cut glass suspended between the pillars running through the centre of the building, of mahogany dining and pier tables, crimson Chinese sofas and chairs, several large pier glasses and mirrors, some tolerable engravings, principally of naval engagements and battles in Europe, likenesses of distinguished persons, &c., and two full-length paintings of Liholiho, taken by an artist attached to the Russian squadron of discovery under the command of Commodore Vasechieff, which not long ago visited this group.

The king was much in the same state as when I saw him after breakfast. Most of the other chiefs, all the principal personages of the kingdom, including the party from Waikiki, having assembled, made a highly respectable appearance; especially the favorite queen Kamehamalu. She was seated on a sofa at the middle of a long table covered with a superb cloth, having a writing-desk open before her, and a native secretary at each end of the table, recording the names and taxes of the inhabitants of a district who were paying tribute. These were entering in single file; and, passing along the table on the side opposite the queen, they deposited their dollars before her, and left the house at another door. Every twenty or thirty of them were preceded and followed by a couple of the king's body-guard, armed with muskets and in a kind of uniform. The only dress of Kamehamalu was a loose pink slip. She left her writing-desk on the entrance of the missionaries, but immediately after receiving them, resumed her seat, excusing herself from farther attentions on account of the public business in which she was engaged. Her manners are dignified and graceful; and her whole appearance that of a well-bred woman, having an unaffected expression of conscious and acknowledged rank. She is a woman of business, and appeared well versed in that before her. She has ordered a roll-book to be opened, in which the names, residence and tax of all the nation are to be registered, and it was the superintendence of this that so much occupied her attention.

Kaahumanu is one of the most powerful of the female chiefs, and attracted particular observation. She joined the company after our arrival, and entered the house with much of real majesty in her step and manner. She was dressed in the native female costume. The *pau* [pa'u] or under garment consisted of about twenty yards of rich yellow satin, arranged in loose and graceful folds, with a full end hanging negligently in front; the upper robe was a purple satin, in as profuse a quantity. It was cast over one arm and shoulder only, leaving the other exposed, and flowed in its richness far on the ground behind her. Her hair was neatly put up with combs, and ornamented by a double coronet of the exquisite feathers so often mentioned in accounts of these islands; colors bright yellow, crimson and blueish green. She appears to be between forty and fifty years of age, is large and portly, still bears marks of the beauty for which she has been celebrated, but has an expression of greater sternness and hauteur than any other islander I have yet seen.*

---

*The Hawaiians had a sense of humor. Rev. Stewart later noted: [46:106] "The pets of the nobles, of whatever kind, have in many cases unlimited privileges. There is at present attached to the palace a hog of this character, weighing four or five hundred pounds, called *Kaahumanu*, after the haughty dowager of that name, which is permitted to range at pleasure, within doors as well as without; and not infrequently finds a bed among the satins and velvets of the royal couches."

The young princess Nahienaena came, seated on the left
shoulder of a stout man, her feet resting on his arms, folded
for this purpose across his chest, and having her right arm
around his head and forehead. This is the way in which she
is usually carried; and is always followed by a train of
twenty or thirty boys and girls, principally of her own age.
Her dress, like most of the others, was in the European
fashion, and of black satin trimmed with broad gold-lace,
with black satin hat and feathers. She is a pretty and well-
behaved child, not as an Indian, but according to our own
ideas of the characteristics of childhood. The prince was
also present in a round coat and pantaloons, of black silk
velvet. They have both learned to read and write, and are
among the most attentive and docile pupils of the mission.

The ceremonies of the last day [of the festival] were
altogether *Hawaiian* in their character, and highly interesting as an exhibition of ancient customs, which it is probable
will soon be lost forever in the light of civilization and
Christianity, now rapidly dawning on the nation . . .

Kamehamalu on this day was, as usual, a conspicuous
object. The *car of state*, in which she joined the processions
passing in different directions, consisted of an elegantly
modeled *whaleboat*, fastened firmly to a platform or frame of
light spars, thirty feet long by twelve wide; and borne on
the heads and shoulders of seventy men. The boat was lined,
and the whole platform covered, first with fine imported
broadcloth, and then with beautiful patterns of tapa or
native cloth, of a variety of figures and rich colors. The men
supporting the whole were formed into a solid body, so that
the outer rows only at the sides and ends were seen; and all
forming these wore the splendid scarlet and yellow feather
cloaks and helmets of which you have read accounts, and
than which scarce anything can appear more superb.

The only dress of the queen was a scarlet silk *pau*, or native
petticoat, and a coronet of feathers. She was seated in the
middle of the boat, and screened from the sun by an
immense Chinese umbrella of scarlet damask, richly
ornamented with gilding, fringe, and tassels, and supported
by a chief standing behind her in a scarlet malo or girdle,
and feathered helmet. On one quarter of the boat stood
Kalaimoku, the prime minister, and on the other Naihe, the

143

national orator—both also in malos of scarlet silk and helmets of feathers—and each bearing a kahile, or feathered staff of state, near thirty feet in height. The upper parts of these kahiles were of scarlet feathers, so ingeniously and so beautifully arranged on artificial branches attached to the staff as to form cylinders fifteen or eighteen inches in diameter and twelve or fourteen feet long; the lower parts or handles were covered with alternate rings of tortoise-shell and ivory, of the neatest workmanship and highest polish.

Imperfect as the image may be which my description will convey to your mind, of this pageant of royal device and exhibition, I think you will not altogether condemn the epithet I use, when I say it was *splendid*. So far as the feather mantles, helmets, coronets, and kahiles had an effect, I am not fearful of extravagance in the use of the epithet. I doubt whether there is a nation in Christendom, which, at the time letters and Christianity were introduced, could have presented a *court dress* and insignia of rank so magnificent as these: and they were found here in all their richness, when the islands were discovered by Cook. There is something approaching the *sublime* in the lofty noddings of the kahiles of state, as they tower far above the heads of the group whose distinction they proclaim—something conveying to the mind impressions of majesty unequaled by the gleamings of the most splendid banner I ever saw unfurled.

The queens Kinau and Kekauonohi presented themselves much in the same manner as Kamehamalu; but instead of whaleboats, had for their seats double canoes. Pauahi, another of the wives of Liholiho, after passing in procession with her retinue, alighted from the couch on which she had been borne, set fire to it and all its expensive trappings, and then threw into the flame the whole of her dress, except a single handkerchief to cast around her. In this she was immediately imitated by all her attendants: and many valuable articles, a large quantity of kapa, and entire pieces of broadcloth, were thus consumed. This feat of extravagance was induced, however, by a nobler motive than that which once led a more celebrated and more beautiful queen to signalize a festival by the *drinking of pearls*. It was to commemorate a narrow escape from death by fire, while an infant: a circumstance from which she derives her name—

Pau, all or *consumed*—and *ahi, fire.* Her house was destroyed by an explosion of gunpowder, which became accidently ignited. Five men were killed by it, and Pauahi herself was much burned.

The dresses of some of the queens-dowager were expensive and immense in quantity. One wore seventy-two yards of kerseymere of double fold—one half being scarlet, and the other orange. It was wrapped round her figure, till her arms were supported horizontally by the bulk; and the remainder was formed into a train supported by attendants appointed for the purpose

The young prince and princess wore the native dress; malo and pau, of scarlet silk. Their *vehicle* consisted of *four field-bedsteads,* of Chinese wood and workmanship, lashed together side by side, covered with handsome native cloth, and ornamented with canopies and drapery of yellow figured moreen. Two chiefs of rank bore their kahiles; and Hoapili and Kaikioewa, their step-father and guardian, in scarlet malos, followed them as servants—the one bearing a calabash of *raw fish* and a calabash of *poe,* and the other a *dish of baked dog,* for the refreshment of the young favorites.

The king and his suite made but a sorry exhibition. They were nearly naked, mounted on horses without saddles, and so much intoxicated as scarce to be able to retain their seats as they scampered from place to place in all the disorder of a troop of bacchanalians. A body-guard, of fifty or sixty men in shabby uniform, attempted by a running march to keep near the person of their sovereign, while hundreds of ragged natives, filling the air with their hootings and shoutings, followed in the chase.

Companies of singing and dancing girls and men, consisting of many hundreds, met the processions in different places, encircling the highest chiefs, and shouting their praise in enthusiastic adulations. The dull and monotonous sounds of the native drum and calabash, the wild notes of their songs in the loud choruses and responses of the various parties, and the pulsations, on the ground, of the tread of thousands in the dance, reached us even at the missionary enclosure.

AUTHOR'S NOTE: Rev. Stewart surely didn't have a good first impression of King Liholiho!

XVII

keopuolani

Levi Parsons Bingham was born December 31, 1822. Sybil was attended by her mission "sisters" as no western physician was available. The baby died sixteen days later, the first death among the mission families. The funeral service was held January 19, 1823 at the thatched mission church at Honolulu. King Liholiho, his queens, and a number of chiefs and chiefesses attended. Rev. Thurston preached an appropriate sermon. Interment of the pathetically small coffin was adjacent to the church.

The only solace for Rev. Hiram Bingham was the bible, and his dedicated work. He concentrated even more than before, if that was possible.

When Rev. Ellis returned to the Hawaiian Islands in early February 1823, he sent a letter to King Liholiho advising his arrival. The Hawaiian alii were rapidly learning to read and write, and delighted in writing letters to one another. Rev. Ellis recorded King Liholiho's answer. When the contents are considered, one suspects that the king had some assistance in preparing the correspondence. As Rev. Ellis put it, "the translation is servile"—it can be considered to represent the then state of the art of reducing the Hawaiian language to writing:[10:480]

Mr. Ellis, eo.
Mr. Ellis, attend.

Aroha ino oe, ko wahine me na keiki
Attachment great (to) you, and your wife, with children

a pau a orua. I ola okau ia Jehova ia
all of ye two. Preserved (have) you (been) by Jehovah they

laua o Iesu Kraist. Eia kau wahi olero ia oe, Mr. Ellis.
two Jesus Christ. This (is) my word to you, Mr. Ellis.

apopo a kela la ku a ahiahi, a ku hoi mai.
to-morrow or the day after when evening, then I return.

I ka tabu a leila ua ite kaua. A i makemake oe e
On the Sabbath then (shall) meet we. But if desire you to

here mai ianei maitai no hoi. Ike ware oe i
come here, well also. Seen indeed (have) you the

na'rii o Tahiti. Aroha ware na'rii Bolabola.
chiefs of Tahiti. Attachment only to the chiefs of Borabora.*

I ola oe ia Jehova ia Jesu Kraist.
Saved (may) you (be) by Jehovah by Jesus Christ.

IOLANI

Revs. Bingham and Ellis devoted considerable attention to King Liholiho. If they could convert him, they were sure that his people would follow. When the king was available, they intensified their efforts (e.g. one day, from 9 AM to sunset). Yet the king's attention did not last too many days in a row, there were so many other things to do (e.g. the king entertained a group of chiefs for hours with accounts of different peoples, parts of the world, and animals which he had heard about). And, of course, he liked to party, and could not be dissuaded when on a course of pleasure. The king had many distractions, not the least of which was the conduct of the foreigners in Honolulu, some good and some bad.

There were such different kinds of foreigners who visited or lived in the Hawaiian Islands! There were the missionaries. There were those who worked for the four well-stocked American merchantile branch establishments. These were also agents for various trading ships. This kind of foreigner was orderly, but always pressed to extend sandalwood credit to the chiefs. Then there were the small number of foreign residents who either worked for the chiefs, or worked some of their properties. They were mostly orderly and loyal. Some grew produce to sell to visiting ships, or distilled intoxicating spirits. Another small group of foreigners operated grog shops, and preyed upon whomever they could. Many troubles were traced to their activities. Business was especially lucrative for them when the whalers stopped for provisions and relaxation (e.g.104 whalers touched at the Hawaiian Islands in 1824). The long-at-sea seamen practically went wild when they came ashore—those who had "hung their consciences on Cape Horn when entering the Pacific". The worst troublemakers were several hundred "runaway sailors and vagabonds" who lived off what Hawaiian generosity gave them, or they could steal.

*The term for the Society Islands.

* * * * *

Sacred Queen Mother Keopuolani had become receptive to Christianity. The missionaries were most pleased, as they had come to understand that her lineage was of great respect to the Hawaiians. Taua, one of the "native teachers" Rev. Ellis had brought with him from Tahiti, became almost her private instructor and "family chaplain." Keopuolani enjoyed peace and quiet and desired to follow Christian principles. Honolulu was not conducive to this, what with the constant excitements and disorders caused by foreigners.

When her husband, Hoapili, made arrangements for them to relocate to Lahaina, Maui, she requested that some missionaries also go to Lahaina and establish a mission station there. The "brethren and sisters" elected Rev. Stewart, and he asked Rev. Richards to accompany him.

The *Haaheo o Hawaii* left Honolulu for Lahaina May 28, 1823, and arrived there three days later.* The departure was well-attended. Rev. Stewart began to amend his opinion of Liholiho as:[46:134]

There was something also in the attention of the king to his mother, when leaving Honolulu, that had a pleasing effect on our minds. This venerable old lady** was the last person that came on board. After we had reached the quarter-deck of the barge, she appeared on the beach, surrounded by an immense crowd, and supported by Liholiho in a tender and respectful manner. He would let no one assist her into the long-boat but himself; and seemed to think of nothing but her ease and safety, till she was seated on her couch, beneath an awning over the main hatch. The king continued to manifest the utmost affection and respect for her till we got under way; and apparently from the same filial feelings, accompanied us fifteen miles to sea, and left the brig in a pilot-boat, in time barely to reach the harbor before dark.

Revs. Stewart and Richards and their families were initially housed at Lahaina in the residence complex of an American named Butler. It was located about a quarter of a mile from the landing place, and in a grove of breadfruit trees. Bananas, taro, potatoes,

*There were some 200 passengers on the 83 foot 191 ton *Haaheo o Hawaii*.

**Keopuolani was but age 43; a wasting illness perhaps?

149

sugar cane, etc., were conveniently planted in the vicinity. Rev. Stewart considered the location "like the delights of an Eden"; Betsy Stockton considered it "East of Eden." The clergymen preached with the aid of an interpreter to Keopuolani and an attentive audience on the beach the morning after their arrival. Preaching and prayer meetings continued daily, and schools were started in the village of some 2,500 Hawaiians. Food was continually provided for missionary tables, and two Hawaiian houses, fifteen feet by twenty three feet, were built for them on the shoreline. A thatched chapel and a thatched schoolhouse were also constructed.

Revs. Bishop, Ellis, Thurston and Mr. Goodrich made a tour around the island of Hawaii June - September 1823. When they arrived at Kailua, High Chief Kuakini was most hospitable. Their arrival at the island of Hawaii probably coincided with the exciting news of the activity at Kilauea volcano, which resulted in a lava flow at Kapapala, district of Kau. The lava was reputed very fluid, and flowed so rapidly to the sea that some Hawaiian inhabitants along the shoreline were unable to even save their canoes.

One can conjecture that this awesome expression of nature could have led to the following conversation between Rev Ellis and High Chief Kuakini. It well illustrates the Hawaiian skepticism then prevalent about Christianity:[10:98-99]

> After dinner, the governor entered freely into conversation on religious subjects, particularly respecting the resurrection of the body, the destruction of the heavens and the earth at the last day, and the final judgement. After listening attentively to what was said upon these subjects, he inquired about the locality of heaven and hell. He was told that we did not know where the one or the other was situated, as none had ever returned from either, to tell mankind about them; and we only knew, that there is a place called heaven, where God makes glorious manifestations of his perfections, and where all good men are perfectly happy; and that there is a place where wicked men are shut up in darkness, and endure endless misery. He then said, "How do you know these things?" I asked for his bible, and translated the passages which inculcate the doctrine of the resurrection, &c. and told him it was from that book we obtained all our knowledge of these things; and that it was the contents of that book which we had come to teach the people of Hawaii. He then asked if all the

people in our native countries were acquainted with the bible. I answered that from the abundant means of instruction enjoyed there, the greater portion of the people had either read the book, or had in some other way become acquainted with its principal contents. He then said, How is it that such numbers of them swear, get intoxicated, and do so many things prohibited in that book? He was told, that there was a vast difference between knowing the word of God, and obeying it; and that it was most likely, those persons knew their conduct was displeasing to God, yet persisted in it, because agreeable to their corrupt inclinations. He asked if God would not be angry with us for troubling him so frequently with our prayers? If he was like man, he said, he was sure he would. I replied that God was always "awaiting to be gracious," more ready to hear than we were to pray; that indeed he was not like man, or his patience would have been exhausted long ago by the wickedness of man; but that he continued exercising long-suffering and forbearance towards sinners, that they might turn from their wickedness and live.

Liholiho visited his mother almost a month later. His arrival off Lahaina on the evening of June 23, 1823 was announced by his brig firing five guns in rapid succession, his regal private signal. The greeting between Liholiho and Keopuolani was affectionate. Liholiho celebrated that night. The next morning the usual assemblage for missionary prayers and religious instruction did not appear. Keopuolani "reproved Liholiho for his habits of dissipation," but Liholiho continued his enjoyments. There became a considerable conflict of interests. On at least one occasion a hula dancing party was broken up by Kamamalu, and the attendees directed to participate in a prayer meeting.

Relations between Keopuolani and Liholiho became strained. King Liholiho left for the island of Molokai July 5, 1823, where he could enjoy himself as he desired without restraints.

Sacred Queen Mother Keopuolani became quite ill September 3, 1823. As it was customary for the chiefs to assemble when an important person was seriously afflicted, swift messengers were hurriedly dispatched to all the islands. Two schooners and a brig arrived off Lahaina the following day—from the islands of Hawaii and Oahu. The some fifty chiefs surrounded Keopuolani's bed and began to wail—in traditional concern and sorrow, and to appease the offended God. Keopuolani became worse the next day, and more messengers were sent to the other islands.

All the important chiefs and chiefesses had arrived by September 8th. Keopuolani's bed was constantly surrounded by tearful King Liholiho and his queens, Kaahumanu and Kalanimoku, Kaumualii and Kealiiahonui, her husband Hoapili, and her other children, Kauikeaouli and Nahienaena. They remained at her bedside day and night. Keopuolani was attended by Dr. Law, a Scot physician then in practice at Honolulu, and Dr. Blatchely of the second company of American missionaries. The doctors were not optimistic.

Keopuolani held on for another week, and finally had a premonition. She assembled the royal family and the leading chiefs for her final words:[42:33]

> I am now about to die. I shall leave my children, my people, and these lands, and I wish now to give you my last charge.
>
> *(to the king)* I wish you after my death to be a friend to all the friends of your father, and to all my friends. Take care of these lands which you have received from your father. Exercise a tender care over the people. Protect the missionaries, and be kind to them. Walk in the straight path. Keep the Sabbath. Serve God. Love him, and love Jesus Christ. Attend also to the word of God, that you may be happy, and that we two may meet in heaven. If you see any of the people going wrong, take care to lead them in the right way, but I entreat you not to follow them in the bad way, when your mother is gone.
>
> *(to the chiefs)* Watch over the king, my son. Exercise a guardian care over him. But particularly I wish you to watch over my two younger children. See that they are brought up in the right way, that they are instructed in reading, that they keep the Sabbath day, that they both love God and pray to him. Protect the teachers who have come to this land of dark hearts. Attend to their instructions. Cease not to keep the commandments of God, to love him, to obey his word, to regard the Sabbath and all the means of instruction, and do not neglect prayer to God. He is a good God. Our former gods were false, but he is the God by whom we may all live forever in heaven. I love Jesus Christ. I hope he has loved me, and that he will receive me.

Keopuolani weakened rapidly during the night. The next

morning she faintly expressed a final desire to become a Christian. Revs. Stewart and Richards were in a dilemma, as they could not speak adequate Hawaiian, and had no interpreter. Fortunately Rev. Ellis arrived from another island. Keopuolani's wish was concurred with by her husband Hoapili, Liholiho, Kaahumanu and Kalanimoku. Rev. Ellis "administered the sacred ordinance which entitles all who receive it to the name of Christian."

Keopuolani died an hour later, at 5 PM September 16, 1823.

The makaainana (commoners) began to flee to the hills so that they would not be candidates for the traditional Hawaiian sacrifices attendant upon the death of an important personage. There were none, as Keopuolani had directed that wailing was sufficient respect. Many began the traditional kumakena (mourning period) riot and license to do anything they wanted. This was stopped by order of Liholiho and Kaahumanu, and enforced by Kalanimoku. Christian prayers were the order of the day.

The hills behind Lahaina resounded for two days with the constant wailing of thousands of Hawaiians. Rev. Stewart recorded:[46:172]

> The word which they pronounce in wailing, is *"au-we!"* *"au-we!"* [alas! alas!]—prolonging the the sound of the last syllable, sometimes for many minutes, with a trembling and agitated shaking of the voice. The tones in which it is uttered by different persons, vary from the lowest to the highest key, and from that which is most plaintive, to that which is most shrill. There being no uniformity in the time of beginning or ending the word, the confusion and discord thus created is terrific. The attitudes of figure are as various as the tones of voice. Some stand upright, casting their arms and faces towards heaven, with the eyes closed and mouth widely distended. Others, instead of throwing their arms upward, clasp their hands and place them behind their heads. Some bend forward, their faces almost to the ground, and their hands placed against their knees, or violently pressed into their sides, as if in excruciating internal agony; others clench their hands into the hair on each side of their heads, as if to tear it out by the roots; and all seem to emulate one another in attempts at the most hideous grimaces and painful distortions, while torrents of tears flow from their heads to their feet.

Rev. Ellis conducted a Christian funeral on September 18, 1823, for this all-important first Hawaiian convert. The service was held in a grove of kou trees and attended by three to five thousand Hawaiians. Following the service, a procession of some four hundred escorted the bier carried on men's shoulders to a newly constructed tomb at Kaluaokiha. The tomb had been expeditiously built of stones carried from a nearby abandoned heiau (temple) and cemented with mud. Four of Liholiho's queens and two "principal women" acted as pall bearers, and carried kahilis beside the bier. The royal family and Hoapili followed. Behind them were numerous chiefs and chiefesses in order of rank. Minute guns were fired from the vessels anchored offshore, colors were at half-mast, and a bell tolled until the coffin was laid to rest. The thousands of Hawaiian spectators were impressed with the simple yet majestic pageantry.

A large stone wall was carefully constructed enclosing the tomb. Each of the thousands of Hawaiians present expressed their individual respect and sorrow—each brought a stone from the old heiau, alii (chiefs and chiefesses) and makaainana (commoners) alike.

Liholiho was disconsolate. Rum didn't bring solace. His favorite Queen Kamamalu could not provide sufficient sympathy to assist his great sorrow. His mother, whose opinion and guidance he had such high regard for, would no longer be there to assist when he was troubled.

Perhaps she had shown the way he should go . . . by her example . . . and by her words "walk in the straight path." Perhaps.

Liholiho just wanted to be alone. To think. To reaffirm his mana (inner spiritual force). For he had his destiny to fulfill. . .

XVIII

let us go . . .
to england

High Chief Hoapili mourned the death of his wife, Keopuolani, for a respectful month. He then married the immense Dowager Queen Kalakua (Kaahumanu's sister, and mother of two of Liholiho's queens, Kamamalu and Kinau.) Rev. Richards performed a Christian marriage ceremony October 19, 1823. The traditional Hawaiian ceremony of taking a wife was also performed. Kalakua took the name of Hoapili-wahine (Hoapili's woman).

The council met perhaps a week later at Lahaina, Maui with probably the following three main agenda items:
Kuhina-nui Kaahumanu spoke at length with concern about the many people who became sick of strange ailments—and many died.

Prime Minister Kalanimoku expressed concern about the chiefs providing inadequate taxes for the operation of the Hawaiian Kingdom and for the welfare of the rulers.

High Chief Boki, governor of the island of Oahu, gave a somewhat impassioned report of disorders at Honolulu caused mostly by seamen coming ashore from the many whaleships there.
The council members stirred restlessly in their reclining positions of comfort. This was bothersome. People dying for strange reasons, taxes (a matter of continual concern), and foreigner seamen causing trouble. There seemed to be no end or solution to these problems.
Kalanimoku spoke quietly, "Yes, these are disturbing things. We must find a way to solve them. Perhaps we should evaluate how we govern the islands and people—there may be a better way—perhaps we can improve on our government and control of the people."

Kaahumanu raised her head quickly and haughtily replied, "No, Kalanimoku, our government cannot be improved. My late husband, Ke Alii Nui Kamehameha, established our pattern of government, and he was correct. He charged me with this policy, and we will carry it out as he willed."

Kalanimoku serenely glanced at King Liholiho, who broodingly sat cross-legged.

Liholiho raised his head and addressed Kaahumanu, "My makua-hanai (foster mother), I must respectfully bring to your attention that conditions have changed since my father died. Yes, he established the policy and pattern of government—but there then were three significant conditions which are not present today."

"First, there was the kapu system, which brought order to all. This system was stronger, much stronger than the kanawai (laws) that the foreigners talk about. And we know that my father imposed very few controls over the foreigners' conduct, except for profaning the heiaus (temples)."

"Second, look offshore at the number of anchored western vessels, mostly American whalers. Why, at the time my father died, this number visited the islands *all that year*—and there are many more at Kona, Hawaii, and even more at Honolulu, Oahu!"

"Third, my father received *all* the taxes, and distributed them as he saw fit."

He concluded, "We have no orderly way of life now, compared with yesterday's way of life, and there are many different things now which impact upon us. Very differing conditions."

Liholiho rose to his feet in one strong fluid motion and began to slowly walk back and forth with his hands clasped behind his back. His head was almost lowered, and he spoke with considerable deliberation. Unconsciously he began to orate—"fire came into his voice." Kaahumanu and the assembled high chiefs raised their heads and began to concentrate their attention upon him. They had never heard Liholiho talk like this before.

"Since my mother, the Sacred Queen Mother Keopuolani, died," Liholiho continued, "I have done considerable thinking and questioning and evaluating. For she of the highest lineage gave me this capability. I am of her blood and lineage." Several of the high chiefs nodded.

"My father," Liholiho went on with deepened voice, "was a marvelous man who did what no other alii had ever been able to do before him. He conquered the islands, and ruled them. We must appreciate that the island of Kauai came firmly under our control after his death." Liholiho stopped, and slightly bowed to Kaahumanu. All knew that he was paying respect to Kaahumanu for the important part she had played in this significant consolidation of their dual Rule. Kaahumanu was not sure that she liked what Liholiho was talking about (without her prior knowledge and consent), but she appreciated the respect. She did not acknowledge the compliment, but Liholiho sensed that she was a *little* pleased.

Liholiho carefully deliberated, and continued, "Let me discuss the three important matters we have gathered in council to consider—sickness and death, taxes, and law and order."

"I am baffled by the sickness and death of so many of our people too. Truly baffled. I recall as a lad the mai okuu* which caused the death of one out of every two of our people. Kaahumanu and Keeaumoku, your father died of this sickness. Koa-Hou, your father died of this sickness. Naihe, your father died of this sickness." Liholiho looked at each named as he spoke their names.

"I have had many lengthy discussions with the foreigner kahuna-lapaau (medical doctors) about this. They are also baffled about the many Hawaiian deaths from sicknesses that they are familiar with and have names for. But I do have a thought. When the foreigners who are Americans first came to the country they call the United States, there were many people there called Indians. Many of these Indians died in large numbers of the same sicknesses that our people are dying of. Maybe the foreigners are accustomed to these sicknesses, for they get them too, but very few die. Perhaps so many of our people die because they are not accustomed to these strange sicknesses. I do not really know. I but present the thought. I do not know of any solution."

Liholiho had completely captured all of the attention of the assembled council members. He had stopped moving, and stood still, looking at each of the council calmly in turn. His usual somewhat soft and hoarse voice had become clear and eloquent. His presence had become more commanding.

"Let us talk about taxes. When my Father was alive, *he* received *all* the taxes, and distributed them fairly, to *you* and yours. What is the situation today? Kaahumanu, myself, and Kalanimoku have to practically plead for taxes from *you*. It was not thus in the time of my Father! I know that times have changed. *You* have been granted the rights to collect and sell sandalwood which the foreigners covet so much. *You* send the people of the areas you control to the mountains to search for the last of the sandalwood. The people have little time to grow their foodstuffs for themselves,

*Cholera or bacillary dysentary epidemic (?) in 1804.

and suffer for it. *You* sell what foodstuffs are available to provision the visiting ships. Do you share (hookupu) with your rulers? A mere pittance is shared! I say this is a great departure from the policy of my Father."

Liholiho stated quietly yet piercingly, "This is not right. Kaahumanu and I have barely enough lands under our own control to support ourselves. I have no more lands to give to your control. It is time you give more of the product of the lands we gave to your control, to your rulers."

The assembled high chiefs looked at one another, and then back at Liholiho. Some appeared defiant, some almost ashamed. High Chief Hoapili started to interject—Liholiho raised his right hand commandingly, and Hoapili shut his mouth. (Liholiho was sure that Hoapili was about to be generous, but this was not the best time.)

"The third matter concerns the law and order of the foreigners, much less our own people. When my Father was alive, the kapus provided law and order. Today we have no such system. To be sure, we have criers who announce to the people what to do or what not to do. But we have no system of enforcement. Each of us insists on compliance as the spirit may move each of us. Our dictates are not followed as they should be, by everyone in the same way. Completely. And this includes the foreigners, too. I must say that I do not know exactly which way to turn, but I have an idea."

Liholiho began to slowly pace back and forth again, and kept his eyes, which had appeared to grow larger, on his attentive audience. He went on, emphasizing attention to the points he was making by indicating a separate finger of his outstretched right hand.

"Most of the foreign troublemakers are Americans, and they are by far the most of the foreigners who come to Hawaii."

"My Father respected the British. And from time-to-time we used the protection of the British flag. Who can forget the great Captain Vancouver?" Liholiho looked briefly at Kaahumanu, for she and Kamehameha had been reconciled at one time by this respected British naval captain.

"The English king is our friend. Did he not send me the *Prince Regent* in response to a promise that Captain Vancouver had made to my Father? I say the British have integrity, are powerful, and have great knowledge."

"Did not my Father, and the fathers of you high chiefs who comprise the council, solicit British protection of the island of Hawaii from Captain Vancouver back in 1794? And did not he and your fathers and my Father agree on British protection? I know that we have seen few British warships since that time, *but that was my Father's and your fathers' policy!*"

"Therefore . . ." Liholiho stopped, and looked squarely at the council members.

"Therefore . . . I have decided that I intend to go and visit the British King George IV and solicit his advice and protection for our Rule. And I have already made a tentative arrangement to do just this with Captain Starbuck of the English whaler *L'Aigle* . . . leaving next month."

Liholiho sat down and calmly regarded the council. There was a hubbub of excited voices at this startling announcement. Kaahumanu and some of the high chiefs were vehement in opposition. Kalanimoku and some of the high chiefs appeared to think that this was a good idea. There was a division of opinion that was vigorously expressed. Liholiho did not enter into the arguments.

One suggested that more knowledge of commercial business as practiced by the foreigners in their own country would be advantageous. Another suggested that British protection could be beneficial for an apprehension that the American traders had expressed—that the Russians coveted the Hawaiian Islands and might try and take them over, as they had the island of Kauai seven years ago. High Chief Boki felt that knowledge of how the British kept law and order in their country would be most valuable. Some were frankly suspicious of the unknown. Several thought that the large number of Americans in Hawaii would not like the idea of British protection.

Kaahumanu had little sympathy with the idea. Liholiho just wanted to "GO," he was looking for adventure and glory, and little good would come of it. Nothing was decided. The council ended on an excited note, and the high chiefs departed in heated discussions.

Another council was held at Kaluaokiha, Lahaina, Maui, on November 15, 1823.[34] Much had transpired since the last council meeting, as behind-the-scenes deliberations was normal practice preceding important Hawaiian decisions.

Kaahumanu had grudgingly concurred with Liholiho going to England for basically three reasons. First, there was no infringement upon her prerogative as kuhina-nui (regent). Second, she was aware of a certain amount of relief from further apprehension about what Liholiho would do for a while. Third, her concurrence was conditional upon High Chief Boki going along as chief counsellor.

And besides, anything that Liholiho *might* be able to secure

159

British agreement on—would be subject to her approval!

The brief council did not formally sanction King Liholiho's trip to Great Britain. There was tacit concurrence following individual consultations prior to the council meeting. First there was the matter of how Liholiho would go to England. Captain Valentine Starbuck, an American from Nantucket, had offered passage in his south sea whaler *L'Aigle*. This ship was English-owned, had set out from Nantucket over a year and a half previous, and was returning with a full load of 2,200 barrels of whale oil. [41:2] Francisco de Paula Marin had suggested that the *Haaheo o Hawaii* be used for the trip. This was rejected as the Hawaiian captain and crew had never made this voyage before. Captain Starbuck's offer was accepted. (It appears that arrangements for return from England to Hawaii received little consideration . . .)

Then came the matter of who would go with King Liholiho. He wanted his Queen Kamamalu to accompany him. All agreed, as Kamamalu was highly respected. High Chief Boki was to go as Liholiho's chief counsellor. His wife, Liliha, insisted on also going. This was agreed upon.

Others were selected:

Kekuanaoa (son of Nahioleu), the Oahu agent for Kalanimo-ku, was to act as the king's treasurer.

Kapihe (Naihe-kukui, son of Hanakahi), commonly known as "Jack" and who was "Admiral" in charge of the king's fleet of vessels, was to go as the king's aide-de-camp.

The king's steward, Manuia (son of Kaulunae), was to go in that capacity.

James Kanehoa Young, the son of John Young ("Olohana"), was to go in the capacity of interpreter.

Three junior alii, Kaunoha'malama (younger brother of High Chief Hoapili), Kaaweawea (or Naaiweuweu, son of Kekumuino), and Naukane (son of Kamanawa) were selected to be attendants.

Rev. Ellis' wife was ailing, and he had determined to return to England. Rev. Bingham suggested that the Ellis family accompany the royal party. This would have the advantage of Rev. Ellis being available as interpreter. For some strange reason, Captain Starbuck refused to take them. Rev. Bingham thought that this was most unusual, as the captain had always been very friendly with the missionaries.

The matter of succession to the Rule, or more exactly, co-Rule with Kuhina-nui Kaahumanu, was firmly established. This had been well-settled prior to the council meeting. King Liholiho announced:[27:255-256]

> Where are you, Chiefs! I am about to sail to a foreign land and I place my younger brother Kau-i-ke-aouli to be your chief (during my absence). I go, and if I return I return; if not, then you are to have my younger brother to be your King," and to Kau-i-ke-aouli he said, "Live in peace with the chiefs; those lands which belong to me are yours, the lands given to the chiefs shall be theirs.

King Liholiho and his party embarked on the *L'Aigle* for the short trip from Lahaina, Maui, to Honolulu November 18, 1823. Departure was near sunset, and was escorted by about a dozen vessels. Rev. Stewart recorded:[46:181] "As soon as she had well cleared her moorings, the whole squadron was in motion, and, with a fine breeze, 'filled away' beautifully, amidst columns of smoke and fire, and a roar of cannon, that the waters and mountains of Maui probably never before heard."

Many were busy in Honolulu preparing for the sudden departure of King Liholiho and suite to London, England. The missionary "sisters" were prevailed upon to make some suitable garments for Queen Kamamalu and Liliha. Rich materials and inexpert Hawaiian seamstresses were provided. The chiefs were prevailed upon to provide a chest containing $25,000. in specie, which was placed aboard the *L'Aigle* in the custody of the captain.

The *L'Aigle* was towed out of Honolulu Harbor and anchored in the roadstead November 25, 1823. Two days later, near midday, the king and his suite made ready to depart at the Pakaka landing at Honolulu Harbor. The travellers were dressed in the height of western clothing. The farewells were emotional. Liholiho's queens who would remain in the islands were crying, and clung to him. Kaahumanu had tears in her eyes as she embraced the departing alii tightly with her huge arms. She had special affection for her foster son, Liholiho. No eye was dry. There were thousands of well-wishers; some were wailing in apprehension.

The cannon of Honolulu Fort, the battery atop Puowaina (Punchbowl), and armament on the many ships anchored in the harbor and offshore were firing continuous resounding salutes. There was a small fleet of outrigger and double-canoes ready to escort the royal party to the *L'Aigle*.

King Liholiho was so choked with emotion that he could hardly speak. He ordered the embarkation by motioning—Let Us Go . . .

161

Queen Kamamalu* was the last to enter a boat at the landing for the short transfer to the waiting ship, which was now standing off and on. She delivered a final farewell message that many could hear in the sudden hush:[27:256-257]

E ka lani e, e ka honua e,
O heaven! O earth!

E ka mauna e, e ha moana e,
O mountains and sea!

E ka hu e, e ha maka'ainana e,
O commoners and people!

Aloha 'oukou.
Farewell to you all.

E ka lepo e, aloha 'oe,
O soil, farewell!

E ka mea a ku'u makuakane i 'eha ai e,
O land for which my father suffered,

Aloha oe,
Farewell,

E ka luhi a ku'u makuakane i 'imi ai e.
O burden that my father strived for.

Ke ka'alele nei maua i ko luhi.
We two are leaving your labors.

Ke hele nei no au mamuli o ko kauoha,
I go in obedience to your command,

'A'ole au e ha'alele i kou leo.
I will not desert your voice.

Ke hele nei no au ma ko kauoha i olelo mai ai ia'u.
I go in accordance with the words you (Kamehameha) spoke to me.

The *L'Aigle* set out to sea at 3 PM. Unknown to those ashore as yet was that King Liholiho's party had increased to a total of twelve people. Jean Rives had secretly gone aboard the ship. He had been of use to Liholiho as secretary and interpreter in the past; his inclusion in the party had Captain Starbuck's approval. There had been no room for the Ellis', but there was for Jean Rives.

*Kamamalu was also known as Kamehamalu, "the shade of Kamehameha" or "under the protection of Kamehameha," her father.

XIX

RIO DE JANEIRO

The excitement of the departure gradually subsided. This was assisted by the steady average seven knot progress of the heavily laden whaleship on a southeasterly course. Liholiho inquired into every small facet of the ship's operation, and scrambled over all the rigging. Kapihe, who had skippered a Hawaiian vessel twice to China, offered to share a watch, which the captain accepted. The captain seemed a different man at sea than he had been ashore—more demanding and autocratic. The king's table was well-supplied with grog and wine, as befitted a royal traveler with known desires and habits.

The weather grew slowly warmer as they day-after-day approached the equator; the winds became lighter and more variable. When the *L'Aigle* day-after-day slowly forged into the south latitudes, southeast trades began to prevail, and the weather gradually became cooler. Captain Starbuck shortened sails to "plain sails" and later "storm sails" at about 45° south latitude when he began to encounter high swells. The weather was westerly, and became progressively raw, wet, windy and cloudy. The temperature dropped to the 40°s, the wind chill made it appear even colder. Liholiho and his entourage huddled together in the creaking cabin for warmth.

Gales began, beginning from the southwest and swinging to end at the northwest, which required "all hands on deck." There would be strange periods of calm, followed by sudden gusts of wind from different directions. The large following seas had to be carefully considered by the helmsman along with the changing winds.

The captain cheerfully assured Liholiho that it was Cape Horn summer weather, and thus milder, *much* milder than Cape Horn winter weather. The captain kept well offshore of Cape Horn in the Drake Passage, as the currents set onshore at about a knot an hour. This was no place to be other than cautious.

It probably took the *L'Aigle* a month and a half to go from Honolulu to the "bottom" of South America, and probably a week to carefully and laboriously make her way through Drake Passage before heading northerly into the Atlantic Ocean.

The *L'Aigle* slowly sailed into the large harbor of Rio de Janeiro February 15, 1824. The narrow entrance was flanked to the left by a huge bare mountain, now called Sugarloaf Mountain, and to the right by the fortress of Santa Cruz. The temperature was warm, in the 75-80°s, which Liholiho and his people appreciated. The several forts guarding the entrance were pointed out to Liholiho. The brilliant colors of the bay and rising hills seemed quite normal to the Hawaiians, as they were similar to their own islands.

A harbor pilot and port officials came aboard. After granting clearance, the *L'Aigle* was directed where to anchor. It was in that portion of the bay in front of the town of San Sebastian di Rio Janeiro. The port officials left and assured that they would inform government officials and the English Consul of the royal passengers.* Several small boats came to sell fresh fruit, which was thoroughly enjoyed by the Hawaiians who were not used to a diet of dried or preserved foods. There was the constant interesting sound of church bells. Liholiho beheld a town whose several story high principal buildings were constructed of brick or stone, covered with plaster which was painted bright colors. How different than Hawaii!

The *L'Aigle* remained at Rio de Janeiro for three weeks provisioning and refitting for the remainder of the voyage to London, England. Liholiho and his people thoroughly enjoyed themselves.

Emperor Don Pedro I invited King Liholiho and suite to a levee at the Palace. Liholiho thus first met a brother sovereign. The Hawaiian royal party landed at the Mole at the appointed hour and were met by a Court Chamberlain. They were escorted across the plaza to the red and yellow painted palace. A military band was playing music strange to Hawaiian ears, and soldiers in bright uniforms lined the passage from the central arch to the grand staircase which led to the State rooms on the floor above.

King Liholiho and Queen Kamamalu wore their best and most impressive western garments. They were attended by High Chief Boki and Liliha, also in western garb. Kekuanaoa and Kapihe escorted, each dressed appropriately in Hawaiian alii ahuula (feather cloak) and mahiole (feather helmet). James Kanehoa Young

---

*Interestingly enough, Diario do Governo, No.38, Thursday, 18 February 1824, page 166, lists the cargo as *olive oil*.

and Jean Rives brought up the rear (in severe plain black) as official interpreters.

Hawaiian eyes darted hither and thither and didn't miss a bit of the splendor. King Liholiho strode more deliberately and pulled himself up to the height of Polynesian dignity. His followers emulated. They were escorted to the Throne Room, which was resplendent with draperies of green damask lined with white and gold, and which sparkled with chandeliers, mirrors and candalabra. The floor was covered with a crimson carpet. Household troops lined the room at rigid attention. There were a number of richly-clad members of the emperor's court and the diplomatic corps standing respectfully adjacent to the raised throne. Yes, the first throne that King Liholiho had ever seen!

Emperor Don Pedro I was standing on the upper step by the throne when King Liholiho was announced. He descended to the floor to meet the Hawaiian king as a fellow sovereign. They slightly inclined their heads to each other in greeting, and took each others measure. The emperor wore a richly embroidered court uniform. He was of medium height, his full black whiskers and mustache added a touch of fierceness to his haughty dignity. His prominent hazel eyes sternly probed King Liholiho. He saw a like dignity, relaxed and smiled a welcome. King Liholiho murmured "aloha", and the Hawaiian and Portuguese interpreters began a fast series of introductions and small talk.

The emperor and his court were very interested in the ahuula (feather cloaks). It was old Brazilian custom to wear feather cloaks, and a brilliant cape of the yellow feathers of the toucon was part of the emperor's coronation dress.

The emperor presented a "most elegant" sword to King Liholiho. It was reported that King Liholiho gave the emperor a feather cape and a small kahili or fan.

On discovering that King Liholiho was enroute to England and for what general purpose, the British Consul-general gave a ball in honor of the royal visitors. The principal Brazilian families and English residents were invited.

The British Navy has always excelled in securing and providing diplomatic as well as naval intelligence. Rear Admiral Sir George Eyre, Commander-in-Chief Brazils (later South Smerican Station) forwarded the following secret despatch to the British Admiralty on the next ship going to England—in the safehand of Captain Starbuck:*

*F.O 58/3/24.

H.M.S. Spartiate
Rio de Janeiro
5 Mar. 1824.

The Secretary of the Admiralty.

The Chief or King of the Sandwich Islands, with part of his family and suite, have embarked in an English South Sea Whaler, called L'Aigle, for a passage to pay his respects to his Britannic Majesty, and to put his Islands, he says, under his Majesty's protection. I avail myself of this opportunity of that ship proceeding to England to acquaint Their Lordships with the circumstances.

He has been well received here by the Emperor, who presented him with a sword, and he seems to know how to appreciate the attentions which have been paid to him here.

(signed) GEORGE EYRE
Rear Admiral, Commander-in-Chief.

United States Consul Condy Raquet included the following in his despatch to Hon. John Quincy Adams, Secretary of State of the United States March 8, 1824:*

His Majesty, Rihoriho, King of the Sandwich Islands with his Queen and a suite of six or eight persons, arrived here on the 15th Feb. in an English ship, on his way to visit the King of Great Britain to ask his protection as I am informed against the encrouchments of his chiefs. I paid him a visit, and signified to him, that he might find it agreeable to extend his voyage to the United States which he probably may resolve upon doing. The captain of the ship is a Nantucket man, to whom the King is much attached.

The stone town of Rio de Janeiro fascinated the Hawaiians. The markets abounded with fresh fruits, including the familiar breadfruit, banana, taro and coconut, which the Hawaiians thoroughly enjoyed. There were numerous religious processions. The Hawaiians were particularly impressed with the little girls wearing artificial wings fixed to their shoulders to represent angels, and who scattered flowers before them. Such strange things—The narrow, dark streets with malodorous gutter channels in the center. The small carriages (seges) pulled by two small mules abreast. The

---

* National Archives microfilm Record Group 59, Microcopy No.T-171, Roll No.2.

numerous churchs and chapels. The street named Ouvidor with its many shops of European goods. The bird feathers, and the large beautiful butterflies. The well-dressed people, and the other extreme, the many African kauwa (slaves)

The Hawaiian interpreters were of considerable importance, as they were the means of fluent communication with these interesting Hawaiian strangers who came from a different ocean. It appears that after a while the English Consul-general refused to have Jean Rives perform this function for him, and turned to James Kanehoa Young. Intrigue began, which was later attributed by High Chief Boki to the efforts of Captain Starbuck and Jean Rives. In any event, Young was given a note ashore one day purporting to come from King Liholiho which forbade his returning to the *L'Aigle*. James Kanehoa Young was thus stranded in Rio de Janeiro when the *L'Aigle* left for England. This loyal and enterprising son of his father managed to follow his king in another ship which shortly sailed for England.

King Liholiho bade a fond farewell to Rio de Janeiro March 7, 1824 and began the almost two and a half month voyage to England. Kaunuha'malama, the younger brother of High Chief Hoapili, may just have seen England before he died of an unknown ailment May 13, 1824. He was buried at sea the following day. This was undoubtedly impressive to the remaining Hawaiians.

The *L'Aigle* rounded the Isle of Wight and anchored in Spithead, offshore of Portsmouth, May 17, 1824—just ten days less than six months from the start of the voyage from Honolulu. Captain Starbuck took the royal party ashore, less Manuia. He was left in charge of the bulk of the baggage and the money chest. The *L'Aigle* soon left and worked her way up the English Channel and the Thames River to London.

Captain Starbuck engaged coaches and transported his royal passengers from Portsmouth to London the next day, Tuesday May 18, 1824. He arranged accomodations at Osborn's Hotel (later called the Caledonian), Robert Street, Adelphi Terrace.

The captain then advised the owners of the *L'Aigle*, Messrs. Boulcott of Wapping-wall, that he had arrived in England with a shipload of whale oil *and* the Hawaiian royal party. They were most surprised. Messrs. Boulcott immediately notified the British government—their first information of the arrival of foreign royalty in England.

XX

London

The London *Times*, Thursday May 20, 1824:[14]

The King and Queen of the Sandwich Islands arrived Tuesday morning at Osborn's Hotel, in the Adelphi, from Portsmouth, at which port they had landed from *L'Aigle*, Captain Starbuck. A person who visited them yesterday found their Majesties amusing themselves with a game of whist, the Queen having for her partner her female attendant, who is the daughter of one of the chief men of the islands, and his Majesty's partner was the governor of the island where the seat of government was held. The ladies were dressed in loose *robes de chambre*, of straw colour tied with rose-coloured strings, and on their heads they wore turbans of feathers of scarlet, blue, and yellow.* The two males appeared in European costume, wearing plain black coats, silk stockings, and shoes. These islanders are of a very large size. The men appear to be above six feet, and exceedingly stout. The females are equally fat and coarse made, and proportionately taller than the men. The whole party are of the darkest copper colour, very nearly approaching to black. The King's name is Riho Riho, but his assumed regal name is Tamehameho; and Wahoo, one of the central islands, is his residence.

When apprised of King Liholiho's unexpected arrival, the British Foreign Office appointed the Hon. Frederick Gerald Byng**

---

*When this article was published, the Hawaiian royal party had been in England for three days. Queen Kamamalu and Liliha wore turbans continually while in London, and turbans became a sophisticated fad. Turbans were not used in Hawaii. Did they pick up this fashion in Rio de Janeiro?

**Mr. Byng was known as "Poodle" Byng because of his unruly hair and his habit of always being seen at odd moments walking his dog. He was a brother of Viscount Torrington, and a Gentleman Usher of the Privy Chamber.

to attend them as official host and advisor. He immediately called upon the Hawaiian royal party, Thursday May 20, 1824, and stated that they would be the honored guests of the British government, and at no expense to the Hawaiian king. Interpretations were through Jean Rives. Mr. Byng took an immediate dislike to the diminutive Frenchman, but had no other choice than to utilize his services.

Mr. Byng asked King Liholiho as to the intent of his visit to England. He was advised that this would be discussed only with King George IV, between fellow sovereigns. Mr. Byng noted that the clothing of the Hawaiian rulers and suite were somewhat less than in London style, and diplomatically arranged for new garments.

Interestingly enough, King Liholiho's visit to England coincided with British Foreign Office research and discussion about the Sandwich (Hawaiian) Islands.

The British merchantile firm of Palmer & Co., was seriously considering opening a branch at Honolulu, as it was a significant enroute servicing location between the Northwest America and China trade. Captain Richard Charlton, a sea captain well-experienced in the Pacific, was contemplated to head the new branch. The Foreign Office was seriously considering appointing him as British representative at Honolulu.

But . . . there was a heavily debated question about the sovereignty of the Hawaiian Islands. This debate continued "behind the scenes" in the Foreign Office while King Liholiho was in London. Ke Alii Nui Kamehameha had "ceded" the island of Hawaii to British Navy Captain George Vancourver in a ceremony at Kealakekua Bay February 25, 1794* This "cession" had never been acknowledged or ratified by the British government. What was the sovereignty status of the Hawaiian Kingdom, of which the island of Hawaii was one of the eight major islands? If Captain Charlton went to Honolulu as representative of the British government, would he be a British Consul, or in some other capacity?

Mr. Byng escorted the Hawaiian royal party on its first public appearance—to Whitsunday service (May 23, 1824) at Westminster Abbey. An unknown English writer recorded:[41]

> The writer, on Whitsunday, 1824, was in the organ loft
> when the king and queen of Hawaii, Sandwich Islands,

*The Hawaiian version of this "cession" was that the British would provide "protection" of the island of Hawaii from external foes.

were introduced by the Dean, and placed near himself in the choir. The king, a vulgar-looking man, perfectly black, dressed in a black coat, white waistcoat, and pea-green gloves, which were not long enough to conceal his sooty wrists, stood up the whole time of the service, gazing with amazement at the roof. The queen, a tall, fine, masculine figure, was so struck with the first burst of the organ, as to be thrown into extreme agitation, so much so that she would have leaped out of the stall in which she was placed, had not her maid of honor (an English lady) prevented her by laying hands upon her. Every time the organ recommenced with its full volume of sound, this frenzy returned, and caused much confusion. During the sermon she settled down into something like composure, and at the conclusion was led out by the Dean and other dignitaries, to view the edifice. Habited in a fashionable morning gown, her majesty was only distinguished from her attendants by her gaunt and gigantic figure, and the sudden ejaculations of surprise, which she was constantly making. The king, however, lost in mute attention, never lowered his eyes from the roof, but kept staggering about the church till he made his exit at the door.

The tour of Westminster Abbey after the service included the Chapel of Henry VII, where a number of earlier kings of England were and are interred. King Liholiho absolutely refused to enter, as he deemed it was too sacred for even a fellow-sovereign to enter and profane by his presence.

Hon. George Canning, Secretary of the Foreign Office, gave a midday reception at Gloucester Lodge, Northumberland House, in honor of the Hawaiian royal party May 28, 1824. Some 200 invited guests attended out of curiosity. Among these were their Royal Highnesses the Duke and Duchess of Gloucester, Prince Leopold of Belgium, the Duke of Wellington, Lord and Lady Stafford, Lord Clarendon, Count and Countess Lievan of Russia, etc. Many of the cabinet ministers and nearly the whole of the diplomatic corps were also present.

Mr. Byng arrived with the honored guests at 11 AM King Liholiho wore fashionable London clothing. Queen Kamamalu wore "a striped gauze dress with short sleeves,* leaving uncovered

---

*One report stated that Queen Kamamalu was dressed partly in European and partly in native costume. [14] It is possible that the "gauze dress" may have been made of kapa (bark cloth).

enormous black arms, half covered again with white gloves; an enormous gauze turban upon her head (*and*) a small bag in her hand."[41] She was attended by Liliha in a modish dress. The Hawaiian king was attended by High Chief Boki and Kapihe in European attire. Kekuanaoa was likewise dressed, but also wore an ahuula (feather cloak) and mahiole (feather helmet), and carried a kahili (staff surmounted with feathers forming a large cylinder indicating who Liholiho was—to the Hawaiians!). Jean Rives scurried around interpreting introductions and small talk.

Those in attendance were a very sophisticated group of people (to whom anything other than pure white skin was black!). One English lady recorded:[41] "One should have pitied them for the way all eyes were turned upon them and for all the observations they occasioned; but it seemed to me that their minds are not sufficiently opened, and that they are not civilized enough either to notice or to suffer from it." Another (lady) recorded:[14] "Everyone stared in the most unparalleled way; only the English can stare so."

Hawaiian alii dignity and presence was at its height. Lord Byron later recorded:[16:61]

> . . . a sort of bustle and crowding round of a well-dressed mob, to look at the strange king and queen and nobles; but the laughter and the exclamations which seem to have been ready prepared for the royal strangers soon died away when it was perceived that not the slightest embarrassment or awkwardness was displayed by them, and that the king knew how to hold his state, and the erees (*alii*) to do their service, as well as if they had practiced all their lives in European courts.

King Liholiho and Queen Kamamalu were introduced to the important guests, and sauntered around acknowledging bows and curtsies. They were particularly entranced with the music being played by the uniformed Life Guards band. After a collation, the

AUTHOR'S NOTE: Meanwhile, back in the Hawaiian Islands, Kaumualii died May 26, 1824. Some of the Kauai chiefs were not satisfied with King Liholiho being Kaumualii's heir-designate, and they rebelled several months later in the Hawaiian tradition. The insurrection was overcome after a short battle at Wahiawa, Kauai. The rebelling Kauai chiefs were distributed among the other islands. Their lands were redistributed to others who were loyal to the Hawaiian Kingdom.

Hawaiian royal party took their leave at 12:30 PM. They enjoyed a carriage ride around Hyde Park before returning to their hotel.

What a curiosity London was! So large, such huge stone buildings, and so many people! Mr. Byng took the king and queen and entourage on drives to view the city and call on various personages. One of the royal party was walking around the city one day and discovered a grey mullet. When he excitedly returned with the familiar fish, the Hawaiians ". . . could scarcely believe that it had not swam hither on purpose for them, or be persuaded to wait till it was cooked before they ate it."[16:60] They found that oysters were available, which they thoroughly enjoyed. As a matter of record, their diet was composed mostly of fish, poultry and fruit. King Liholiho delighted in a new taste, cider, and Mr. Canning provided a good supply.

What a curiosity the Hawaiians were! Their appearance and color was so singular and intriguing! And they spoke such a strange and different language. It was a wonder they could understand each other. Their decorum, dignity and moderation made the Hawaiian visitors acceptable to Londoners. They became "quite the thing," and an interesting topic for conversation. Many personages called on them. Portraits of the king and queen were made, and copies appeared for sale in the shops.*

Mr. Byng was indefatigable with hospitality. The royal box at Covent Garden Theatre was made available in the evening of May 31, 1824, and the royal visitors enjoyed "Pizarro". There was applause when they entered the box, and "God Save the King" was played. The play was interpreted by Jean Rives; Queen Kamamalu shed tears at some of the scenes.

They attended the horse races at Epsom (they said that the horses *flew*!). They enjoyed a presentation of "Rob Roy McGregor" from the royal box at Drury Lane Theatre June 4, 1824. The following day they went to Fulham and returned by boat on the Thames. They were escorted to Chelsea Hospital and to the Royal Military Asylum. They also witnessed a balloon ascension at White Conduit Gardens. Mr. Byng took them to the British Museum June 8, 1824. They had few comments while there, but there was much discussion later between the Hawaiians. That night they went to the Opera House to see a French ballet. Queen Kamamalu wore ". . . a

---

*Alfred Frankenstein wrote a delightful phamphlet, *The Royal Visitors*, about these portraits (number 14 in the bibliography).

white silk dress of European fashion, her sash was of scarlet silk, and her head-dress was of the same color, decorated with silver spangles and embroidery."[14]

Mr. Byng repeatedly queried King Liholiho as to what he intended discussing with King George IV to no avail. The Foreign Office reluctantly made an appointment for King Liholiho to see King George IV on June 21, 1824.

Meanwhile, Manuia, the king's steward, had arrived at London on the *L'Aigle* with the remainder of their baggage. The money chest was taken to the Bank of England. When it was opened, there was only a little over $10,000. in specie remaining of the original $25,000. Captain Starbuck was queried, and could account for but some $3,000. expended at Rio de Janeiro and the expenses of transporting the royal party from Portsmouth to London. The difference could not be accounted for. Jean Rives seemed to be involved in some strange way. King Liholiho, High Chief Boki and Kekuanaoa were extremely disturbed, but they had no clue as to what had happened to the missing money. Besides, King Liholiho liked Captain Starbuck,* and Jean Rives was their only interpreter.

*King Liholiho and Queen Kamamalu appreciated Captain Starbuck so much that they gave him a feather cloak and a kapa (bark cloth) dress. (A descendant of the captain returned them to Hawaii in 1927.) Captain Starbuck's employer, Messrs. Boulcott, did not like his using the *L'Aigle* to transport the royal party instead of pursuing commerce. They fired him.[14]

XXI

Liholiho and kamamalu

And then . . .

Amidst all this excitement, interest and gayety . . .

Manuia the steward became ill June 10, 1824, and King Liholiho cancelled a scheduled visit to a brewery out of concern for his fellow-Hawaiian. Manuia was better the next day, and several of the royal party went out. The following day Manuia was worse. Dr. Hugh Ley was called, and diagnosed measles.

King Liholiho became ill on June 13, 1824 while at the Royal Academy Exhibition in Somerset House. This illness was diagnosed as also measles. Within a week the entire Hawaiian royal party was taken severely ill—with measles. Unseasonable cold and damp weather didn't assist Hawaiian comfort.

King Liholiho's audience with King George IV was cancelled.

Dr. Henry Holland was called in consultation on June 21, 1824. Sir Henry Halford, a king's physician, consulted several days later. They had never seen such virilent cases of measles before. The solicitous Mr. Byng arranged for other well-known doctors to assist: Dr. M'Gregor, who had lived in "hot climates and (had) consequent knowledge of the disorders prevalent there", Dr. Peregrine, Sir Matthew Tierney (another king's physician), and Dr. Alexander.

Some of the royal party began to recover. High Chief Boki, Kekuanaoa and Manuia got well enough to go outside the hotel. King Liholiho was seriously, but not alarmingly, ill. Kapihe, who had been the most ill, had begun to rally.

The illness of Queen Kamamalu, however, began to worsen, and her lungs appeared to be seriously affected. Liliha was constantly at her side giving what comfort she could. The doctors made continuous calls, and became very concerned.

King Liholiho had recovered sufficiently to receive Captain Richard Charlton July 4, 1824. The Foreign Office had ended its

175

debate on Hawaiian sovereignty, and had appointed the captain as the first British consul at the Sandwich Islands.

The king also wrote a letter to be carried by Captain Stavers of the ship *Offley* who was soon to set sail for Hawaii:[29]

London, June (July 4), 1824.

To Paalua, Kaahumanu, and my younger Brother.*

Much love to you all:

In the month of (Kaaona) May we arrived in England. One of our number Kaunuhaimalama, is dead; he died just outside of England. He was taken sick Tuesday (May 11) and died in the night of the 13th night of the moon; the following day (Akua), the 14th night of the moon, he was buried at sea. On Friday (Tuesday) May 18th, we arrived in England. We got into carriages and in one day we reached London, and went to the Hotal. On Thursday the king's man (Mr. Byng) arrived, and told us he was to see to all our wants, and the King was to pay all our expenses. We are having everything we want. The King of England has taken a great liking to us. We have not yet seen the King. We were all taken sick in June, but have all recovered except three of us, Kamehamalu, Kapihe and myself.

If the commander of the vessel (Captain Stavers) should ask you about building a wooden house in Oahu, you must grant him his request. You are not to charge him any harbor fees for he is taking our letter to you., Give him five pigs, ten boxes of potatoes. I love you all dearly. We will remain till we see the King and receive from him that which will be of great benefit to us, then we will return.

Aloha,

(signed) IOLANI

Four days later, the afternoon of July 8, 1824, King Liholiho was informed that Queen Kamamalu was critically ill, beyond the help of the doctors, and that she was dying. He insisted that he go to her, was placed in a wheelchair, and was taken to her bedchamber. At his order, he was lifted upon her bed and placed by her side. They embraced . . . and both wept. King Liholiho dismissed the doctors and his attendants.

*Kalanimoku was also known as Paalua.

"O, Kamamalu, my love, this I have done to you for I brought you to England."

"No, no, Liholiho, my love . . . do not reproach yourself for I would have been long-dead without you by my side. I insisted on coming." Kamamalu spoke weakly, and gently stroked Liholiho's hair.

"Kamamalu, the kahuna-lapaau (medical doctors) tell me that you shall soon leave—to rejoin our Father. If this does happen, I do not desire to remain here. I must be at your side, for I have loved you since we were small children. Life without you would be meaningless. If this does happen . . . I shall follow you."

Kamamalu wept, and faintly said, "No, Liholiho, my love, you have so much to do, to see King George, to return to our people, to bring them good—for you are our ruler."

Liholiho almost muttered, "Ruler . . . nay . . . but part ruler. Kaahumanu and my younger brother Kauikeaouli, with Kalanimo-ku's help, can do better than I. For I was always trying to be a bigger man than I actually was . . . and am."

"You are your Father's son and your mother's son. You have accomplished much." Kamamalu barely whispered.

Liholiho shook his head slightly. "But even more, I am your husband, and you are my love."

"I tell you, Kamamalu, my love, if you leave me, I shall follow. This I must do, for without you I am nothing . . . this I shall do."

Kamamalu sighed . . . and just lay in Liholiho's welcome embrace, breathing slowly and heavily. Both wept, and tightened their embrace.

Their hearts beat together . . . as one.

About an hour later Liliha opened the door quietly and peeked in. Liholiho beckoned, and was taken back to his bed. The Hawaiians continued their vigil at Queen Kamamalu's bedside, all except Liholiho.

King Liholiho lay in his bed without speaking . . . for the longest of long time, which was measured by each heartbeat. His spirit was elsewhere . . . with Kamamalu.

Suddenly Liholiho sat up . . . with agony on his face, and tears in his eyes. It was 6:30 PM. Kamamalu, his love, had started on the long unknown journey to rejoin their Father. But one heart remained beating . . . and it was lonely . . . terribly lonely.

Lord Byron recounted:[16:67]

Liliah, whose dutiful and affectionate behaviour to her
friend and mistress had been most exemplary, now took
charge of her body, and disposed it after the manner of her
country, unclothing it to the waist, leaving also the ancles
and feet bare, and carefully dressing the hair and adorning it
with chaplets of flowers. The king now desired the body
might be brought into his apartment, and laid on a small bed
near him: that being done, he sat up looking at it, but
neither speaking nor weeping. The medical attendants
observed that the state of Riho Riho was such as to render it
highly improper to keep the queen's body near him, and it
was therefore proposed to him to allow it to be taken away;
but he sat silent, and answered no one, only by gestures
showing that he forbade its removal. At length, after much
persuasion, and then leaving him to himself for a time, he
suddenly made signs that it might be taken away; which was
accordingly done, and the queen was again placed on her
own bed.*

Mr. Byng, who had become quite fond of his strange charges,
consulted King Liholiho about final arrangements for Queen
Kamamalu. It was decided that the body would be embalmed with

---

*(Bulletin). The queen of the Sandwich Islands departed this
life about half-past six this evening, without much apparent
suffering, and in possession of her senses to a late moment. The
king, in the midst of this deep sorrow, manifests a firmness of
mind which has penetrated every body about him with a feeling
of respect. Though very anxious to express his grief in the
manner of his country, and to show the marks of deference
which are usually paid to the dead there, he submits with good
sense and patience to every suggestion which our habits dictate.
We have every reason to believe that his anxiety and depression
of mind have aggravated all the symptoms of his disease, which,
but for this cause, might ere now have terminated prosperously:
but we hope, in a day or two, that he will be better.*

> *(signed) HENRY HALFORD.*
> *HENRY HOLLAND.*
> *HUGH LEY.*

> *Thursday evening, July 8, 1824.*

all the odoriferous scents that could be obtained, and interment would be ultimately in the Hawaiian Islands.

Queen Kamamalu's coffin lay in state in High Chief Boki's bedchamber for three days. It was covered with a black satin pall and a red and yellow ahuula (feather cloak), and a chaplet of yellow feathers was placed on the head of the coffin. A kahili stood at the foot of the coffin. Two lighted candles were on a table at the foot of the coffin.

King Liholiho remained apathetically in his bed. His spirits were low, his cough increased, and "he himself declared he should not long survive."[16:68] Mr. Byng became very concerned. He endeavored a good diversion—he had the Hawaiian royal party relocated to a different section of the hotel on the other side of the street overlooking the river. This did not comfort Liholiho. The king's health began to fail rapidly.

The realistic Mr. Byng strongly urged King Liholiho to make a simple will that would be recognized by English law and would provide for his followers. This was prepared for him by Jean Rives on the morning of July 13, 1824. He bequeathed whatever property he had in England to High Chief Boki for the benefit generally of his entourage. He expressed the desire that his and Kamamalu's bodies be taken back to the Hawaiian Islands. King Liholiho was able to feebly make his mark, and it was witnessed by all present.

Dr. Ley was called that afternoon and found Liholiho in a very low state, and death appeared near. It was Hawaiian custom to gather around a critically ill person—out of respect, to appease the offended God, and so that the afflicted one would not be alone at the second great occurrence in that person's life. All of the Hawaiians remained at his bedside. All except Kapihe, who was in disfavor for some reason. He remained in the adjoining room, heartbroken.

The vigil was long and strained. Liholiho did not seem to recognize anyone commencing about 2 A.M. July 14, 1824.

"From that time till four o'clock A.M., he kept continually saying, 'I shall lose my tongue' and just before he breathed his last his Majesty faintly said, 'Farewell to you all, I am dead, I am happy'. After uttering these words he expired in the arms of Liliha."[41]

Kalani-nui-kua-liholiho-i-ke-kapu, King of the Hawaiian Islands, began the long unknown journey to rejoin his Father . . . and his love, Kamamalu.

epilogue

Jean Rives, the king's interpreter, was dismissed by High Chief Boki. The British Foreign Office (gladly) financed his return to France. Rives took the king's gold watch with him.

No trace was ever found of the missing almost $12,000. in specie.

The remaining Hawaiian visitors were given an audience by King George IV, September 11, 1824, with James Kanehoa Young interpreting. No record was kept of this interview. Kekuanaoa later provided the Hawaiian version of the audience in the following testimony:[*]

> King George IV stood before Boki and said to him and we heard it.
>
> I exceedingly regret the recent death of your King and his wife. The chiefs and people will think perhaps that I have been inattentive to your King, but it is not so, for the same medicine and the same Physicians have been employed as are employed by the chiefs of this nation. On account of the severity of the disease he died.
>
> Then James Young, the Interpreter told all these words to Boki and we all heard them.
>
> Then King George asked Boki the chief thus.
>
> As you have come to this country, and the King has died here, who will be the King of the land?
>
> Boki answered thus to him—His Majesty's younger brother will be King, but it is for Kaahumanu and Kalaimoku to take care of the country.
>
> The King then asked Boki what was the business on which you and your King came to this country?

[*]Archives of Hawaii F.O. & Ex. 1824.

Then James Young interpreted the words to Boki and we all heard the question of the King to Boki.

Then Boki declared to him the reason of our sailing to Great Britain—We have come to confirm the words which Kamehameha gave in charge to Vancouver thus—go back and tell King George to watch over me and my whole Kingdom. I acknowledge him as my landlord and myself as tenant (or him as superior and I inferior) should the foreigners of any other nation come to take possession of my lands, then let him help me.

Then James Young told all these words to King George, the ancient words which King Kamehameha I gave in charge to Vancouver. These he told to King George.

And when King George had heard he thus said to Boki—I have heard these words. I will attend to the evils from without.* The evils within your Kingdom it is not for me to regard: They are with yourselves. Return and say to the King, to Kaahumanu and to Kalaimoku, I will watch over your country, I will not take possession of it for mine, but I will watch over it, lest evils should come from others to the Kingdom. I therefore will watch over him agreeably to those ancient words."

The British Foreign Office expended £5,400 hosting their unexpected Hawaiian royal visitors.

The British government arranged that the bodies of King Liholiho and Queen Kamamalu, and the remainder of the Hawaiian visitors, were returned to the Hawaiian Islands on the 46 gun frigate *H.M.S. Blonde*, Captain The Right Honorable Lord Byron. The *Blonde* sailed from Spithead September 29, 1824 and arrived at Lahaina, Maui May 4, 1825. Interment of the king and queen was at Honolulu May 21, 1825.

Among Lord Byron's instructions were the following: [14]

If any Disputes as to the Succession on the Death of the late King should unhappily arise, you will endeavor to maintain a strict Neutrality, and if forced to take any Part, you will

*This is borne out by a letter from Mr. Byng to Undersecretary Planta. F.O., Pacific Islands, 58/4.

espouse that which you shall find to be most consistent with the established Laws and Customs of that People.

You will endeavor to cultivate a good Understanding with the Government, in whatever native Hands it may be, and to secure by kind offices and friendly Intercourse, a future and lasting Protection for the Persons and Property of the subjects of the United Kingdom.

On the question of the Rights of Great Britain to the Sandwich Islands, you will pay greatest Regards to the Comfort, the Feelings, and even the Prejudices of the Natives, and will shew the utmost Moderation towards the Subjects of any other Power, whom you may meet in these Islands.

His Majesty's Rights you will, if necessary, be prepared to assert, but considering the Distance of the Place, and Infant State of political Society there, you will avoid as far as may be possible the bringing these Rights into discussion and will propose that any disputed Point between yourself and any subjects of any other powers shall be referred to your respective Governments.

Lord Byron attended an important council meeting at Honolulu June 6, 1825, almost a month after his arrival in Hawaii. The council reaffirmed the succession of Liholiho's younger brother, Kauikeaouli, as king—to share the Rule with Kuhina-nui Kaahumanu. Kalanimoku was appointed kahu (guardian) of the 12 year old king. High Chief Boki officially reported on the interview with King George IV. Lord Byron was called upon, and he carefully offered the following basic suggestions:[16:156-157]

1. That the king be the head of the people.

2. That all the chiefs swear allegiance to the king.

3. That the lands which are now held by the chiefs shall not be taken from them, but shall descend to their legitimate children, except in cases of rebellion, and then all their property shall be forfeited to the king.

4. That a tax be regularly paid to the king to keep up his dignity and establishment.

5. That no man's life be taken away except by consent of the king, or the regent, for the time being, and of twelve chiefs.

6. That the king, or regent, can grant pardons at all times.

7. That all the people shall be free, and not bound to any one chief. (*This was normal Hawaiian practice.*)

8. That a port duty be laid on all foreign vessels. (*This was being done, but had become excessive.*)*

There was discussion among the council about these suggestions. They were accepted by the chiefs.

Lord Byron was asked if the British had any objection to American missionaries being in the Hawaiian Islands. He replied, no objection, providing they did not interfere with Hawaiian Kingdom governmental affairs. He had heard that the missionaries had suggested some laws (akin to the Ten Commandments). Rev. Bingham stated that their Instructions precluded interference in the political or commercial concerns of the Hawaiian Kingdom.

King Liholiho's visit to England achieved what he had intended. The Hawaiian Kingdom became more firmly established.

---

*Resultant port regulations were printed. They also provided a penalty for seamen left in Hawaii without permission.

appenðices

LIHOLIHO'S AGE AND GENEALOGY

Early Hawaiians did not use our familiar Gregorian calendar time scale prior to their literacy. Hawaiian age was measured as stages of maturity, and related with significant events. Liholiho may have been born in 1797 (Kamakau, Fornander, Alexander, etc., estimates) or in 1796 (Stokes, based on contemporary estimates). When Liholiho died in England, a plate was affixed to his coffin which read (in Hawaiian and English): "Tamehameha II., King of the Sandwich Islands died, 14th July 1824, in London, in the 28th year of his age. May we ever remember our beloved King Iolani." (Iolani was a symbolic name for Hawaiian royalty; literally, the soaring flight of Io, the Hawaiian hawk, high in the heavens.) The Kamehameha crypt at the Royal Mausoleum, Honolulu, does not indicate Liholiho's dates of birth and death.

The year 1796 has been arbitrarily considered by the author as the year of Liholiho's birth—thus he is stated to have been 23 years old at his accession and 28 years old at his death.

The alii (chiefs) were very conscious of their genealogies. There was a wide gulf between the alii and the makaainana (commoners) as the class structure was similar to feudal societies elsewhere: lords, peasants or serfs, and slaves. A member of the alii class could not be degraded to that of a commoner—provided he knew who his forebears were, and could convince those skilled in genealogies.

Like the early ruling Incas and Egyptians, the more powerful alii (chiefs and chiefesses) of all the islands closely intermarried for dynastic purposes. They would usually have several marriages (e.g. five) during their lives, which makes relationships difficult to follow.

Before Hawaiian written records, genealogies, as well as myths and traditions, were handed down from memory to memory. We who depend upon the written record sometimes give insufficient credence to those of old who were trained and skilled at memorizing. Fortunately, farsighted individuals, such as Judge Abraham Fornander, researched and reduced as much memory knowledge as possible to writing and thus preserved it for today. Liholiho's genealogy and relationships were developed and reproduced mainly from Judge Fornander's *"An Account of the Polynesian Race,"* 3 vols., London: 1880.

Liholiho's genealogy starts with Pili, an alii who was the first of the second migratory period chiefs from the south (probably Samoa) to establish rule over the island of Hawaii circa 12th–14th Century.

Appendix

1.	PILI KAAIEA (k)	Hinaauaku (w)	KOA (k)
2.	KOA (k)	Hinaaumai (w)	OLE (k)
3.	OLE (k)	Hinamailelii (w)	KUKOHOU (k)
4.	KUKOHOU (k)	Hinakeuiki (w)	KANIUHI (k)
5.	KANIUHI (k)	Hiliamakani (w)	KANIPAHU (k)
6.	KANIPAHU (k)	Alaikauakoko (w)	KALAPANA (k)
7.	KALAPANA (k)	Makeamalamaihanae (w)	KAHAIMOELEAIKAAIKUPOU (k)
8.	KAHAIMOELEAIKAAIKUPOU (k)	Kapoakauluhailaa (w)	KALAUNUIOHUA (k)
9.	KALAUNUIOHUA (k)	Kaheke (w)	KUAIWA (k)
10.	KUAIWA (k)	Kamuleilani (w)	KOHOUKAPU (k)
11.	KOHOUKAPU (k)	Laakapu (w)	KAUHOLANUIMAHU (k)
12.	KAUHOLANUIMAHU (k)	Neula (w)	KIHA (k)
13.	KIHA (k)	Waoilea (w)	LILOA (k)
14.	LILOA (k)		

LEGEND (k) *kane, man*
(w) *wahine, woman*

187

The following genealogical chart depicts descent and relationships from Liloa (14th generation), king of the island of Hawaii circa 16th Century, to Liholiho.

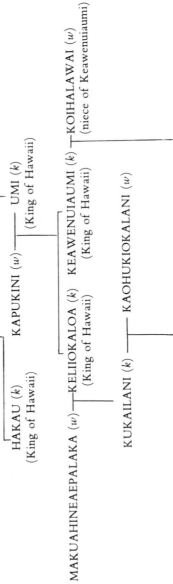

14.

PINEA (w) ——— LILOA (k) ——— AKAHIAKULEANA (w)
(King of Hawaii)

15.

HAKAU (k)   UMI (k)
(King of Hawaii)   (King of Hawaii)

KAPUKINI (w)

16.

MAKUAHINEAEPALAKA (w) ——— KELIIOKALOA (k)   KEAWENUIAUMI (k) ——— KOIHALAWAI (w)
(King of Hawaii)   (King of Hawaii)   (niece of Keawenuiaumi)

17.

KUKAILANI (k) ——— KAOHUKIOKALANI (w)

18.

KAIKILANI (w)   KANALOAKUAANA (k)
                             (Half-brother of King of Hawaii)

19.

KEAKEALANIKANE (k)   KEALIIOKALANI (w)
(King of Hawaii)

20.

KEAKAMAHANA (w) ——— IWIKAUIKAUA (k) ——— KAUAKAHI KUAANAAUAKANE (w)

21.

KANALOAIKAIWILEWA (k) —— KEAKEALANIWAHINE (w) —— KANEIKAIWILANI (k)
(Queen of Hawaii)

22.

KEAWE (k) —— KALANIKAULELEIAWI (w) —— KAULAHEA (k) —— PAPAIKANIAU (w)
(King of Hawaii)   (Half-sister of Keawe)   (King of Maui)   (Niece of Kaulahea)

23.

HAAE (k) —— KEKELAKEKEOKALANIAKEWAE (w)   KEKUIAPOIWA I (w) —— KEKAULIKE (k)
(Brother of Alapainui,   (King of Maui)
King of Hawaii)

KAMEHAMEHANUI (k)   *KAHEKILI (k)
(King of Maui)   (King of Maui)

24.

KEKUIAPOIWA II (w) —— KEOUA (k)   KALOLA (w) —— KALANIOPUU (k)
(Half-brother of Kalaniopuu)   (King of Hawaii)

25.

KEKUIAPOIWA LILIHA (w) —— KIWALAO (k)
(King of Hawaii)

26.

KAMEHAMEHA (k) —— KEOPUOLANI (w)
(First King of the Hawaiian Kingdom)

27.

LIHOLIHO (k)

LEGEND
(k) kane, male   (w) wahine, female
*reputed sire of Kamehameha

APPENDIX 2

THE KAPU SYSTEM

The kapu system provided the social order throughout Polynesia and was developed to a high degree in the Hawaiian Islands. It directed the "way of life" for all Hawaiians and was the "law of the land." The kapu system was complex (like our present day laws!) with many regulations and penalties, both secular and religious. Violation was not only a crime but a "sin" (fault, state of evil). Death or disfigurement was the usual Hawaiian penalty.

Dr. E. S. Craighill Handy described kapu as follows: [19:3]

> The Polynesian word kapu, tapu, or tabu, as a verb, meant to prohibit or restrict, or to be prohibited or restricted; as a noun, a prohibition or restriction; as an adjective, prohibited, restricted. The ultimate source of all prohibiting authority was psychic. Natural law, in the mind of the Polynesians, was motivated by psychic force manifest in spirits and phenomena, men and things. Kapu may therefore be defined as personal and social discipline by immanent supernormal agency. Specifically, kapu related to prohibition or restriction for one of two reasons: because of sanctity, or because of defilement. A thing kapu was a thing isolated and hence to be avoided, in some cases because it was sacred, in others because it was defiling.

The kapu system also served as the feudal caste enforcement system of the alii (chiefs). Dr. Handy further stated: [19:5]

> For the alii (chiefs), the kapu of sanctity was at once a wall of protection and the source of prestige and authority. The same kapu determined for the commoners their social and economic relationship to, and the reverential attitude towards their overlords. As for the kauwa (slaves), their segregation and exclusion from the social organism was due to a kapu of defilement.

The alii had established numerous prestigious kapus dependent upon lineage. The few highest chiefs, being almost divine, had kapus that required the makaainana (commoners) to prostrate themselves upon their appearance. Other alii of lesser lineage had kapus which required the people to at least squat when they appeared. Others had lesser kapus, or privileges denied the common people.

W. D. Alexander wrote of respect for a king that: [1:26]

Death was the penalty for the slightest breach of etiquette. For example, it was death for a common man to remain standing at the mention of the king's name in song, or when the king's food, drinking-water, or clothing was carried past; to put on any article of dress belonging to him; to enter his inclosure without permission; or even to cross his shadow or that of his house. If he entered the dread presence of the sovereign, he must crawl, prone on the ground, kolokolo, and leave it in the same manner. The chief's head was especially sacred, and for any one to touch it or occupy a position above it would be treasonable. No subject dared to appear on the deck of a vessel when the king was in the cabin.

Some kapus were permanent, some temporary for specific purposes. Some were based on ancient or everyday-living logic, some on caprice. Some were religious in nature and venerated the Gods, heiaus (temples), or idols; some were in respect to the alii, and some were imposed by the king for any reason. Certain fish would be kapu-ed for periods of time, either for their sacred character or for conservation, as the case might be. For a time there was even a kapu against warfare during seven months of the year (this is strikingly similar to western European 10th-11th Century Christian Peace and Truce of God).

Kapus on the people would establish such arbitrary restrictions as: no canoes could set out to sea or land on the shores, no fires could be lighted, no kapa (bark cloth) beaten or poi (taro paste) pounded, no sound permitted (dogs and pigs would be muzzled and poultry shut up in calabashes), etc. Death was the usual penalty for non-compliance.

Religious rites, pursuits of life such as fishing, farming, crafts, etc., were established on a daily basis using the lunar month as time frame. Each lunar month had four kapu periods of two nights and one day, each period in veneration of one of the four principal Hawaiian Gods: Kane, Kanaloa, Ku and Lono. During these religious periods there was no work permitted, intercourse was prohibited, women were restricted from entering canoes, etc. The king usually venerated the God honored by remaining within the confines of a heiau (temple) and praying to the God.

A most onerous kapu was that the sexes were not permitted to eat together or have their food prepared together. Thus each residence had separate eating houses for men (hale-mua) and for women (hale-aina). Women were not permitted in the hale-mua, under penalty of death. The poorer men who could not afford several houses usually formed mens' eating clubs to comply with the kapu.

Women were further restricted from eating certain foods under the kapu: pork, bananas, coconuts, turtles, some kinds of fishes, etc.

The arrival of westerners beginning with Captain James Cook in 1778 abruptly stimulated the thinking and questioning of the long-isolated Hawaiians. They began to question their inherited respect for the kapus. The foreigners were men like themselves, all but in shade of color, but men who knew nothing about the kapu and did not adhere to them. Kapus were violated by these foreigners with apparent impunity. The "why" of this was impossible to answer. The prestige of the foreigners with their (comparative) marvelous possessions increased the confusion caused by their disregarding numerous kapus. The many Hawaiians who shipped as seamen worked equally with the foreigners aboard ship. They returned to Hawaii and told about life and customs on the ships and in other lands—where the kapu system had never been heard of.

The Hawaiians had become demoralized primarily due to considerable population decimation caused by intruded diseases. The estimated 300,000 population of the Hawaiian Islands in 1778, when Captain Cook arrived, had been drastically reduced to less than half that number by the year 1819. The old sense of values was disrupted by the flow of western goods into the islands, and the strange new economy of sandalwood and trade. The report that King Pomare of the prestigious former alii fatherland, the Society Islands, no longer worshipped the old Polynesian Gods, had a profound effect upon the Hawaiian chiefs.

The kapu that seems to have been most irksome and oppressive was that which required separate male and female eating, and the choicest foods being prohibited to females. This restriction, and the discontent of the powerful Dowager Queen and Kuhina-nui (Regent) Kaahumanu with Hawaiian male-female inequalities compared with the foreigners, provided the final impetus for the overthrow of the kapu system. There were some secret violations of the kapus, and there was no vengeance by the all-seeing Hawaiian Gods upon the culprits.

The powerful Ke Alii Nui (The Great Chief, King) Kamehameha, who had adhered to the ways of old, died in 1819. The time became ripe . . . the kapus were overthrown. There was nothing to replace them, either religious or secular, and further Hawaiian social disorganization took place.

The first company of American Protestant missionaries arrived less than six months later. The timing was most fortunate for them.

APPENDIX 3

SELECTED HIGH CHIEFS RELATIONSHIPS

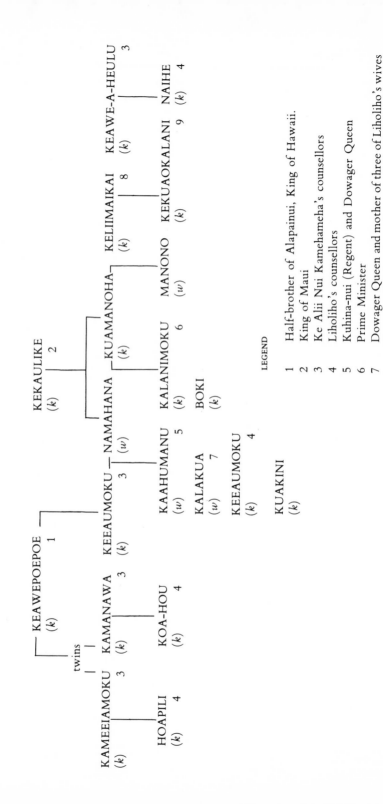

LEGEND

1   Half-brother of Alapainui, King of Hawaii.
2   King of Maui
3   Ke Alii Nui Kamehameha's counsellors
4   Liholiho's counsellors
5   Kuhina-nui (Regent) and Dowager Queen
6   Prime Minister
7   Dowager Queen and mother of three of Liholiho's wives
8   Younger full-brother of Ke Alii Nui Kamehameha

(k) kane, male   (w) wahine, female

APPENDIX 4

LIHOLIHO'S WIVES

KAMAMALU   Liholiho's half-sister. Kamamalu was a daughter of Ke Alii Nui (The Great Chief, King) Kamehameha by Kalakua (younger sister of Kuhina-nui (Regent) Kaahumanu). She was born at Kawaihae, Hawaii in 1802. From a young age she lived in Liholiho's household as his betrothed. They were married when she was 12 and he was 17-18. Kamamalu was Liholiho's favorite wife. She accompanied him to England where she died July 8, 1824. She was also known as Kamehamalu. No issue.

KINAU   Liholiho's half-sister. She was Kamamalu's younger sister, born on Oahu in 1805. Date of marriage not known. No issue. After Liholiho died in 1824 she married Kekuanaoa, governor of the island of Oahu and had children: Moses Kekuaiwa, Lot Kamehameha (King Kamehemeha V), Alexander Liholiho (King Kamehameha IV), and Victoria Kamamalu. Kinau was kuhina-nui (regent) 1832-1839. She died April 4, 1839.

PAUAHI   Liholiho's step-niece. Pauahi was a daughter of Pauli Kaoleioku, who was the first-born son of Ke Alii Nui Kamehameha when he was a youth. Date of marriage not known. No issue. After Liholiho died in 1824, she married Kekuanaoa* and had children: . . . (Princess) Ruth Keelikolani.

KEKAUONOHI   Liholiho's step-niece. She was the daughter of Kahoaku Kinau (son of Ke Alii Nui Kamehameha by Peleuli) and Wahinepio (sister of Kalanimoku and Boki). Date of marriage not known. No issue. Several years after Liholiho's death, this "mischievous girl" ran away with Kaahumanu's husband, Keliiahonui. She then married Haalelea in mid-1849 after Keliiahonui died. She was governess of Kauai 1840-1851.

KEKAULUOHI   Liholiho's cousin. She was the daughter of Ke Alii Nui Kamehameha's half-brother, Kalaimamahu, by Kalakua. Kekauluohi was the older half-sister of Kamamalu and Kinau. She was born in 1794, and in her childhood had been offered in betrothal to a son of King Pomare of Tahiti. She became the wahine palama (wife to warm old age) of her uncle, Ke Alii Nui Kamehameha. Kekauluohi married Liholiho when he became king in 1819. No issue. She was "given to" and married Kanaina in 1821 and had children: . . . younger of whom was Lunalilo, who became

*Kekuanaoa first married Pauahi, and later Kinau.

king of the Hawaiian Islands in 1873. Kekauluohi was kuhina nui (regent) 1839–1845. She died in 1845.

KEKAIHAAKULOU   When Liholiho went to the island of Kauai in 1821, he was "given" King Kaumualii's wife, Kekaihaakulou. It was at this time that he "gave" his prior fifth wife Kekauluohi to his friend Kanaina. It would appear that this marriage of Liholiho and Kekaihaakulou was considered to be a "state" marriage.

CONTRACT FOR THE PASSAGE OF
THE MISSIONARIES TO THE HAWAIIAN ISLANDS

Know all men by these presents, that it is agreed by the owners of the Brig Thaddeus, and by Capt. Andrew Blanchard, the Master of said Brig, on the one part,—and by the subscribing Regents of the American Board of Commissioners for Foreign Missions on the other part, that the following persons shall be taken as passengers on board said Brig, and safely conveyed to the Sandwich (*Hawaiian*) Islands, in the Pacific Ocean, (the danger of the seas, and other unavoidable evils not preventing) viz. the Rev. Hiram Bingham and the Rev. Asa Thurston, Messrs. Daniel Chamberlain, Thomas Holman, Samuel Whitney, Samuel Ruggles and Elisha Loomis and their wives, five children of Mr. Chamberlain, Thomas Hopoo, John Honooree, George Tamoree and William Temiooe natives of said islands; and that said passengers shall be found with a sufficient supply of wood and water for their health and comfort during the voyage, and shall have their provisions suitably cooked and prepared at the expense of said owners; and on their arrival at said islands, shall have a reasonable time to confer with the King, or Kings of said islands, with respect to a residence there, and to fix upon an eligible place for such a residence; in consideration whereof the said owners are to receive a compensation at the following rate viz. One Hundred Dollars for each adult passenger, and Fifty Dollars each for the five children of Mr. Chamberlain, to be paid within ten days of the sailing of said Brig: and an additional sum of Two Hundred Dollars for extraordinary labor in loading and taking out a part of the frame of a house and other articles.

Although an abundance of provisions for the passengers is put on board, still, should their supplies unexpectedly become deficient, (other than wood and water,) either from the length of the voyage, or any other cause, it is engaged by the parties, that provisions shall be furnished by the captain of said Brig, at the rate at which said articles can be bought at the Sandwich Islands, the price to be agreed upon between the said Captain and a majority of the seven passengers, first named, and said supplies to be paid for on demand at Boston.

And it is agreed to be reasonable, that if said passengers should not think it best to land at Owhyhee (*Hawaii*) they shall be conveyed by said Brig to Woahoo (*Oahu*) with all convenient dispatch, and thence in like manner to Atooi (*Kauai*), if they desire it: provided, however, that if it should be found necessary, in the opinion of the master, to the successful prosecution of the voyage, for said Brig to return to the windward islands, and he should actually return with this view, then such compensation shall be made to said owners for the time taken up in sailing to Atooi and returning therefrom to the windward islands, as shall be declared to be just by the referees hereafter named.

And it is further agreed, that the captain of said Brig shall unite his exertions with those of the passengers to obtain a quiet landing and permanent residence for said passengers, at such place in the islands as shall be deemed eligible by the passengers: and if, contrary to the expectation and desire of all the parties, it should be found impracticable to obtain a permanent establishment, a united attempt shall be made by the master and the passengers to obtain permission for a temporary residence, till a passage can be obtained to the Society Islands. And should it be found ultimately impracticable to obtain a permanent residence, and should the passengers, from well grounded fears as to their personal safety, be compelled to give up the design of residing at the Sandwich Islands (*Hawaiian Islands*), the master will use his best endeavors to procure for them a safe and comfortable passage to the Society Islands, on reasonable terms: and said master will not, in any case, abandon said passengers to imminent danger of personal violence. Should (it) be found necessary, in order to avoid this painful alternative, to proceed with said Brig, and thus convey said passengers to the Society Islands, then a statement of all the facts shall be laid before the following gentlemen, who are merchants well acquainted with the business prosecuted in these seas, and who are hereby agreed upon as referees: viz. Thomas H. Perkins, William Sturgis, William H. Boardman, and Nathan Winship, and it shall be decided by said referees, or the survivors of them, what shall be a just and reasonable compensation to said owners for the detention of said Brig, while on said voyage from the Sandwich Islands; and such sum as shall be thus awarded, shall be paid to said owners in Boston within sixty days after said award. If said referees cannot agree upon an award they shall select a fifth referee, and then the decision of the whole shall be binding.

And it is further agreed, that on the arrival of said Brig at the Sandwich Islands, the passengers shall use all diligence in fixing on a place for residence and shall make no unnecessary detention of said Brig: and that said master whenever said passengers are ready to disembark, shall put them on shore with all convenient dispatch, and with all their baggage, furniture, boxes, implements, boards, planks, all that may remain of their ship and cabin stores, and all property of every kind on board said Brig, as belonging to said passengers, or for their use.

And it is hereby agreed that if either of the parties shall complain of having sufficient damages in consequence of a non-compliance with the agreement by the other party, then the question of damages shall be decided by the above named referees, and their award shall be final.

Signed, sealed, and delivered at Boston this 23rd day of October 1819.

GLOSSARY

Aha, religious ceremony, also sennit cord used in pule-aha
'Aha'aina, feast
Ahuula, feather cloak
Ai kapu, eating with opposite sex forbidden
Ai noa, eating with opposite sex permitted
Ai-oeoe, "Long necks," sobriquet of the missionaries
Akua, night of, night of the lunar month when the moon was first fully round
Alii, chief and chiefess ruling caste
Aloha, love, greetings
Amama, finish of a prayer, literally offer in sacrifice
Anaana, sorcery praying to death
Au-we, alas
Halau, open-sided long house with thatched roof
Hale mua, men's eating house
Hale noa, sleeping house
Haole, foreigner
Heiau, place of worship
Hilo, night of, first night of the new moon in the lunar month
Holua, sled
Hua, night of, thirteenth night of the lunar month
Hula, dance
Hunakele, to hide in secret
Ikuwa, month of October
Kau, semi-annual season, May to October
Ka'ai, sennit casket
Kahili, feather standard indicating alii lineage
Kahu, guardian
Kahuna, priest or expert in any profession
Kahuna kuni, sorcerers who used fire
Kahuna nui, high priest
Kahuna pule, priest
Kapa, cloth made from wauke or mamaki bark

Kapu, forbidden
Kapu moe, prostration kapu
Ke Alii Nui, great chief, king
Keiki hanai, foster child
Kihei, kapa mantle or cloak
Kohala, whale
Kuhina nui, regent
Kukailimoku, Kamehameha's war god
Kukui, candlenut
Kumakena, mourning period
Lauhala, pandanus leaves
Lei, garland
Maikai, good
Mahiole, feather helmet
Maile, fragrant leaves of a twining shrub
Mai oku'u, cholera or bacillary epidemic of 1804
Makaainana, commoner caste
Makahiki, annual festival and tax time
Makalii, month of December
Makawalu, order of battle emphasizing flanking movements
Malo, loin cloth
Mana, inner spiritual force
Mele inoa, name chant
Mohalu, night of, twelfth night of the lunar month
Moku o kohala, whale ship
Muku, night of, thirtieth night of the lunar month
Niaupio, offspring of a brother and sister or half-brother and half-
    sister
Olohana, John Young sobriquet
Pahu, drum
Pa'u, skirt
Pili, grass much used for thatching
Poi, cooked taro corm pounded and thinned with water
Pule, prayer
Pule aha, religious prayer which required absolute silence
Pule hui, prayer in unison
Taro, colocasia esculenta
Ti, cordyline terminalis
Uki, sedge
Uku, deep sea snapper fish
Wahine, female
Welehu, month of November

BIBLIOGRAPHY

1. Alexander, W. D. *A Brief History of the Hawaiian People.* NY: American Book Co., 1891.

2. ——"Overthrow of the Ancient Tabu System in the Hawaiian Islands." *Twenty-fifth Annual Report of the Hawaiian Historical Society.* (1917)

3. Arago, Jacques. *Narrative of a Voyage round the World . . . 1817-1820.* London: Treuttel & Wurtz . . ., 1823.

4. Ashley, Clifford W. *The Yankee Whaler.* 2nd Edn. Boston: Houghton Mifflin Co., 1938.

5. Ballou, Howard M. and Carter, George R. "The History of the Hawaiian Mission Press with a Bibliography of the Earlier Publications." *Papers of the Hawaiian Historical Society No. 14.* (1908)

6. Bassett, Marnie. *Realms and Islands, the World of Rose de Freycinet in the corvette Uranie, 1817-1820.* London: Oxford University Press, 1962.

7. Bingham, Hiram. *A Residence of Twenty-one Years in the Sandwich Islands . . .* Hartford: Hezekiah Huntington, 1847.

8. Bradley, Harold W. *The American Frontier in Hawaii.* 2d Edn. Palo Alto: Stanford University Press, 1944.

9. Dibble, Sheldon. *History of the Sandwich Islands.* Lahainaluna: Press of the Mission Seminary, 1843.

10. Ellis, William. *Narrative of a Tour Through Hawaii . . .* 2d Edn. London: H. Fisher, Son, and P. Jackson, 1827.

11. Emerson, Nathaniel B. *Unwritten Literature of Hawaii.* DC: Smithsonian Institute, 1909.

12. Fornander, Abraham. *An Account of the Polynesian Race.* 2d Edn. 3 Vols. London: Trubner & Co., 1880.

13. ——*Fornander Collection of Hawaiian Antiquities and Folk-lore.* (Memoirs of the Bernice P. Bishop Museum Vol. IV Part I) Honolulu: Bishop Museum Press, 1916.

14. Frankenstein, Alfred. *The Royal Visitors.* Oregon Historical Society, 1963.

15. Captain Louis de Freycinet's Account of a Voyage Around the World in the French Ship *l'Uranie.* Translation of the section relating to the Hawaiian Islands in the Archives of Hawaii.

16. (Graham, Maria) Capt. The Right Hon. Lord Byron. *Voyage of H.M.S. Blonde to the Sandwich Islands, in the years 1824–1825.* London: John Murray, 1826.

17. Halford, Francis John. *9 Doctors and God.* Honolulu: University of Hawaii, 1954.

18. Handy, E. S. C. *Polynesian Religion.* (Bernice P. Bishop Museum Bulletin 34) Honolulu: Bishop Museum Press, 1927.

19. ——*Cultural Revolution in Hawaii.* American Council Institute of Pacific Relations. (1931)

20. *Hawaiian Almanac and Annual for 1880.*

21. Artemus Bishop to Jeremiah Evarts, November 30, 1826. Missionary Letters Vol 2 (typescript) page 626, in Hawaiian Mission Childrens Society library.

22. *Historical Statistics of the United States, Colonial Times to 1957.* DC: U.S. Bureau of the Census, 1960.

23. "History of Hawaii, written by Scholars at the High School, and Corrected by One of the Instructors. Lahainaluna: Press of the High School, 1838." *The Hawaiian Spectator.* Vol 2 No 2. Honolulu: 1839.

24. *Instructions of the Prudential Committee of the American Board of Commissioners for Foreign Missions to the Sandwich Islands Mission.* Lahainaluna: Press of the Mission Seminary, 1838.

25. Jarves, James J. *History of the Hawaiian or Sandwich Islands.* Boston: Tappan & Benney, 1843.

26. Judd, Laura Fish. *Honolulu, Sketches of Life, Social, Political and Religious in the Hawaiian Islands from 1828 to 1861.* NY: Anson D. F. Randolph & Co., 1880.

27. Kamakau, Samuel M. *Ruling Chiefs of Hawaii.* Honolulu: The Kamehameha School Press, 1961.

28. ——*Ka Po'e Kahiko (The People of Old).* (Bernice P. Bishop Museum Special Publication 51) Honolulu: Bishop Museum Press, 1964.

29. Kelley, Antoinette. *Liholiho, His Life and Reign.* (1924) Typescript in University of Hawaii Library (Hawaiian).

30. Kuykendall, Ralph S. *The Hawaiian Kingdom, 1778-1854, Foundation and Transformation.* Honolulu: The University of Hawaii, 1938.

31. Levin, Stephanie Seto. "The Overthrow of the Kapu System in Hawaii." *The Journal of the Polynesian Society.* Vol 74 No 4. (Dec. 1968).

32. Lydgate, John M. "Ka-umu-alii, the Last King of Kauai." *Twenty-fourth Annual Report of the Hawaiian Historical Society* (1915).

33. Malo, David. *Hawaiian Antiquities (Moolelo Hawaii).* (Bernice P. Bishop Museum Special Publication 2) 2d Edn. Honolulu: Published by the Museum, 1951.

34. Extracts from the Journals of Don Francisco de Paula Marin. Typescript in Archives of Hawaii.

35. *Missionary Herald.* Vol XVI (1820).

36. ——Vol XVII (1821).

37. ——Vol XVIII (1822).

38. ——Vol XIX (1823).

39. Montgomery, James (comp). *Journals of Voyages and Travels by the Rev. Daniel Tyerman and George Bennet Esq . . . 1821-1829.* 2 Vols. London: Frederick Westly & A. H. Davis, 1831. Vol I.

40. Morgan, Theodore. *Hawaii, A Century of Economic Change, 1778-1876.* Cambridge: Harvard University Press, 1948.

41. Pleadwell, Frank Lester. The Voyage to England of King Liholiho and Queen Kamamalu. (Essay read at the meeting of the Social Science Association June 2, 1952) Typescript in University of Hawaii library (Hawaiian).

42. (Richards, Rev. William) *Memoir of Keopuolani, Late Queen of the Sandwich Islands.* Boston: Crocker & Brewster, 1825.

43. *The Sailors Magazine and Naval Journal.* August 1834.

44. Sanderson, Ivan T. *Follow The Whale.* NY: Bramhall House, 1956.

45. Schmitt, Robert C. *Demographic Statistics of Hawaii 1778-1965.* Honolulu: University of Hawaii Press, 1968.

46. Stewart, C. S. *A Residence in the Sandwich Islands.* 5th Edn. Boston: Weeks, Jordan & Co., 1839.

47. Sullivan, Paul. The Way of Wisdom. (1971) Typescript in Punahou School Library.

48. Taylor, Albert Pierce. "Liholiho: A Revised Estimate of His Character." *Papers of the Hawaiian Historical Society No 15 (1928).*

49. Thrum, Thomas G. (comp). "Sandalwood Trade of Early Hawaii." *The Hawaiian Annual,* 1905.

50. ——"Extracts from an Ancient Log." *The Hawaiian Annual,* 1906.

51. Thurston, Lucy. *Life and Times of Mrs. Lucy G. Thurston, Wife of Rev. Asa Thurston . . .* Ann Arbor: S. C. Andrews, 1882.

52. Walch, David B. "The Historical Development of the Hawaiian Alphabet." *The Journal of the Polynesian Society.* Vol 76 No 3. (1967).

53. Webb, M. C. "The Abolition of the Taboo System in Hawaii." *The Journal of the Polynesian Society.* Vol 74 No 1. (1965).